The Vanitas

& Other Tales of Art and Obsession

Jake Kendall

The Vanitas

& Other Tales of Art and Obsession

Jake Kendall

NEEM TREE
PRESS

Published by Neem Tree Press Limited, 2024
Copyright text © Jake Kendall, 2024
Copyright illustrations © Neem Tree Press, 2024

1 3 5 7 9 10 8 6 4 2

Neem Tree Press Limited
95a Ridgmount Gardens, London, WC1E 7AZ
United Kingdom
info@neemtreepress.com
www.neemtreepress.com

A catalogue record for this book is available from the British Library.

ISBN 978-1-911107-72-9 Paperback
ISBN 978-1-911107-73-6 Ebook
ISBN 978-1-911107-01-9 US Ebook

Printed and bound in Great Britain.

To all the suffering artists

Contents

Impression, Sunrise

L ucien edged through the brine-suffused darkness. Before him the black ocean lashed the shore with waves that hissed as they beat back in retreat. He stepped cautiously over slick jagged stones and around the glimmering outlines of silvery rock pools. His hand-me-down boots from his older brother were well-worn by now, their torn leather unable to prevent the shrinking tide from seeping into the fabric of his socks and chilling his feet.

He stopped by the ghostly outline of the jetty where the fishing boats were tied. He pulled his threadbare coat tight against the wind and the biting cold of the pre-dawn morning, his breath emerging in small puffs of warm mist that were swallowed swiftly by the night. Except for Lucien, the seafront was completely deserted. Likely all of Normandy was sleeping at that hour. He knew that he should be too—chasing memories and fleeting fantasies from the warmth and safety of his bedsheets.

The distant declarations of the church bells chimed four times, causing Lucien's stomach and throat to clench hard. He could see it now, a solitary distant orange orb, floating down from the cottages to join him on the beach. The man holding it was not from the village. Lucien had observed him keenly

1

the day before and listened as he entreated the fishermen on their return to shore. The Stranger had been wearing clothes quite unlike any that Lucien had ever seen—frilly and delicate, they were alien artefacts belonging to another world entirely, an urbane life far removed from salt, spray, and fresh-gutted fish. Paris could be glimpsed in those clothes, even at a distance they smelt of money.

The Stranger's approaches to the fishermen had appeared unsuccessful. Certainly he had cut a disappointed figure as he left the beach and traipsed back towards the village. Lucien had raced after him to query his purpose, and learned that the Stranger wanted to be taken onto the water under darkness and that he was prepared to pay twenty francs to any person willing to take him.

Almost five weeks before, Lucien's father had fallen from a ladder while repairing their rooftop. He had broken his left leg and been bedridden ever since. Lucien's father was a skilled fisherman, but the inexperience of his sons had shown when they worked the waters in his stead. Their catches were insufficient to live off, let alone sell. The family had already exhausted what meagre savings they once had and were living like scavengers. Their mother was feeding them charitable offerings from the villagers, supplemented by seaweed, garden snails, garlic, and mushrooms foraged from the woods nearby. Too often Lucien had seen his parents go to bed hungry so that he and his younger siblings could eat. He had informed the wealthy stranger that seven of his thirteen years had been spent out on the cove, and had assured him that he could deliver as safe passage as any. The Stranger had looked him up and down; with a smile and a ruffle of Lucien's hair he had agreed to meet at the jetty just after four that morning.

The orange orb neared, and a shadowed face peered out from behind a gas lantern. Something was attached to the man's back, a large bundle that was covered and strapped. As he approached the jetty, the Stranger called out, "*Salut?*" in a voice soft and uncertain. Lucien summoned his courage and replied in kind, waving his arms to draw the man's attention.

The Stranger was eager to be taken immediately to sea. Despite this, Lucien held out his hand and made a faltering request for payment before they took to the water. When the twenty francs were all accounted for, they stepped onto the jetty. Lucien forewarned the Stranger of the looseness of the fourth board, not because the board truly was loose, but because it occurred to him that such instruction might lend an appearance of deep familiarity with the jetty, and, by implication, the entire cove around them.

He found the familiar outline of the family boat, bobbing with the lapping waves. Having never removed its fastenings in the dark before, the boy asked for the gas lantern to be raised above the mooring post as he began untying the bowline knot in the lines. He apologised silently to his family as he did so. They would be sick with worry to discover him gone. If his father found the strength to stand later, he might even reward the enterprise by thrashing the boy with leathers until the skin on his back broke—though, hopefully, the sight of twenty francs might assuage his father's fury.

Lucien held the lines and took hold of the gaslight with his free hand. He ushered the Stranger onto the gently rocking boat and watched as the man removed the bundle from his back and placed it onboard gingerly. Lucien passed the Stranger the gaslight and moved toward the prow. He took an oar, pushed the boat off the jetty and slid through the rippling water—

away from the shoreline and toward the moon, to where the pale pewter water met the star-speckled sky.

*

Lucien grunted and strained with each slow stroke. He steered the boat starboard, where the cove was deepest, offering tacit prayers that nothing would catch and damage the keel. His eyes pooled with tears in the icy air, tears that stung his skin as they streamed impassively down his face.

His passenger sat transfixed. The gas lantern flickered at their feet between them, illuminating them both from below. The inky countenance of the Stranger appeared sinister; a shadowy face, hovering, disembodied in the dark. He was relatively young, around thirty perhaps. His face was framed by a thin strip of facial hair that descended from his sideburns, to around his chin, and up to his bottom lip in a neat line. The small moustache that sat above his lips was imperfect, thicker at the corners of his mouth than it was under his nose. His thick black hair was slicked back to emerge again from behind his ears. A long coat was draped loosely over his shoulders, covering his entire body.

Lucien's gaze perhaps lingered too long. The Stranger caught the look and returned it, his dark eyes shining with some indecipherable, burning purpose. Lucien found his mind involuntarily recalling stories read by his schoolteachers of that vengeful revenant Monte Cristo.

"Do you like the night?" asked the Stranger.

Lucien shivered, his breath shallow, his eyes alert. His family's dire situation had made him rash. He had not truly stopped to consider who this man was and what his purpose could be out on these waters. He saw the Stranger briefly as a vampire, one intent on luring a hapless victim out beyond the reach of civilisation, where escape was impossible. More likely, the Stranger was mortal: an assassin, a pirate, or a smuggler. Perhaps Lucien was inadvertently abetting an act of treason, or a vital mission to support some secret cause. Perhaps the mysterious bundle protected so preciously by the Stranger was filled with money, jewels, or some other substances that could be traded with another boat. Who knew, the Stranger might harbour no intentions of returning to the village at all, or of leaving a living witness. They might spot a second vessel on the horizon—there might be no warning then, just a blade run across his throat.

"I like the night," the Stranger continued wistfully to fill the silence. "The colours! But sadly, it is quite impossible." His voice was articulate and refined, yet his base accent remained northern French—likely the Stranger hailed from a place not far from Lucien's own village. He kept rowing, the oars swooshing rhythmically as they sliced through water.

"Where are we going?" Lucien asked after a while.

"Take me there," the Stranger replied, pointing towards a limestone arch that protruded just outside the cove.

When they reached the place indicated by the Stranger, the sun had sent out its first overtures to the day, ringing the eastern horizon with a luminous pale strip. The Stranger reached into his pocket and drew out an ornate silver pocket watch. He then took tentatively to his feet.

"Can you keep us still?" he asked.

"I will do my best," Lucien squeaked.

"Good enough," the Stranger replied. "Apologies, this will take some time."

"What are we doing out here?"Lucien stammered hesitantly.

"We are here to capture something," the Stranger said softly.

It was an answer ripe with intrigue. New possibilities continued rushing unbidden into Lucien's mind. Perhaps the national authorities might reward any reports of illicit behaviour on the English Channel. Perhaps he might even find himself positioned to double-cross the Stranger and have his family paid twice-over. These were possibilities that could perhaps be favourable—presuming, of course, that his life was not sacrificed on the altar of whatever grim purpose had compelled his enigmatic passenger to ride this paltry vessel across the treacherous nocturnal waves.

Beneath the long coat, the Stranger was wearing dark overalls, not unlike those worn by the village fishmongers. He began working the straps and fastenings of his bundle and produced a long, dark instrument. The boy found himself crying aloud for his mother, half-expecting to be struck. The Stranger looked up and regarded the boy with wry silent amusement. Placing the object between them, the Stranger pulled it out onto three legs before producing, not a telescope, nor a gun, but a blank white square, and mounted it on top of the tripod.

"We have come out here to capture…" the Stranger added in a breezy drawl "…the rising sun."

Several brushes and metallic tubes followed the tripod out from the bundle. Lucien's sense of deep dread rapidly dissolved. After everything, his passenger was an artist, a mere artist!

"Absurd, isn't it?" the Stranger exclaimed, squeezing paint out onto a slate palette, "to think people choose to sleep through such colours!" His amusement at the thought appeared to be quite genuine.

Lucien was stupefied. Indeed, it was absurd: the boy had risked the fury of his family, their boat, and perhaps even his life—all so some reckless poseur could make a painting of the sunrise. Absurd was far too small a word! A host of obscenities bubbled in his mind. Were it best not to provoke the insane, Lucien would have aimed a furious eruption of relieved outrage in the direction of the lunatic sharing his boat. He held his tongue instead and sulked in silence.

"Have you ever witnessed such a sight?" asked the Stranger, nodding back to the horizon.

Lucien had indeed seen the daybreak before. He said so bluntly, finding himself in no mood to indulge the saccharine whimsy of a sophomoric dandy with little regard for human life.

"Your eyes are closed, my young friend," the Stranger insisted as he commenced his work. "Nature opened mine. She taught me how to see...Look again."

Lucien shook his head and turned his attention back east. They would float there into the day, the Stranger painting like a man possessed, Lucien thinking that he should probably take him to the nearest asylum the very moment they landed. Nevertheless, Lucien eventually conceded—privately at least— that in some ways he was glad to have been shown such a vision.

He had indeed seen the daybreak before, but never one such as this. He saw the morning sun, resplendent in a magnificent shade of deep coral red, rising like God's own gas lantern to peel back the darkness and reveal the vibrant splendour of the world once again. Surrounded by a haze of mottled vaporous light, their boat was engulfed by an exquisite symphony of orange, salmon, and violet, that danced across the waters and mingled with the vanishing mist.

Thirty-Seven Neugrabenstrasse

The world's unhappiest billionaire was born on 12 April 1974, in a hospital in Vienna. He was named Markus. His mother was named Katja. His father remained at home.

Home was Thirty-Seven Neugrabenstrasse, an inauspicious flat on the top floor of a Viennese suburb. The flat may as well have been the entire world, for it was a place that the family very rarely left.

As the years passed, every inch of those eight rooms impressed themselves deep within Markus's memory, from the fading paint on the walls of the pale blue living room and mint-green bathroom, to the peeling yellow wallpaper in his bedroom, the patterns in the hallway woodgrain, and the shape of each watermark in every ceiling.

Through Markus's early years, his family was supported by their friends—a rotating cast of extremely serious people who would come and go quickly and quietly, speaking exclusively in hushed voices, as they brought provisions and money with them into the flat. Markus found them all so featureless and interchangeable that he could only remember them as ghosts: faceless, sombre, and grey. For the most part, they had no interest in talking to a child. The only real exception was an older woman named Jule, who spent three days a week home schooling Markus. Jule taught him essential skills, such as reading, writing and arithmetic. She also taught other subjects such as geography and history. She told him that they were all German, though they lived in Austria—*which is Germany's neighbouring country*. She would emphasise that it was the duty of all good neighbours to live polite and quiet lives, just like the old man on the floor below. Jule was not unpleasant, though she did lack warmth. Markus could feel obligation in their interactions; he understood on an instinctive level that their relationship was transactional by nature.

Markus would watch other children playing from the window. Yet on the rare occasions he encountered them in person—those times in which Katja would take him out for groceries, doctors, dentists, and occasional play-parks excursions—the other children frightened him. They were like wild animals, bounding impulsively with alien joy. He found their laughter and shrieking abrasive. Markus would cling to his mother and quietly plead to return home.

If his shyness saddened Katja, his father Heiner remained unmoved. Markus once overheard him saying that *a billionaire simply does not need friends*, as quietly as his frustration would allow.

Heiner said that word, "billionaire", often. It was a word that lit up his eyes and, at times, made the grip of his fingers so tight on Markus's arms that it caused bruising.

When Markus asked what the word meant, Heiner told him it meant they owned one billion schillings—so much money that it would not physically fit inside the flat. He would try to explain the value to his young son by writing down all the zeros on paper, or else he would say that the weight of their wealth would probably prove heavier than a whole herd of African elephants. When his son was unable to comprehend any of these attempts to conceptualise their wealth, Heiner grew irritated, summarising that being a billionaire means, in short, that they were exceptionally fortunate, and would want for nothing in their lives.

As Markus grew older, he began understanding one thing about his family's wealth. It seemed to make their lives a paradox of sorts. Their exceptional fortune seemed to weigh heavily on both of his parents. Heiner would twitch behind curtains, sometimes demanding total silence while he listened with skittish intensity, his head cocked, his palms damp. Katja would sometimes hold Markus in the kitchen while she wept silent tears. His parents would argue in the night too. That was a strange thing to hear; two people shouting in whispers and furiously scribbling letters to each other in the same room.

Markus read everything he could find in the flat, many books on art history, artist biographies, and a handful of old novels. He read them all, over and over, until he could recite whole chapters by memory. Whenever he was not reading, he spent his time among the many paintings owned by his parents. He would sit in these rooms filling his imagination and his heart as he left his childhood behind.

In the summer of 1988, aged fourteen, Markus began writing a diary. There was little of his days that merited recording; nevertheless, it was an occupation, and a means of expressing his thoughts.

5 May 1988. Mother is tired of me complaining. She has given me this old notepad with the suggestion that I keep a diary of my thoughts and share them with her before bedtime. We have been talking about art a lot recently, and she has procured several books on the subject for my education. I am currently learning about the history of one of her favourite painters: Pablo Picasso.

The late nineteenth century ushered in an age of constant artistic revolution. The artists of the early twentieth century felt compelled to charge boldly through the doors of modernity, cast open by groups such as the Impressionists. Two groups, both represented in my father's collection, emerged almost like competing aesthetic schools. The Fauves, such as Matisse, took their inspiration from vibrant colour. However, despite their radical innovations, the Fauves were essentially Expressionists by nature, acolytes of the school of Paul Gaugin and Vincent van Gogh. The second school, led principally by the Spaniard Pablo Picasso, turned their attention elsewhere. In doing so, they invented an even more revolutionary visual style called Cubism, compositions built from abstracted details and visual riddles that interrogated conventional understandings of space and time.

For example:

Mother sprawled. Hugging peas. Frozen. "Oscillating fan." Ceiling watermark in the shape of a cloud. Art and Illusion, *by Ernst Gombrich. Potato salad with pickles, ham and bread. 98.6 degrees. A blue fractured body with divorced shadow. Neck protruding oddly. Head atop the canvas. .ratiuG Strings slashed diagonally*

across

the

canvas.

This is how I think Picasso might have described our living room today. As a style, I find it emotionally detached. When I put this observation to mother, she said that it is precisely this coldness that appeals to her, and that she thinks sometimes detachedness is best.

19 June 1988. Today I started reading Crime and Punishment *by Fyodor Dostoevsky. This will be the fifth reading. My last reading took four days and six hours. Mother tells me there is an even longer Russian novel called* War and Peace. *She promises she will get it for me soon. She swears that it will keep my mind busy for at least a week.*

I wonder if all old novels follow the same titular pattern of balanced and diametrically opposed concepts. The pattern is pleasing. The concepts cannot co-exist, for they are defined by their contrast. A person cannot experience Freedom and Confinement simultaneously. Nor Happiness and Sadness.

One of the grey ghosts visited us today. His name is Götze. He has a very dour face, like it has been painted by Otto Dix. Even though Götze looks miserable, his visit made father happier than I have ever seen him. He was laughing, hugging mother and myself. He produced a bundle of schillings from the vault in his bedroom and sent mother out to the shops for wine. Father even allowed me to put the radio on quietly while we waited for her return. He hummed along to the music: Beethoven, Chopin, Wagner.

recant   behooving   nephew
benign   cenotaph   however
newborn   pathogene   chive
whatever   nonbeing   epoch
venerating   hebrew   pooch.

When mother finally returned, she gave me a glass of an Italian wine called Vietti Barolo that I did not like at first. We ate an untitled dish, made of sausages and beans, garlic, onion and tomatoes, tubes of pasta and a bowl of salad. I separated out the constituent parts and tried to find the dish's title through interrogation and rearrangement. Mother told me to stop that at once.

Father talked incessantly about returning home, about buying a cabin in the Alps, and about buying something called a Porsche.

Mother was also crying, though she also said that she was fine. Finally, it is almost over, she said.

    This picture is incomplete.

2 August 1988. Something has happened, but I do not understand what. All I have are abstracted details and visual riddles.

    Götze returned two weeks ago. Shattered plates on the floor. Hushed voices in the kitchen. 'Fallen through, cannot be sold on.'

o	g	i
l	A	e
o	p	s

No one comes for me all night. "Sometimes detachedness is best." Rumbling stomach. Mother crying. Father observing a composition only he can see, deep within the ceiling. Everything is different. Father is withdrawn, mostly in his bedroom repeating his new favourite word:

a	e	B
t	a	l
y	!	r

Mother tells me it is time to stop reading books all the time, it is time for me to learn how to be a man around the house. She shows me how to cook several dinners and how to complete necessary tasks around the flat: changing light bulbs, wiring sockets, cleaning glass, and brushing canvas.

Last night there were noises: more hushed arguments, things moving inside their bedroom. 'Fallen through.' All fern though. Fall on her thug. Go far hell hunt. Though in feral. Ran fought hell. Ghoul in father. "Cannot be sold on." Cloned nanobots. Let noon abscond. Anon blonde Scot. Lends onto bacon. Bald connotes no. No nascent blood.

6 August 1988. This morning, I woke to find my parents waiting in the kitchen. Mother was fully dressed, her bags and suitcases packed already by the door. Father's head was in his hands. Mother said she cannot stay any longer. She is not strong enough to endure number

Thirty-Seven Neugrabenstrasse,
and
everything
it
contains.

"Stop crying and quiet our voices." Father is angry.

Mother would not take me with her and cannot stay. "You are a man, Markus, this comes with rspnsblty, nd dty."

I was told that the family, the money, the sacrifices made so far, all meant my place was here: at number

Thirty-Seven Neugrabenstrasse.

'Listen to your father. Do not go outside, and do not talk to anyone without permission.'

Knock at the door. Grey ghosts. Mother gone. Sometimes detachedness is best.

The flat is quiet without Mother. Father did not know what else to say to me. After lingering silently for some time, he said that the fridge has been left full, and that he would like lunch around twelve. He left me alone in the kitchen until I ran out of tears. I do not fully understand what has happened. All I know is that this will be my last diary entry, and that I am tired of Cubism.

No doubt, the diaries of other fourteen-year-olds are quite different.

*

With his mother gone, Markus was responsible for the flat and his father. Heiner seemed to shrink over time. He became so thin that his old and ragged clothing hung loosely around his frame. Still, the billionaire would not leave his flat to purchase anything new. Heiner's beard and hair grew long, matted, and speckled with skin flakes. Markus frequently offered to trim and groom his father, but Heiner always refused, insisting that he was uninterested in vanities. He did allow Markus to clip his nails though, whenever they curled inwards sufficiently to cut his fingers and toes.

On his eighteenth birthday a letter arrived informing Markus he had been given a job with a maintenance company in Germany. Markus never visited their offices, or indeed left Vienna, and yet once a month money was paid into an account that had been set up for him. His wages were enough to pay off the utility bills, buy food for them both, with a little for other amenities. Heiner insisted to Markus that this money was payment for all the tasks he completed around the flat and informed him that they should expect fewer visits from the family friends.

Markus used the leftover money to buy new books. And newspapers. He loved newspapers. Pictures and stories from the outside world fascinated him: the travel pages showed images of the mountains of Nepal, of Caribbean beaches and igloos beneath the Aurora Borealis. Heiner promised that one day they would go see it all.

Markus also liked the sports section. Germany, he was told, is the greatest footballing nation in the world; *Die Mannschaft* won the Euros in 1996. Markus and Heiner followed and memorialised the tournament through newspaper cuttings, one game at a time. The day after the final, they drank cold beer together in victory, Heiner sitting back with his eyes closed as Markus read the journalist's account of the match. Heiner promised that one day they would go and watch a game in person.

The thought of television and film also fascinated Markus. He would read those sections of the newspapers excitedly, pleading for one to be brought into the flat. Heiner strictly forbade the notion, fearing anything that could send out signals into the world. All Heiner could give his son was yet more promises of another day.

Katja wrote letters. They came to the flat indirectly, their envelopes addressed to a location in a city called Hamburg in Germany. These letters arrived in erratically timed bundles, pushed into a letterbox downstairs during the night. Markus would read them aloud to his father. Sometimes Heiner wept. Other times he stared impassively into the distance. Then,

Katja wrote e*nough was enough*, and that Heiner *should stop living this life, go to the police and...* Markus never found out anything further, the letter was snatched from his hands. After that, Markus vowed he would hide any further letters from his mother, though no more ever came.

As a young adult, Markus was permitted brief trips away from the flat. He was required to go venture out for groceries and reading material. Heiner would warn him to exercise frugality, insisting that money was not limitless.

Markus began to get irritated, asking why they had to treat each schilling so preciously when, apparently, they had so many that they could not fit it all within the flat? Heiner proudly declared that they owned a billion schillings, easily, but that, for the time being, it was getting harder and harder to access their money.

As Markus would put on his coat and shoes, Heiner would loom in the hallway, scratching at his bleeding wrists, visibly panicked, and saying things such as: *don't forget the eggs. I want eggs for lunch today. And don't be too long. You are much slower than your mother was. You like to stroll, don't you? Gorging your eyes on shop windows, and parks, and the pretty ladies too. Don't you think I want to be doing these things as well? Come back, Markus, quickly.*

At night, the flat transformed. There were faces in the walls, faces in the ceiling, faces in the shadows, and eyes that always followed.

Outside the windows were the Bird-People. They patrolled the streets below, they swooped through the sky, cawing malevolently, their beaks opening and filled with sharply pointed teeth.

In those hours, Markus searched frantically, opening every door, looking for an escape. Each room contained only disembodied screaming. Heiner stalked languid in pursuit: long-legged, taloned, and scaly, his beard and hair turned to feathers, a long robe of plumage billowing as he moved, his pale blue eyes cold and glassy as he scanned for any trace of Markus.

One night, Markus opened the letterbox and called for help. A man crawled up the staircase outside, grey-green in complexion, with hair made of flames, hissing like a snake. It slithered up through the letterbox and coiled on their floor before pulling itself upright onto its one stumped toe, unfurling itself up to full height as it moved along the hallway walls. The malevolent creature had tiny arms, at the end of these arms were gigantic hands with claws like knives. It began to claw maniacally at its torso, ripping away at its skin, tearing at its flesh, and shrieking in wordless agony.

Markus felt his teeth falling from his face. He tried to push them back in, but every tooth that he touched detached weightlessly from his gums. He would clean his father's paintings, only for the oil to run and for the canvas to tear. Heiner somehow knew of these mistakes immediately. He would hurtle out from his lair, screeching Markus's name, forcing him to flee beneath the floorboards. Markus found a system of tunnels beneath the flat, tunnels that twisted and turned in the cold wet dark, only to lead him back inside Thirty-Seven Neugrabenstrasse.

His adolescent mind strained, trying to satisfy his hormonal urges, trying to build a convincing image of a woman. It had no point of reference. The women he constructed stared back at him with dead and vacant eyes. They were static images.

They were fluid abstractions, or they were provocative and crude. They were two-dimensional vaginas that flowed into thorny flowers. They were cubist compositions, their features randomised and angular. They were bare-breasted mocking skull-faces like in his father's Magritte.

When a woman finally felt real, Markus felt warmth and affection as she held him close. The woman said that she loved him. She said she had a sister though, and her sister wanted to hurt Markus. Markus simply had to meet her. The sister mocked him. She said that she had left him and was never coming back. They had *both* left him and were never coming back. Confused, Markus asked who they were. The sister asked Markus if he was so stupid that he could not see. Suddenly, Markus realised the two women had the same face, that they were both his mother. The realisation jolted him awake, and he found himself crying.

*

In the autumn of 1996, the quiet old man downstairs passed away. Markus and Heiner peeked out from the corners of their curtains, watching as his body and possessions were removed from the building. Soon after, a young couple moved into the vacant flat.

Two days later, the young couple ventured up the stairs and knocked. Markus opened the door and haltingly introduced himself. The couple were named Simon and Esme. They had brought a gift of a loaf of home-baked bread. Markus, grateful for the gesture, began to invite the couple inside for coffee. Heiner came charging through the flat immediately, his eyes wide and brows sweaty. He told the couple that he was sick and that his illness was contagious. Heiner spluttered and feigned snivelling as he closed the door.

Markus asked why his father had been so hostile, but Heiner refused to listen. He pressed his ear against the keyhole until he was certain the couple had walked downstairs.

"We do not talk to strangers, Markus. This is quite simple. It is how we have always been. You know this."

"But why father?" Markus pushed, clenching his fists in frustration. "They seemed friendly, and we could benefit from some company. They brought us this."

Markus passed the loaf of bread to Heiner.

"Simon. He said his name was *Simon.*" Heiner muttered, tossing the bread into the dustbin.

Markus did not understand. Heiner was worse than ever. He was convinced of vermin in the flat. He had Markus lay traps around the skirting boards. He seemed terrified of the new neighbours, though other times he laughed about them too, broken notes of sharp, acid amusement.

"It is fate," he would say, "now it is we who hide in attics, and Simon—*Simon!* - who lives downstairs."

Heiner requested that Markus shop for food during the night-time. He was losing his mind, repeating the same requests over and over, and forgetting the hours kept by normal society. His skin was sore, his body small and emaciated. Heiner coughed endlessly, sometimes leaving blood on tissues. He desperately needed to see a doctor, though, when Markus suggested it, Heiner declared theatrically that he would never again leave his flat, even if it meant dying there. Markus found himself increasingly in one of two places. If Heiner was locked in his bedroom, Markus would window-watch, staring out at the passers-by, happy families, and loving couples. If Heiner roamed the flat, Markus would sit beneath the Klimt.

His father owned one large Klimt. Over the years, it had become Markus's favourite painting in the family collection. A depiction of two lovers entwined, painted in soft oils and gold flakes. Markus took a pillow from his room and recreated the pose, embracing the pillow tightly. He closed his eyes and imagined the scent of perfume he had smelled on ladies in the street. He imagined the pillow breathing with him. He imagined a heart beating inside it. He imagined what it would be like for the pillow to have a collarbone, a neck with jewellery, a head, and a face. He imagined the pillow turning to him to brush his lips with soft kisses.

It was futile. Markus could not hope to even imagine love. Not by clutching a pillow on a hardwood floor. When he opened his eyes, he saw the shimmering gold of the painting and felt a rush of anger coursing through his body. His family were supposed to be so wealthy, and yet their wealth had created so little happiness. Their fortune had broken both of his parents and made a freak of him.

For years now a current of deep unease had coursed through his spirit. He knew that something was profoundly wrong in their lives. As he turned off the lights that night, Markus resolved to find out what it was.

*

Keeping secrets in such an enclosed space was always going to be difficult. However, with careful planning and a little patience, Markus used what little autonomy and privacy he had to sneak new books into the flat. These contraband works were neither novels nor biographies of artists; they were books on European history. When he was certain that Heiner was asleep, Markus would sit in his bed, reading about the World Wars. When, for the first time in his twenty-one years, he encountered the names of Adolf Hitler, and the Nazi Party, an apoplectic rage burned within him. He had been denied so much knowledge and understanding of the world.

He held his tongue at first and kept reading. Markus's anger turned to horror as he learned of the persecution of Jewish people, about the murder of millions, of the banality of evil, and the active and passive complicity of the general population as a nation chose to look away. He read of property and wealth, including thousands of artworks, stolen and not returned to the rightful owners. He read the stories of minor Nazis and Gestapo officers fleeing Germany to hide in other countries, his horror transfiguring into revulsion as he came to understand it all— the paintings, the network of family friends, their reclusiveness and secrecy, his father's paranoia, and his mother's shame.

Heiner had not banned the subject of his own father outright, but neither had he ever encouraged any discussion on the matter. As a child, Markus had naturally and innocuously inquired about his grandparents once or twice. He had been informed that Heiner's father had played a role within the German armed forces at a time of war. It was over breakfast one morning in February 1997, that Markus resolved to ask Heiner exactly who his grandfather had been.

"My father was a war hero. For the fatherland."

"Was he a Nazi?" Markus replied, blunt in his reply. A long pause followed this question, the air in the room curdling.

"Markus, where have you heard this word? Who have you been talking to?" Heiner rose to his feet and paced the kitchen. "Have you been talking to the couple downstairs? Has *Simon* taught you this word?"

"No father... I have been reading."

"Reading?" Heiner let out a deep sigh. "My son. Every book is a story, even history books are stories. You see, every book comes from a *writer*, and every writer has a *side*. You must understand, we were on the losing side of a war. *The* war."

"How did you acquire all of these paintings father?" Markus asked. "And why do you never leave the flat, if there is no reason to fear leaving them? Why must we always be quiet?" Heiner said nothing, he leaned against the kitchen counter and narrowed his eyes. "Is this our money?" Markus pressed, "All of it contained in stolen art? Sixty-seven paintings father, I know them all. Is this why you tell me that we are *billionaires*?" The accursed word was so bitter in Markus's mouth that he could barely speak it.

"Schillings, Deutschmark, American dollars," began Heiner, waving his hand dismissively, his skin like the petals of dead violets. "It is easily a billion wherever we sell them. The Klimt alone could sell for a hundred million! I read that one just like it reached that price at auction. The Picassos—thirteen Picassos!—they are worth tens of millions, each!" There was something like passion in Heiner's eyes once again. Markus had not seen such a look in years. It was the hope that kept his father tethered to this miserable existence. Heiner leaned close, his voice straining. "We can still be rich men, my son; we will send for your mother. We will buy everything we ever wanted."

"We have nothing father," Markus interjected, "worse than nothing. These paintings are not yours; they belong with other people. They are a cursed inheritance. They have wasted your life and destroyed your family."

"My father bequeathed these paintings to me on his deathbed, along with this flat. *I* have committed no crime.

These paintings are mine, Markus. I keep them for you. I will sell them for you. Please." Heiner's voice trembled. "*Please* do not lose faith."

The moral argument failing, Markus tried a practical one instead. "You will never sell these paintings without getting noticed. These names: Picasso, Ernst, Klimt… You will be arrested if you even try to sell them now."

"Jail? Pah."

"Who would you even sell to? If your family friends knew of buyers, they would have sold them years ago. Mother was right…"

"Your mother betrayed us!" Heiner shouted, raising his voice and his hand to Markus for the first time in their lives. Markus was not scared however, for Heiner's rage was impotent, and hollow. He was too weak to hurt Markus now. They both knew this. "What are you going to do?" Heiner asked softly in retreat. "Will you abandon me too? Go and tell *Simon* downstairs? Tell the police? I am too weak for another such betrayal. It will be the death of me, Markus. You do this and you will kill your father."

Markus looked at his father and beheld a truly pitiful sight. Heiner was a paranoid lunatic. A bearded vampire. A thing of darkness and obsession. He had lived too long upstairs at number Thirty-Seven Neugrabenstrasse to walk away from it now.

"I will not tell a soul," Markus declared, standing purposefully. "That responsibility is yours. I hope you will see sense. Phone the police. They will surely show leniency towards a man of your age, trying to make amends for the sins of the past."

Heiner remained petulantly silent as Markus made for the door.

"Markus," Heiner barked after him. "Markus, I *command* you to stay."

For the first time in his life, Markus ignored a direct command from his father, and he opened the front door.

"Please," implored Heiner softly. "I promise you this is the death of me, son. The death."

Markus looked back one last time. He knew that Heiner was correct, he could not continue alone. He wondered if his departure would force his father to change his mind and join him, if he would sulk for a few days before handing himself in, or if he would see things out to the bitter end. He realised that it did not matter which, for Markus also knew that he could not stay here another minute. Whatever Heiner chose to do, number Thirty-Seven Neugrabenstrasse would soon be free of him and his stolen paintings, the works rediscovered and returned to their rightful owners.

"Here, you are dead already father," said Markus from the hallway, "this is no longer a flat, it is a grave. Mother could not live here, and neither can I. See sense. It is over. Do the right thing. Please?"

Heiner lingered, downcast in the doorway. Saying nothing in reply, he stepped back and shut the door behind him.

Medusa

For the attention of Mr Alexandre Corréard and Mr Henri Savigny,

I am deeply honoured to make acquaintance with men such as yourselves. Despite every odious effort that has been made to silence and discredit your voices, the tale of the Medusa reached me one recent evening at dinner. My companion had not recounted even half of the horrific rumours surrounding the story of your survival when realisation struck—I have been waiting for you my entire life.

Your ill-fated expedition gnaws at my conscience. My bed is now disarrayed and drenched with sweat. The remorse I feel turns each morsel of food so bitter and so foul in my mouth that I cannot bear to swallow, and when I hear the sweet melody of *La Marseillaise*, my shame transfigures each note until all I hear is the splintering of wood and dire screams in the darkness.

How can I begin to soothe such sorrows as these? How can my talents, limited as they are, and the great privileges of my birth help to cultivate justice in this world? Sirs, although society does not yet know me as such, I am an artist, and—with your blessing—I would use everything I have learned and what skill I possess to serve the subjugated and to cast the culpable into eternal damnation.

I have heard that already some have used your pain to service their own ends—that the Bonapartists have made a sabre from your suffering and thrust it towards the monarchist heart. Such flagrant self-interest would surely cast doubts in your mind about the intentions of other concerned parties. Let me now clarify my own to you: The artist looks only for fidelity, with a scope that extends beyond the petty politicking of our current day. Should you grant me the generosity of your blessing, we shall work together to banish both base speculation and ignoble deceit. We shall discover the true meaning of suffering and situate it in so prominent a place that no citizen of our great nation could ignore it or dare to forget.

Yours in sincerity,

Théodore Géricault

*

We met the artist in the doorway of his home, a spacious townhouse on the outskirts of the city, where he embraced us in turn as if we were brothers. He was an intense young man who looked to be in his mid-twenties. His mournful eyes were like pools of wet hazel and his dark uncombed thatch of hair contrasted sharply against a neat-trimmed beard. He greeted us that afternoon wearing a burgundy shirt of lustrous satin and black leather boots that were so polished that they dazzled, and I found my arm shifting instinctively to cover the rip in the side of my jacket.

He led us down a long corridor and into a room to seat us at a table before taking his leave to source refreshments. The room, which appeared to be something like a drawing room, was elegantly decorated with floral wallpaper patterned with snaking branches bearing vibrant crimson blossoms and petals of verdant green. Mounted on the walls were several portraits of grey and brown horses and one large Italian vista with the name *Claude Lorrain* inscribed onto an ornate silver-leaf frame. A striking bureau of bright blue lacquer was richly decorated in the oriental style, with the silhouettes of huts, trees, and several human figures dressed in billowing far-eastern robes, wrought finely in gold across the top. At our table two candlesticks were shaped like cherubs.

He returned to us then, accompanied by a retainer who offered us pastries, coffee, fruit, and brandy, while the artist delineated his thinking. Afterwards he took us onto the lawns located behind his home, past the sculpted waters and lilac blooms of his Japanese garden, to reveal a large white outhouse that he had constructed to facilitate the painting of his epic. He seemed to grow quite excited as he showed us inside this bespoke studio, for doubtless he recognised an opportunity for great fame in such a scandalous and tragic story—perhaps fame enough to launch a great and celebrated career.

We were told that a painter of reality—such as he—requires the physical presence of his subject. Therefore, we returned two weeks later to help take delivery of a considerable amount of timber. We spread the wooden slats and poles across the floor and began the long process of lashing and nailing them together. As the form of a raft emerged from the material, the smell of saltwater started to seep impossibly through the bricks and plaster of the studio. The slats beneath my feet started to buck and roll across phantom currents, and the vile flavours of garlic and lemon set themselves upon my tongue and down my throat. All strength drained immediately from my legs, and I found that I was falling—falling straight through the studio floor, back to the Medusa, and back amidst the merciless blue.

*

Our ship, the Medusa, was one of four charged with the reclamation of French interests in Senegal. An aristocrat and former exile, by the name of Hugues Duroy de Chaumareys, was made first captain of the expedition. His appointment had been one of political expediency, the newly restored King rewarding those who had demonstrated loyalty to the throne, and yet none among the crew could ever have believed that any person commanding so high a rank could ever have proved so profoundly incapable. The captain's blustering orders had betrayed his ineptitude with every directive—which sometimes proved a source of amusement to the crew. For instance, on July first, de Chaumareys spied Cape Blanco and ordered us to make the cape. Those of us able to distinguish a rock from a cloud were confused, for we saw nothing but a great mass of vapour. Some of the more mischievous persons on deck elected not to contradict the order and we sailed fully into the fog, making disingenuous preparations for landing while our captain's face flushed red. Many of us found little mirth in his incompetence, however; the ocean is not a place for frivolous games and the threat of ruination hung over us constantly. Our captain chartered a route that belied all nautical sense. We sailed through shallow waters and over sandbars, hugging the western coast of Africa perilously close to conceal his inability to navigate over open water.

The expedition left France as four ships. The other three slipped away unnoticed in the night to make their own safer passage south. Yet for those of us aboard the Medusa, nothing short of a full mutiny could have freed us from the authority of a man who had not stepped aboard a ship in twenty-five years and had never once commanded one.

Tensions boiled as we approached the Anguin Bank, a strait so treacherous that the experienced sailor shows it the respect of sixty miles. The captain, determined to shorten his time on the ocean, ordered us to halve the distance of this passage. Sure enough, the water around the ship soon changed to a lighter hue and mud and seaweeds began to cling to the keel. Some among the crew began to vocalise their doubts and their dissent. The captaincy arrested these men, charged them with sedition and lashed them with the nine tails.

The banking of the Medusa was inevitable. We had sailed over reef for almost half a day before the changing tides immobilised us. The shock of the impact threw most of us to the decking and everywhere I looked stupefied horror was etched onto the face of every man aboard. An unnatural silence descended upon the ship for several long minutes before the air filled with a deluge of despair and futile rage.

We took to the longboats and spent two days pulling at the anchors to shift the great ship. Our efforts were thwarted both by uncooperative winds and by the new Governor of Senegal, who refused our requests to lighten the load by jettisoning his precious provisions of quality European flour, cheeses, and wine. It was proposed then that a raft be built and that, should the Medusa be lost, the crew would be towed safely back to shore by our officers, who would take the barges and the longboats.

As one of the ship's engineers, I oversaw the construction of the accursed raft. A first foundation was composed of the top masts of the frigate. These different pieces were joined together by our strongest ropes. Four other masts were joined two-by-two at the centre of the machine creating flexibility without sacrificing much-needed solidity. The rest of this first tranche was made of nailed boards and the same material formed a kind of parapet around the perimeter of the raft, which would have been of great service to us had we built it higher. The raft was made still more solid by use of long planks of wood, which were placed across the foundation and lashed together with strong rope and cord. When it was finished the raft measured at least twenty metres from one extremity to the other and was about seven in breadth.

After three days suspended between the unmoving rocks and the constant trauma of the elements, the inflexible Medusa finally broke. Water flooded the keel at an alarming rate and reluctantly we abandoned ship. First the governor, the captain, and the other officers embarked upon their barges and lifeboats taking with them the few women and children who had taken part in the expedition. The soldiers and sailors remaining—a tally of around one hundred and fifty men—were forced to climb down onto the raft as it danced a ferocious tarantella upon the waves. Quickly we were forced to confront a crucial flaw overlooked in our plan. The raft's surface proved just large enough to host us all upon it; however, no one had truly considered the sheer weight of human cargo it would be attempting to carry. Saltwater began pouring over the shallow parapet when just thirty souls were aboard. Each hesitant passenger pushed the craft further and further below sea level until around seventy of us stood aboard, engulfed to our knees, with around a hundred scared faces looking down from the deck of the sinking frigate.

There was no time to execute an alternative plan, and we had no means of preventing the sea from spoiling our provisions—for all were immediately ruined but the water-tight wine casks. The captain gave command of the raft to an aspirant of the first class by the name of Lieutenant Coudin, who had some days earlier suffered a severe laceration on the fore part of his right leg while exploring the Isle of Aix. The lieutenant climbed dutifully onto the raft, though the biting pain of sea water flooding into his open wounds robbed him of his composure, causing him to spasm and shriek in agony.

Around twenty stragglers remained on the Medusa when the forward order was issued, tarrying tentatively between two terrible fates. Some jumped into the waters and swam after the departing flotilla—and we welcomed them aboard our raft, for we had not yet jettisoned our civility along with our useless supplies. The few that stayed on the Medusa were likely the first of us to die. Embracing oblivion, they drank deeply from the wine casks atop the slow-doomed deck, grateful for the chance to surrender their lucidity as they waved farewell.

*

I begged the artist's pardon for fainting in the studio and gave assurances that, given time, I would manage to reconcile myself with the presence of a raft. Géricault waved the apology aside and vowed to exercise the patience of a saint until the labour was complete. We agreed to spend two days per week with him, furnishing the developing work with every detail of incident and mood.

"I have been working with great zeal and application, often drawing long into the night," Géricault informed us upon our next visit to the studio. "There is now not an angle from which I cannot accurately depict our raft." He presented a series of good-quality sketches on his easel as he addressed us. "All the while I have been contemplating which moment is best able to capture the true essence of the story. In the first version recorded in the public papers you described how the original plan failed. It was reported that the tow ropes were stretched so tightly between the longboats and the raft that the tension coupled with the constant impact of the waves broke them."

"A lie," countered Mr Savigny at once, "a sequence of deplorable revisions made by perjurious cowards."

"We submitted our full testimony to the ministry the moment we reached Paris," I explained to the artist. "The version that was printed shortly afterwards bore our names, but our words had been much changed by the censors."

"What version would you tell me now?" Géricault asked.

His expression was occupied by a singular earnestness, and he spoke in a soft voice that made him seem quite considered and quietly courteous. I felt as if we could trust him to be receptive to the truth.

"We were still in the process of building the raft even as our ramshackle armada began to inch slowly out into the open water," I replied. "Our progress was immeasurably slow and arduous. Stacked vertically beneath the burning sun, those upon the raft were sent crashing into each other as the swelling ocean cast waves at us and pulled the tow ropes tight. The officers in the longboats were attempting to deliver masts and sails taken from the sinking Medusa so that we might use the force of the wind to aid our movement."

"I was positioned at an edge close to the officer's boats," Mr Savigny interjected, "and although initially we were grateful for the assistance, we could not help but notice that the officer's boats could have each quite comfortably accommodated several more of us. And Sir, the sight of sanctuary squandered tears at the souls of desperate men. We begged for the refuge of just some of our number. When they refused our pleas, we cursed them and some of the men reached for their weapons. The cowardly officers let loose their tow ropes and swiftly rowed away. I recall one of them appealing to the common decency of his comrades, imploring them to turn back to retrieve the ropes and to resume the escort." I might have witnessed Mr Savigny giving this account a hundred times since our rescue, and yet still his voice began to crack. "They did not. And as the waves crashed and fell with indifferent fury upon our wretched fleet, the other officers piloting the other boats also began to sever or drop their connections with the raft, until, at last, the air filled with a disbelieving refrain. We *forsake them!*—our officers cried—*we forsake them!*"

"The false story published in the papers was plausible and very persuasive," I said, "so much so that the officers whose axes had cast us adrift used it to defend themselves in court."

"We must have been like ghosts to them," remarked Mr Savigny, "furious revenants, returned from the water to wreak vengeance upon the duplicitous dogs."

"Sirs, I have no reason to disbelieve you," Géricault said eventually. "I believe too that this would be the most incendiary image we could paint. It will shock and forever shame those who have done so grave an injustice to you both—we *must* paint it. We shall position you at the front, Mr Savigny," the artist said, taking up a position on the edge of the replica raft. "Sinking to your knees in horror, your arms outstretched, like so." He held his palms open and upwards, as if he were beseeching the heavens. "And you, Mr Corréard, you will be standing behind, your arm reaching out in a manner that will recall the great David's Horatii. The other models we shall position similarly, or perhaps some shall be turning away in disgust and fear."

"Sir, at that moment there was barely room enough to stand, let alone fall to their knees or turn in disgust," observed Mr Savigny.

In the quiet safety of the studio those words must have seemed almost outlandish to the artist who scanned the vast dimensions of the empty replica.

"There were one hundred and fifty of us still when the ropes were cut." I reminded him.

"I cannot possibly paint so many figures!" Géricault exclaimed, "and how will I show any of the raft?"

"The raft would not be at all visible at that moment, sir. We were at our heaviest weight for the first two days. The raft was submerged to the depths of around one metre, and we were in water up to the middle."

Géricault was muted by these words. Perhaps he was lamenting the many hours he had wasted in building a studio big enough to house the replica and learning to draw it; or perhaps he was envisioning the scene as we described it from God's perspective. From above, the moment would have been a peculiar maelstrom of torsos and faces emerging implausibly from the surf. The displeasure that rippled across the artist's face indicated that God must have deemed us a wretched and ridiculous spectacle—too impractical to elicit pity.

*

When next we visited the artist, we found that he had shaved his thick hair, leaving his head entirely bald like a monk. Inside his studio Géricault replaced the dandyish affectations he wore in his home with a dark smock worn over an old shirt and britches. From that point we were joined by thirteen other men hired to pose upon the replica, burly men wearing scant clothing chosen to display their muscular arms and backs.

We did not believe that these heroic and muscular men reflected us accurately, though Géricault ignored our reservations and insisted that he had chosen his models well.

"All those that suffer are heroes," he clarified, "for society purchases progress dearly with their pain." After much deliberation he had decided against abandonment as the theme for the work and wondered instead if wrath lay at the heart of our story. "No man—no reasonable man—would condemn your mutiny following such betrayal," he insisted. "Your ship must have been named by a poet. In the stories, Medusa was once a beautiful priestess. Her beauty caught the eye of the sea God Poseidon one day as she walked beside the shore, and he arose from the waves to ravish her. Athena, the Goddess she served, cursed her for this loss of purity and transformed her into a terrifying Gorgon. In this monstrous form Medusa stands for the wrath of the victim—*your* wrath following the cutting of your tow ropes."

"Sir, at that time we were numb to wrath," Mr Savigny began, and annoyance flickered across the artist's face as his hypothesis was contradicted. "Your supposition is entirely reasonable of course; but reason does not govern the hearts of those forced to endure such ordeals as these."

"Besides which, there were some officers among us—including Lieutenant Coudin," I added, "and, initially, all aboard the raft shared solidarity, for officers, soldiers, and civilians had all been forsaken together and would live and die the same. Yet a violent storm visited us on the first night, sending torrents of water to buffet the raft from every angle, pelting us from above and surging up from below. The raft was thrown erratically by the storm and several men were thrown screaming into the frenzied pitch that thrashed against our every side. The edges of the raft were all but impossible to discern in the darkness and so—ignoring all appeals for calm—the men panicked, pushing through each other to retreat to the centre. Our fraternity vanished in the tumult, along with any sense of order. I waded through the confusion as best I could. Next to me, one man called out for assistance. His feet had gotten entangled between the slats, and he required assistance. I located the man, though a great wave hit us before I could pull him loose, and we were sent tumbling onto our backs amidst froth and throes. I was able to pull myself upright once again, but the poor unfortunate soul had drowned beneath the crush. Dumb fortune led me to a mast pole, and I clung tightly to it throughout the storm and beseeched the heavens for respite and for mercy."

Géricault directed us around the replica raft as I spoke, arranging his models in the foreground as he experimented with several ideas. Swiftly he rejected them all.

"Respite came with the daybreak," I continued, "though the sun brought no mercy with it. The storm had passed, but we remained alone and mired in the ocean without oars, rudders, charts, or compass and we could neither determine our course of travel nor our place on the map. Ten or twelve men had died trapped between the pieces of our raft. Several others had been taken by the sea. Those that survived were half submerged in water and half burning beneath the sun. There was no rest to be found beneath the fervid sky, the water prevented us from sleeping, and when the men urinated, defecated, or vomited due to sunstroke, they did so in the water they stood in."

"Every fear of thirst and famine quickly arose within our imagination," said Mr Savigny, "yet the only food with us were several barrels of biscuit that the sea had turned into a salted paste. That morning we mixed the biscuit-paste with a little wine and distributed it to the men." Géricault looked quietly repulsed by the thought. "This was our first meal together on the raft—and it was the best we would have."

"Many of the soldiers cherished thoughts of vengeance upon the officers who had so basely abandoned us, and in vain they voiced a thousand violent fantasies. Others were sure that we would soon spy sails coming over the horizon for our rescue, or that we would see the coast once again. These voices lost their certainty as the day drifted in the boundless blue. As dusk approached one soldier became convinced that we would all soon die. He declared his intention to end his life on his own terms and was soon joined by two other men. These three bade farewell to their friends and comrades at the raft's edge before closing their eyes and falling backwards into the waves. Perhaps, given all that followed, one might recognise the wisdom of that decision. The first storm was eclipsed in ferocity by a second that raged during the subsequent night. Precipitous waves reared and smashed against the raft, threatening to capsize the crowded vessel and feed the ocean with every soul onboard. Even I, who had been involved in the construction of the raft and knew it to be solid, could not be certain that it would withstand so much tension and weight."

"Perhaps these storms might have forced the officers to abandon the towing of the raft," Géricault reflected, somewhat thoughtlessly aloud.

"Perhaps, they would have," Mr Savigny spat, "but at least then we should have had only the elements to accuse!"

"Lieutenant Coudin and his officers took the centre," I said quickly, lest Mr Savigny's temper flare further. "They called out to the men surrounding them to run from one side to the other to counterbalance the sections of the raft raised up by the sea. Death never felt closer. The dread words of the soldier who had elected to take his own life must have rung in the ears of other men during that second storm, for certainly they did in mine. Some of the men were possessed by terror. They fell into a destructive hysteria that compelled them to begin cutting at the ropes holding the raft together. This faction rallied behind a colossal Asiatic man with long matted hair, who commenced to roaring wordlessly like a cornered bear. The Asiatic giant took up an axe and swung it wildly at those in his way, overthrowing several men from the raft and when an officer commanded him to stop, the giant killed him outright with a single savage blow to the skull. It was Lieutenant Coudin who saved us all then. He rallied his remaining soldiers and ordered them to stop the sabotage by any means necessary. Anguished and horrified cries soon mingled with gunshots and the sound of sabres slashing and clattering in the dark as combat ensued."

"How could anyone discern friend from foe?" asked Géricault.

"We couldn't," said Mr Savigny, "and so, to survive the night, Mr Corréard assembled the workers and civilians on the front of the raft and raised a wall of bayonets and sabres, forbidding us to engage anyone unless they attacked first. The mutineers fell upon us in several waves—fighting like madmen as they demanded the head of captain Hugues Duroy de Chaumareys, refusing to hear or believe that he was not among us. Some of our adversaries were without arms and still they fought—biting and clawing at us like rabid beasts. I witnessed one man tear open the throat of another with his teeth, and a companion being beaten to death by the mutineers who used the butts of carbine rifles. The giant was eventually brought down when a rifle shot tore through his face. I was bitten in the heel by a man I presumed dead— he bit right through skin and sinew—and again he bit my shoulder. My right arm was stabbed through with a Genoese knife, rendering it useless for some weeks afterwards. One of the loyal workmen informed Mr Corréard that a young comrade, named Dominique, had joined the mutineers and had just been thrown into the sea. Forgetting the treachery of the man, Mr Corréard threw himself into the sea after him, risking his own life to save his erstwhile friend. Fortune prevailed, and Mr Corréard not only located the man, but was also able to drag him back aboard the raft.

"You see," Géricault interjected, "your actions are worthy of the bravest of heroes."

"There was no valour and no honour to be found on Medusa's raft," I reflected, "merely chaos. Dominique seized a blade and re-joined the mutineers the moment he recovered his strength. I saw him ran through with a bayonet when he resumed hostilities with the men who had just saved his life. When the fighting finally finished the brutal legacy of the night was illuminated by the dolorous silver of the moon. Our complement of one hundred fifty men had been reduced to around sixty. Several of our officers and many good men were dead. The prone bodies of the slain floated in the shallow water still covering the raft, their black blood calling to the sharks who swam in our wake."

Each working lunchtime the artist took us into his garden. His retainers would prepare a great buffet and arrange the feast on a wooden table painted pale blue that had been placed beneath a blossoming cherry tree. Most days there were cheeses and fashionable crusty breads that were baked to look like batons. There were cold cuts of ham, hard-boiled eggs, dressed leaves, buttered potatoes, and sometimes hot stews of hare and rabbit. Mounds of fruit were assembled, as were platters of custard pies, jam tarts, and cinnamon pastries. The jugs of water they brought from the kitchen were always cool and garnished with mint leaves and strawberries. We would take our plates and glasses onto the lawn and the models would eat with great delight. Géricault rarely ate anything himself. The cooks proudly produced a whole salmon one hot afternoon, baked with lemon and garlic. The smell of the dish made me acutely nauseous. I tried to talk to the artist and request that the fish be removed from the table, but the lemon scent stuck to the back of my throat, and I collapsed to heave and spit bile in the grass.

*

The weeks became months and still Géricault had not discovered the true meaning of suffering. His mania manifested in a carpet of sketches that covered his studio floor, showing thousands of muscular men battling and pleading theatrically across a hundred rafts. He looked gaunt and tired, as if the endeavour was beginning to stretch him. His physical condition looked all the worse when he was surrounded by the brawny surrogates that he had chosen to model for us—indeed, if anyone at all inside that studio resembled us in the moment of survival, it was him.

The foetid stench of death permeated the hot and stifling room, turning each painstaking moment of the labour into a new test of our endurance. The artist's unflinching commitment to fidelity had compelled him to slowly transform his studio into an abattoir, and he filled the room with human limbs and a severed head borrowed from the morgue, all so that he could immerse himself within every sensation of miasma and rot.

"Sirs," the artist began, his unease palpable, "sirs, I must ask—is there any part of your narrative that you would prohibit the use of?"

"How can we tell the truth of our story if we prohibit parts of the narrative?" I asked.

"Because…" he started before allowing silence to insinuate. We both knew what he was tacitly referencing of course, yet neither of us chose to liberate him from his discomfort. "…because the truth is less flattering in some moments than in others."

"Flattery neither concerns nor interests us," replied Mr Savigny.

"I do not sit in judgement," Géricault insisted as his face began to crimson, "I am simply content to exclude the more sensitive rumours, should you wish to shield the sensibilities of the public."

"Those sensitive rumours are facts, and they are known already," replied Mr Savigny.

"These rumours—these facts—are indeed known," replied Géricault hastily, "but knowing is quite different from understanding. There will be many who will say that they would rather have died than survive in the manner that you did. I have no wish to shame you."

"There is no shame in living," declared Mr Savigny. "It is easy for the innocent to stand resplendent in purity when they have not felt the torments of an endless hunger consuming their entrails."

"By our third day we were reduced to eating our belts, our scabbards, and cartouches," I added. "We suffered a raging thirst that could not be quenched by seawater and so we urinated into tin cups and began drinking it—it thickened in the intense heat and developed an intensely acrid flavour. Some men fashioned hooks from spare sabres and fished inefficaciously for sharks. I even witnessed one man weeping as he tried to consume his own excrement—though he found that he was unable to do so. As the sun rose upon the fourth morning, we saw that ten or twelve of our companions had expired during the night. The sight of their lifeless bodies stretched out across the rail induced a deep despair within us, forcing us all to reflect upon our diminishing vitality and the inexorable conclusion that soon the Atlantic Ocean would host a silent raft of bobbing corpses."

"The first flesh was eaten only by a reluctant few," said Mr Savigny. "Those men harvested the accursed amenity to a chorus of revulsion and outrage. Most among us refused it at first; and yet, when it became clear that those who ate the dead were gaining strength and nourishment, our options became quite clear—live and eat or expire and be eaten."

"The shame is not ours," I insisted. "When we were finally taken to Senegal some among our compatriots there greeted us with fear and revulsion, knowing or suspecting some of what we had done to survive. Yet I was not afraid to meet the gaze of those with disgust in their eyes, and I prayed that those who spoke in appalled whispers would choke on their judgements. Where shame exists it exists because of those who appointed so incompetent a captain to lead us, and with the dishonourable cowards who abandoned us to suffer these disasters and degradations."

"I should not have even been aboard the raft," Mr Savigny laughed bitterly, "I was allotted a place on one of the longboats, but I was certain that we would be towed safely back to shore, and I felt duty-bound to my colleagues aboard the raft. I could not help but reflect upon this as circumstances forced me to break the great taboo."

The artist began to position the models for a new composition. He placed most of them around the mast pole of the replica. Two lay slain in the foreground. At the centre, one man stood over another slicing his throat while both stared outwards to meet the viewer's gaze. Beside them another man knelt, lifting the arm of a dead man close to his face, poised as if he were about to tear into the meat like a savage dog. We told him that this was not the way we consumed our comrades. We cut strips from their bodies and cured them in the blazing heat of the sun, disguising the flavour with the last of our scant supplies—the juice of lemons and thin slices of garlic—but the artist did not want to hear us.

"Sirs, there are several kinds of truth," Géricault explained, "there is God's truth, and there is the artist's truth. We are

47

searching for that singular image capable of telling the whole story. We wish to create an icon to ignite the ire of a nation and sear itself indelibly within the public imagination!"

The artist sketched the scene in full and we contemplated the image. To my mind it seemed more a melodramatic tableau than *an icon to ignite the ire of a nation*. Perhaps Géricault concurred with my silent appraisal, for he shot to his feet and declared the project a failure amidst an eruption of curses and—stopping only to kick his easel to the floor—stormed out from his studio, vowing never to return.

*

Summer arrived and peaked without further word or invitation from the artist. Mr Savigny and I eventually concluded that he was keeping to his impassioned words and had discarded the project. The disappointment we felt was somewhat tempered by a string of donations from several sympathetic parties. These donations enabled us to purchase a printing press, granting us another means to tell our story free of the censors. We moved into the press, located at 258 Palais Royal, and named it *The Sinking Medusa*. Just as soon as we had settled into our new office, we sent a letter back to Géricault, thanking him sincerely for his efforts and requesting one of his old sketches for use as a sign.

The reply came quickly with a frantic knocking at the door of our new press. Géricault had crossed town, and with a triumphant air he removed a rolled canvas from his carriage and brought it into our office.

"Sirs," Géricault began, "forgive my many frustrations and my long silence. Our project has not been in vain after all, it merely needed a little rejuvenation. I remained certain that our problem could be answered and that the meaning could be found. I have immersed myself for many hours in books and galleries until finally I recognised the elusive solution to our problems in the work of the Old Masters—I just needed to see with fresh eyes! Time and time again they demonstrated that the adept artist expresses their theme through composition. Sirs, I needed only to discover our structure and the meaning would surely follow."

He unfurled the canvas he bore, revealing a muddy-brown sketch depicting an incident we had once described to him. The incident occurred on our thirteenth day aboard the raft as the long ordeal was nearing its end. The sketch showed the raft emerging from the water, a tattered sail bending backwards as the choppy motion of the waves raised the front. On the left, an older sailor sat, his head in his hands, as he mourned a prone man resting between his legs. A dead man lay next to those figures, clutching at white cloth. Ten other survivors were clustered together looking towards a ship, one of our sister ships, the Argus, that had appeared. It had been the master gunner of the frigate who had first spotted the ship. *Saved!*—he had rasped—*see the brig upon us!* Even those of us robbed of all ability to stand due to the accumulative toll of our wounds and exhaustion had then crawled to the front section of the raft that we might confirm the realness of the vision. When all the men agreed that we were, in actuality, looking at a ship, we embraced each other and wept with joy. Strength found us then. We pulled ourselves to our feet, exalting and waving whatever material we found near to hand in the direction of the brig.

"Do you see how the work is staged?" Géricault asked expectantly. "Starting from the point of despair and death on the left, we read the image like text, moving left to right until we rise in a crescendo of hope."

We paused to consider his words.

"Do you believe that is the true meaning of suffering—hope?" asked Mr Savigny.

"Sir, you once told me that those on Medusa's raft were numb to wrath, but surely hope was with you, impelling and sustaining all who survived. And when the crew of the Argus returned for you, did they not do so in hope?" asked the artist, his confidence visibly faltering in the face of such a perfunctory reception. "Hope is our greatest virtue and our deliverance—is this not the truth that we were seeking?"

"Hope had indeed been with us on the raft," I said, feeling my head gently shake, "though it had felt neither like our greatest virtue, nor our deliverance. Hope had conspired with sunstroke and dehydration to mock us, creating false visions of dry land or the sails of rescue boats approaching over the horizon. Hope was a white butterfly that flew around the raft and settled upon our sail, causing the men to rejoice at the sight—as if they believed merciful God was present within those pale wings, or that the tiny creature might be somehow directing us back towards dry land—yet, when the butterfly flew away, neither land nor God had materialised. When our ever-dwindling supplies ran critically low, it was our desire to live that gave voice to the most horrific of thoughts," I continued, finding myself unable to swallow the sudden outburst, "and if you were paying close heed to our number, you might have counted that we were then more than the fifteen men found by the Argus. The others had been pushed beyond any reasonable chance of survival. These most wretched and broken comrades may have consumed thirty or forty bottles of wine before expiring—bottles of inestimable value to the healthier among us. We debated the unthinkable and voted almost unanimously to execute it. Three of your heroes then took it upon themselves to push the weakest of us into the sea while the rest of us turned aside our faces and wept—and we wept both for the unjust ends of our fellows, and for our own souls which might yet be found but were quite beyond saving."

For the first time it seemed as if Géricault had heard my words and understood why his more heroic interpretations were so objectionable to us. The truth, when discovered, is too ugly a thing to paint. Fifteen men survived the ordeal, sunken hollow-eyed shades, long bearded and naked, our emaciated bodies scorched by the relentless sun. We were the wild faces of tragedy, curled up beneath the drying morsels of human flesh that hung from the masts. The artist, with all his learning, his poetics and aesthetics, had constructed little more than a romantic proxy, designed to inspire feelings that a story such as ours does not naturally inspire. The arrival of mutineers, cannibals, and murderers had inspired horror in our compatriots when we finally reached Senegal—and whatever else those feelings were, they were at least honest. In Senegal we were advised to outcast ourselves from France and travel to London where our misfortunes would have been treated like a victory of sorts, and where we might have wanted for nothing. We ignored this advice and returned to Paris, where the Minister for the Marine informed us that we had set sail of our own free will and were therefore owed no apology and no reparations, and where our first account of the voyage was stolen, doctored, and printed beneath our names.

"The moment you have painted was not the moment of our rescue," reflected Mr Savigny. "The first time we spied the

Argus, the brig was further away, and none among us could say for certain which direction it was travelling. We watched and hollered through cupped hands until the ship disappeared over the horizon. From ecstatic relief we fell into agony and despair, and we collapsed, one by one, to await death. Hope had been every bit as futile as our wrath had been. Emotions have no value for the powerless. That is what the raft taught me about suffering."

"Then, sirs, I believe our work needs just one alteration," said Géricault after some consideration.

"And what alteration would that be?" queried Mr Savigny.

"The alteration I suggest is a matter of proportion. In some way, we are all of us with you on that fateful raft. Nothing you have told me has ever diminished our *need* for hope. If anything, I believe that need should be magnified even further. However, the salvation we strive towards is far, far in the distance. Unobtainable. Little more than a shrinking speck. The human spirit endures—forever suspended between hope and despair, drifting into the uncertain future."

Under Shimmering Constellations

A falling plate remains complete for only for as long as it is in motion. Each moment that the fall is prolonged provides a precious respite before it shatters. In principle, should someone discover a miraculous method of prolonging the fall indefinitely, the hapless plate could defy its fate.

Kee prolongs her fall through industry. She defies despair by occupying both her mind and her hands. This afternoon she is making a broth from chicken bones and cabbage leaves. The pungent concoction bubbles now on top of the stove. She snaps from her reverie and walks to the window to watch Johannes and Vincent at play.

Her son is hiding behind the apple tree and is doing it very poorly, half of his body juts out visibly beyond the trunk—not only that, but he is also moving, convulsing with nerves and laughter. Vincent roams the garden, pretending he cannot see the boy. He searches ineffectively this way and that. He takes in the potato patch and the chicken coop despite the obvious futility of both endeavours. He scans the distant horizon with theatrical aplomb, taking in just about every conceivable location in the garden except for the most obvious one. Johannes is greatly amused. Two full decades separate the pair, and yet at this moment they are just like children playing together.

Vincent meanders past an apple tree, seemingly on his way to inspect the distant cowshed. This farcical ruse proves one too many, Johannes breaks cover—screaming wildly—and leaps onto Vincent's narrow back.

The sight almost forces a smile onto Kee's lips. It is the first time her mouth has come close to forming a smile in several months. Shame courses instantly through her. She is still wearing black—to smile would be *profoundly* incongruous.

Kee steps away from the window and looks for other chores to satisfy her restless fingers. The bread needs to be unwrapped and taken through to the dining table and there is butter in the pantry and milk to drink. She takes two bowls from her cupboard and places them on the table. She starts back to the kitchen before a thought occurs to her—although she cannot recall seeing Vincent eating a meal in many months, she should at least offer him lunch. She takes a third bowl from the cupboard and places it on the dining table.

When Kee returns to the kitchen, Vincent is standing in the hallway door with wet patches across his shoulders. Kee can hear it now, a burst of rain that has arrived rudely and without forewarning.

"Where is Johannes?" she asks instinctively.

"The rain started. I sent him to his room to practise his letters," Vincent replies tentatively. Vincent is a voracious reader. He reads not only the Bible but also poetry and novels. He speaks and writes fluently in five languages. With Vincent's help, Johannes can now draw the entire alphabet and recite lengthy passages of Scripture. "Was that right of me?" he continues, "or would you like me to call him back down?"

He seems nervous. He always seems nervous. He twitches in the doorway, moving from one pose to another, as if ease forever eludes him.

"No. It is good for him to practise. Thank you."

Vincent's face breaks into a bashful smile before her gratitude, and the blood rushes to his cheeks. He is a strange man. Everyone in their village says as much. He walks the streets barefooted, wearing dirty clothing, clutching his ragged Bible, and preaching—always preaching. He had been sent away to Borinage last year. Borinage had quickly returned him. Rumours were that he had proved too zealous in both belief and action even for the evangelicals. However, despite his eccentricities, Vincent is generosity itself—a man who treats time and possessions solely as means for charity.

"Will you eat with us this afternoon?" Kee asks.

In truth, she is indifferent to his answer. Like so many others, she does not truly relish time spent around such an intense presence. Yet Vincent has done much for her and her son since Christoffel's passing, so much that she cannot begrudge him their company. He stares back at her in silence, almost as if he is trying to ascertain the honesty of her offer. Kee feels herself blushing slightly, wondering if her mind is being read. He says nothing. "Forgive me," Kee continues, correcting herself. "I meant to say, I *want* you to eat with us. You are skin and bones! Please, you are most welcome, stay, and eat a good, hot meal."

"You are blushing," Vincent declares, moving tentatively towards her.

Now it is Kee's turn for silence. Her blushes emanate from her struggle against the ingratitude of her thoughts, against the shame she feels in acknowledging just how much effort it takes to like the person trying hardest to help her and Johannes in their time of greatest need.

"Can it be?" he asks. "Do you feel it too?"

The question is unexpected.

"Do I feel what?"

Vincent removes his straw hat. He is staring into her eyes, unblinking. He is searching ineffectively once again, only this time in earnest. Kee is at a loss to know what Vincent might possibly be experiencing.

"What?" she queries, unable to endure the protracted silence.

"There," Vincent replies softly. "Want, love, the *desire* that lives between us."

Kee wonders if this is a poorly conceived joke, though Vincent rarely jokes. As always, he radiates sincerity, and real need. She can blush no more.

"Vincent…No…No, I am deeply fond of you. Sincerely grateful for everything you have done for us…" She falters.

He cocks his head slightly to one side. "I am fond of you also!" he says. He begins to look around her kitchen with inexplicable purpose. "Can you see it?" he asks forlornly. "That fondness. It is here, swirling and rippling, filling the room."

"Vincent. Must I…need I say why that…*that* is wrong?"

"You are not long-widowed," Vincent speaks in a voice cracked and wavering as he draws close. "You see only impropriety in a new love. Yet in love, you will—to your *amazement*—find God's force. That which compels us to action: feeling! God's love is the only true propriety."

He continues, though the particular of his lust wash over her like the spray of some miserable storm. He speaks of Christian duty, of the importance of family, and of his new passion for painting and drawing—of how work devoid of love can only ever be austere and joyless. He becomes almost frenzied, pressing until Kee loses patience and slaps him hard across his face.

"*Cousin!*" she demands in a raised voice, "have you lost your mind?"

"If my mind is lost, it is lost in thoughts of you...And love is the sweetest lunacy! Want has rendered me insensible. I am left to wallow in obsession, groping blindly through pink mist."

"Adulterer! Drunk! Incestuous degenerate!" Kee's accusations come with fresh blows, wild ones that are easily parried. "It is not God's love you feel. It is a bestial perversion—a carrion desire for a grieving relative—a lust to shame Gomorrah!"

Vincent looks confused. He steps back from Kee and her wrathful palms.

"Mother, why are you hitting Uncle Vincent?"

There is a note of fear in Johannes' voice—or if not fear, then at least alarm. Vincent turns his head to the boy and does his best to reassure him.

"Please do not be overly concerned, Johannes. I simply raised the possibility of moving into this house, to live with you both."

Vincent glances ruefully back at Kee.

She only wants him gone.

"Your mother is cold to the notion," he mutters in a voice soft and uncertain, "though perhaps, in time, she may thaw."

Vincent lingers in her kitchen. He is a different man to her now. Kee understands why he was unable to join the priesthood. She sees behind the veil of innocence to where a sinful heart resides. He does not seem to yet understand this of himself. He returns her attention with a dumbstruck expression, as if the rejection of his perversions had come as a genuine surprise. He retrieves his hat and makes his way out of the kitchen. He stops to rustle Johannes' thick hair and, for the first time, Kee feels uneasy about their contact. In this second, she knows there will be no more play between them, and no more tuition.

Vincent walks out of her house, moving quickly through her garden. He cannot look back. He takes the path outside, the one that leads out of Kee's garden and away from her home. It is a long and lonely path, one that will eventually take him through cypress groves and fields of radiant sunflowers, beneath liquid mountains, and under shimmering constellations.

Composition #5

The gallery was filled with the sharp odour of floor polish, and when the tourists and day-trippers flittered by in casual chattering cliques, there came fleeting fragrances of perfumes and colognes, or the chalk-and-coconut scent of suntan lotion.

I had landed a summer job as a Gallery Attendant at the newly opened Tate Modern and took to my duties at a leisurely pace. I would linger in air-conditioned corners and observe the monotonous circling of fat bumblebees that somehow wound their way inside, seemingly bored by their thwarted efforts to locate an exit. Or, with my black long-sleeved shirt clinging tightly to my back and beads of sweat trickling down my thigh in the stifling heat, I would walk among the milling visitors, eavesdropping on idle conversations and soaking in the vivacious enthusiasm of modern art's champions and the droll observations of the sceptics.

Largely I sided with the champions and grew to love many of the works within the collection. My favourites were a sequence of four pieces all created by the same artist. These gorgeous and radiant visions were set starkly against sterile white walls—symphonies of urgent colour that shimmered and danced with the viewer as they moved around the room. No other painter could have ever hoped to breathe more life and humanity into abstract imagery. Her canvases pulsated with such pure and tangible feeling that I came to view every stroke as an invitation to connect with her, an invitation sent from the brush of the artist directly into my soul, a welcome invasion of alien emotions that somehow synthesised with my own. In the quiet moments of the day I would stand, breathless before them, feeling my skin prickle, almost rushing off that deep sensation of connectivity. Perhaps I was imagining things, but when other people stood before them, I felt odd pangs of jealousy—as if the artist painted for me alone, and those unwitting interlopers were intruding upon a private conversation.

That fateful afternoon, one such woman stood obscuring my view of these beloved works to an intolerable degree— leaning in far too closely and lingering before them for far too long—when I noticed that she was ready to raise a camera. I tore myself forwards with a triumphant air, certain that our strict 'no photography' policy would encourage this irritating presence to finally move herself along.

I addressed her formally at first, straining for the most authoritative tone that a twenty-four-year-old gallery attendant could muster. The woman turned to answer, but seized by some conceited charm, I did not let her speak—asking her instead how she supposed the multi-millionaire artists of the Tate could possibly fill their swimming pools with Champagne if we did not make the postcards and other gaudy merchandise sold at the gift shop a necessary purchase.

"I don't love Champagne," she replied with a smile that suggested that she relished cutting through this absurd diatribe. "If anything, I'd swim in Barolo," she added, raising her camera, and ignoring my directive. "Though that does seem wasteful—not to mention sticky."

Her casual dismissal rendered me speechless. I looked back to the paintings and to the name written on the information cards beside them.

Abebi Oladele Isah. 1967 -

I may have adored her paintings but back then I knew nothing of the woman behind them. She had existed to me then only in scant and esoteric terms—a name, a birthdate, and four paintings mounted on a wall.

I looked back at the woman standing before me. She looked to be around the right age. She wore a sleeveless saffron dress with a headscarf of deep sapphire, and her pretty face was framed by beads and jewels. She looked confident, expensive, and extraordinary. She smiled playfully and winked, confirming that the penny should drop.

I was no longer able to meet her gaze. I apologised to the floor for my poor attempt at humour in a voice that was small, star-struck, and blathering. I should have walked away then and perhaps hidden in a cupboard until closing time, and yet I found myself lingering. When I finally found the courage to look up once more, she lowered her camera and turned to face me. She stared deep into my eyes, and I wished I could retract every stupid and facile word that I had uttered so far. Instead, I thanked her for bringing such beautiful art into the world.

"Do you mean that?" she asked eventually.

I wondered how many times in a lifetime a person would find themselves able to offer their admiration directly to their favourite artist. Hoping that my face did not betray my nerves, I told her, in all honesty, that I visited her works every single day I came to the Tate, that no one else could possibly appreciate her art the way I did, and that it felt as if, somehow, she and I shared a relationship already—one not yet consciously understood.

"But you didn't know who I am?" she asked, arching an eyebrow.

"I knew your name, nothing more," I replied. Here too, I was being honest. The gallery did not provide a likeness, and these were the days before smartphones, when all the information of the world did not live within a pocket. "I'm not obsessive," I giggled weakly, hoping that my insufficiencies as her fan could be masked with something that resembled nonchalance. "Besides—who cares about faces anyway? Surely, art and artists are completely different things."

"How little you know!" she laughed. "Well, you may not care about my face, but I think I like yours…I am going somewhere that makes the best Whiskey Sour in London. Come and join me as soon as you're free." She was already writing her phone number on the back of a business card as she asked.

I agreed to meet her, as if there could have been any other answer to give.

The remainder of that afternoon dragged. I swallowed all mention of the encounter before my colleagues. It was too unreal. Abebi Oladele Isah was one of the most famous, and wealthiest, painters in the country and now that I had seen her in the flesh, she also seemed to me almost preternatural in her self-assurance and beauty. Simply put, I had never met anyone like her in my young life.

In the final rotation of my shift, I read and re-read the information plaque situated beside her works:

Abebi Oladele Isah was born in Hackney, London, and studied at the Glasgow School of Art. Her degree exhibition was purchased by Charles Saatchi who supported her while she created six linked works for his gallery. The series, titled 'Joy,' (1989), won Isah the Turner prize aged just 22. Her paintings are Neo-Expressionist, blurring the line between representative and abstract art. For Isah, "Painting, like music, is a transpersonal dialogue. I aim straight for the heart. I would spiritualise our age."

*

She had given me a card with the words, 'The Owl—The London Speak-Easy,' printed in elegant gold type against a black background. The address was on the reverse. I walked the street two or three times in an increasing state of panic until finally I located a golden owl sketched against a black background sitting above a crooked arrow that pointed down a flight of stairs. I walked down into a small white room that contained nothing but a mechanical owl sitting on a perch with its back to the entrance. The bird shuddered into life, the cogs and motors quietly purring as it began rotating its head until it reached the spot where I was standing. The robot opened its eyes, and, with a juddering snap, it raised a wing to point towards an unassuming door on the right. I shook my head and, for the first time in my life, entered somewhere affluent, exclusive, and quite removed from the dim roar of the city outside.

The lounge was bathed in the light of a dozen red-tinged lamps that hung from a ceiling. The armchairs and couches seated only fabulously dressed people who talked and laughed quietly over a playlist of classic soul. The well-groomed staff greeted me with impeccable professionalism and smiled politely as I, a young man then, entered their luxurious and aspirational world wearing cheap clothing and carrying a tattered rucksack slung across my shoulder.

The grand bar was made of dark mahogany, the drinks behind it illuminated by red bulbs. Isah was sitting on a stool there, her finger working languid circles around the rim of her cocktail glass. She was engaged in conversation with a grinning barman with a sculpted moustache who was standing alert in a white shirt and a waistcoat of golden paisley. I almost lost my nerve there and then—my every instinct telling me to turn and quietly flee far away from her and her world—when the barman noticed my presence and invited me towards them with the sticky-warm welcome of judicious customer service.

Isah turned her head to follow the barman's greeting. "He showed up!" she exclaimed smiling, her white teeth shining in the half-light.

"No way!" laughed the barman. "This is your gallery guy?"

"He's heard everything," said Isah. "I told him about your little joke, and how horrified you looked when it backfired—we were sure that you wouldn't come."

I was thankful that the red light covered my blushes as the two of them laughed together like old friends. Isah pulled out the stool next to her and told me to get a drink. Seeing no beer taps, I scanned the shelves behind the barman and saw an array of expensive-looking whiskeys. I dithered, hoping to spot one moderately priced option among the bar's offerings.

"Do you have a house vodka?" I asked. The barman nodded. "Then I'll take one with lemonade."

"No—" Isah interjected, a pleasing expression flashing across her face that resembled something like moral outrage. "I did not bring you here—to The Owl—to drink cheap mixes. The

Owl serves *the* finest Whiskey Sour in London—and mine is what you can call an informed opinion on the matter."

She had clearly taken several drinks in the three hours or so since we had last spoken. She ordered two sours and told the barman to pour a double measure of Yamazaki for me, insisting that I catch her up. He nodded at the request and obliged her before melting into the background. I tipped back the whisky and held the liquid for a moment. To this day, I can still remember the clean quality, and the crisp, clear flavour. Quite simply, it was the best alcohol I have ever drunk, and I told her as much.

"It better be good," she laughed. "It's worth quite a few postcards at the Tate."

I stared at the empty glass, aghast, wondering just how much the double shot might have cost me.

"Relax," she insisted, "I invited you. I'm paying."

"Thank you," I replied. "Sorry—I should have savoured that more."

"Should you?" she shrugged. "Sometimes I think we are still the children of puritans—so apologetic about everything, so terrified we might accidentally enjoy life once in a while."

"It's not that," I insisted, "I just don't get to experience the finer things. I don't have much."

"Don't you? How old are you?"

"Twenty-four."

"And what do you think you have?"

"Right now, a room in a shared house and a salary that just about covers the month. Everything else fits into two suitcases."

"Girlfriend?"

I shook my head.

"Just checking," she said with a wink. "A boyfriend then? Children?"

"No—nothing," I said, a little laughter trickling through my pursed lips.

"Then it's a matter of perspective," she insisted. "Some would say you have everything worth having."

I disagreed with that perspective. Indeed, between thoughts of my menial job and the bedroom I rented in Peckham—a mouldy rectangle that was damp during winter—and the deep feelings of inadequacy I felt before her, I pushed for clarification.

"You have nothing that you could not walk out on tomorrow," she explained. "No ties and no responsibilities. You could pack your two suitcases tomorrow and follow any possibility that interests you. You can spend whole nights under the stars or fall in love a dozen times over with whoever you please. Young bodies absorb everything. They can endure a little discomfort. They are strong enough to survive a few indulgences. You have youth, freedom, and a pretty face too. Never, ever, undervalue these things—when they leave, they leave forever."

"It's easy for you to be philosophical," I replied, ignoring the baited compliments, "you're Abebi Oladele Isah."

"*The* Abebi Oladele Isah," she giggled, stressing her 'the' with mock-grandiosity. "And not so long ago, that meant absolutely nothing too."

"And now?"

"And now Abebi Oladele Isah has obligations. She has lots of work to do and expectations to meet. She has pressure, and headaches, and sometimes cannot sleep without a glass of wine or three. And she is allowed to look affectionately back on simpler times without being accused of hypocrisy."

I liked her face even more when she smiled.

She held my gaze, and my skin began to prickle once again.

"Yeah?" I said playfully, wondering how far I could push my luck. "Then how about we swap lives for a little while? I can swim in champagne on weekends, and you can remember the virtues of earning five-sixty an hour."

"Fuck off," she replied, snorting into her drink.

"See," I replied, "it's just empty talk."

"I worked hard to get where I am," she said, her smile softening a little. "Nothing was ever given to me."

"I believe you," I said, "I was joking, mainly."

"I know that. I don't take myself that seriously. Most people do. Pride is the original sin you know—it's what makes our world so ugly and dull." As she spoke, her hand brushed my thigh briefly before she pulled it away. "But...also, getting anywhere worth going requires sacrifice," she added slowly, her statements drifting incoherently on waves of inebriated logic. "And we must all suffer for our dreams and passions."

I didn't truly consider those words at the time—I was too busy wondering how my face looked when she was speaking, if I was managing to maintain a smile properly, or if I was blinking at natural intervals. The arrival of our cocktails offered me a welcome chance to focus elsewhere. The glasses were sparkling and heavy, and the pale brown liquid within was garnished with a cherry and sliced lemon. Abebi tipped back her drink and pushed the empty vessel back to the barman. She pointed too to my empty shot glass and, before I could make a feeble show of protest, another double measure was placed before me.

"You like art then?" she asked as I sipped at my cocktail.

"On a passing level. I'm no expert."

"Keep it that way. Our world is filled with experts, those brilliant people gifted with *exhaustive* insight. Personally, I am more interested to hear what a person feels than what they've learned, or which dead artists they think the living should be compared to—as if we wish to be an echo of someone else's music... Painting is expression beyond language, beyond culture. It is communication without prejudice. If you allow it, it can bypass everything that the tedious adore—all that dull history and dry theory—and establish a language of the heart." Her tone seemed almost forlorn, though if that were an effect of the drink, I could not tell. "Beauty," she contemplated softly aloud, "true beauty, ends where intellectual expression begins."

For someone uninterested in intellectual expression she seemed to be doing lots of it. I remember wondering how seriously she truly took herself and if she would be amused by my observation. Deciding quickly that she would not, I found myself simply repeating my words from earlier and telling her that I loved her work.

"I didn't invite you here for admiration" she snapped, refocusing her attention sharply on me, "I don't need a fan tonight."

"Then what do you want?" I began, momentarily hurt.

Isah knew the precise moment to say nothing. She stared directly into my eyes, patient until I understood that her gaze was an invitation to connect.

"Your face is pretty too," I said eventually.

We were kissing then, a kiss that was unlike any kiss that I had experienced before. Abebi Oladele Isah kissed exactly how she painted—urgently, ferociously, and demanding of my whole self.

That night we gave ourselves to each other in total mutual acquiescence, our hearts beating out a fevered duet. I felt no trace of nervousness around her. It was almost as if we were not strangers at all but familiar lovers, somehow reunited after an absence not consciously understood. Our mouths explored our interlocking bodies hungrily, my skin alive to her every touch. I moved with her, achieving near-perfect understanding, as we co-constructed a gorgeous vision of desire and need, breathlessly together.

When we lay next to each other she would look deeply into my face, stroking my cheeks and hair, her eyes burning with the same want and longing that I felt for her. I could not help myself then. I had to kiss her until her mouth prickled and came up in slight rashes where it rubbed against my stubble. The darkness crept through the window, turning our writhing forms into silhouettes. We were drunk already, but still she poured out glasses from a bottle of pink wine during our tired lulls. I vaguely recall trying to tell her which of her works in the Tate was my favourite. She laughed at such trifling talk and returned us quickly to our wild states, kissing and licking every bit of each other's bodies, each taking turns to lead the dance.

The rain began to pelt against her Knightsbridge penthouse with an almost biblical ferocity. We held each other close and watched the water awhile, listening to the drain pipes gurgling and the rooftops playing out a symphony of storm, punctuated by rolling thunder and flashes of lightning. When the air in the room finally cooled, she raised the bedsheets up from the floor to cover our legs. I pulled her close and kissed her again. Finding a source of energy denied to dispassion, I moved my mouth down her body until our exhausted bodies were ready one last time. She closed her eyes and urged me to listen to the rain falling between her soft stuttering gasps of breath.

*

I woke in half-light and found the bed beside me empty. When I remembered where I was and how I had got there, it seemed like some strange fantasy.

I fumbled through the gloom until I heard muffled laughter coming down the corridor from behind a closed door. Of all the memories of that first day, blurred as they are by time and by alcohol, I recall vividly the strange qualities of her laughter that morning—it wasn't a happy sound, it was more an expression of maniacal energy, a high-pitched eruption almost like a boiling kettle. In truth, it was almost unpleasant, and I did not like it one bit.

Behind the door was a large room with a hard wooden floor and white walls, much like a gallery. Canvasses and paper were strewn everywhere. Sketches and drafts. Lamps and models. Tubes of paints and brushes. Isah was inside, still drinking and slurring self-affirmations aloud as her brush caressed purple squares onto the canvas. She had not noticed me. When I cleared my throat she jumped, as if she had completely forgotten that anyone else was in her flat.

"You can't be here!" she shouted, "get out at once."

I put up my hands and backed out immediately. Returning to her bedroom, I decided to leave. Throwing on my clothes, I drank greedily from the tap of her ensuite sink and churned some minted mouthwash. When I stepped back inside the bedroom, she was waiting in the doorway.

"I couldn't sleep," she explained, "I was lying in bed so alive with feeling that I had to work. That's my studio—I didn't mean to snap, but no one else can ever be in there."

"Understood," I replied. "Look, I better get moving."

"I can think of a better idea," she replied, reclining playfully against the doorframe.

"I bet you can, but I'm due back at work this morning."

She furrowed her brows. "No," she said, her tone flat and irrefutable. "No, that can't happen."

I was laughing then, an awkward giggle that was neither self-assured nor nervous but somewhere in-between. I said that I was more than willing to return, but that I had to work to make rent.

"No, you don't," she replied. "That's a choice. You could also choose to quit everything else and stay here instead." I remember searching for sarcasm in her expression and finding none. In time, I would learn that Isah might be many things, but disingenuous was never one of them.

"That's…" I began, losing the confidence to finish the thought with a word such as *mad* or *stupid*. "You want me to just quit my job and move in with you? That's…too much to ask. I can't do that."

"You're not asking anything. We agreed last night that you are free and untethered, that means you can choose whatever options are available to you. I am making this option available to you."

"Oh, I get it—you're still drunk."

"I'm not drunk, and you're not leaving."

She was right of course. Two options were available to me. I could either spend my day in the galleries of the Tate, preventing tourists from taking photographs and directing them towards the toilets, or I could stay in bed with a beautiful and brilliant woman with enough money to make anything we desired a reality. I agreed to stay with her, as if there was any other answer to give.

"You must understand why I want you here," Isah began as she sat us on the bed. "I've been blocked. I haven't painted anything worth showing in a long time… I've used different materials, I've rented news spaces, painted drunk, painted stoned, anything to catch myself out as it were. Nothing was working." She opened her hands out as she spoke, looking at them as if she imagined that the problem might have been physical. "Somewhere in all the money and the fame, I think I lost my soul. It's as if the world has created some new kind of success—one that is vulgar, empty, and void…The easier the success became, the less I felt like an artist. Instead, I felt like a well-paid employee of a global money-laundering scheme." She looked quite different as she spoke those words, she seemed almost vulnerable, scared even. "That's why I was in the Tate yesterday. I was looking for that *thing* that used to be mine alone. And then I met you and everything felt uncomplicated and good. I felt my confidence returning—I know I can paint again. So—you must stay, the money is nothing. Nothing matters but the painting."

I remember failing to keep a straight face as I phoned my manager at the Tate and telling her that I was quitting the day job to become a kept mistress. I clowned around on her bed sheets afterwards, posing naked on her bed in homage to Titian's Venus—or perhaps I was thinking then of Kate Winslet—and declaring myself her muse. I remember Isah pushing me back into her bed and how we made love before we drifted off to sleep contentedly in each other's arms. I remember taking the Tube to Peckham later that day to pack my belongings and load them into a taxi back to Knightsbridge. I remember all the joyful details of that day, the fun and excitement of embarking on some great adventure into the unknown, like an unwitting passenger, waving a gleeful farewell to the shore as they departed on some doomed expedition.

*

What can I tell you about our time together? Well, it was good for us both, for a while at least. The first months passed by in a sensuous and exuberant blur. I was never happier. I lived a life of borrowed grandeur. Her flat was enormous, her living room was filled with interesting and beautiful things—ceramics, statues, paintings, drawings, and photographs—made mostly by Isah and her many friends in the art world.

Three photographs took pride of place on her mantelpiece. On the left side, a twenty-two-year-old woman in white maxi dress nervously collected the Turner Prize. Next to it the middle image showed her three years older, still slightly wide-eyed as she collected the Roswitha Haffmann—but smiling this time and holding the award high in triumph. By the time she received the Wolfgang Hahn prize at 26 she looked much more like the Isah I knew, comfortable on stage in all her eye-catching vibrancy. I adored those images; between them they showed a process of glorious self-actualisation evolving through artistic expression and success.

Abebi left me a credit card for spending money. I used it to buy myself a silk dressing gown and ensured that her kitchen was forever filled with fine wines and spirits. I ordered us takeout whenever we grew hungry, or else we lived off bowls of fruit, frozen pastries, and coffee. Almost nightly I filled a bathtub almost large enough to swim in. By day, we drank cocktails, and discussed her work. She told me, for example, that the mutable and dynamic qualities of her canvases were achieved through careful layering of gloss and matte paints— an exhausting technique, she assured, one that demanded much time, energy, and concentration to achieve.

One morning I awoke to find her lying beside me and staring into my eyes.

"I don't do portraits," she said. "But since you're so pretty, I'll draw you."

I was deeply honoured. She had me sit upright in her bed, the sheets cascading casually from my shoulders, my hair wild and long as it was back then. She sat at the end of the mattress with drawing paper and graphite, completely lost in focus.

"Every passing moment takes a little more from us," she reflected as she worked. "Art preserves the fragile and fleeting things. It immortalises everything that was beautiful in our best moments—you must promise me that you will never sell this drawing."

When she revealed the finished image, I nearly cried—it was gorgeous, intimate, and deeply familiar. I could see the different tones and textures of flesh and hair. I could make out the moisture on my lips and eyes. I could see it moving. I could hear the phantom sound of breathing emerging from the lips of my two-dimensional duplicate. I had given myself completely to Abebi, and there in my hand was the combination of my likeness and her talent—proof of our synthesis.

Things never felt normal—how could they ever feel normal? We lived in a vast shrine to her talent, and the world that she knew outside revered her. Believe me, such lovers subsume you completely. They destabilise every room they enter. They are the centre of the universe and everyone else is merely in their orbit. I found myself lying to friends and family whenever we spoke, or at least telling only partial truths about what I was doing. Those conversations went like this: I had met someone, she was an artist, and it was going well. I found myself declining meet ups and phone calls. I concocted false reasons why I could not attend social occasions. I let every tangential relationship in my life wither and die in the cold air of my indifference to anything but her. Nothing mattered but her.

Abebi had an assistant back then, a French girl with short blonde hair, who visited most weeks, usually bringing with her a white lockbox filled with bags of various intoxicants. The three of us would sometimes binge for days on end, filling the flat with music and laughter and dancing. When we tired, Abebi would have us eat brownies and smoke hookah. She would talk aloud about art, pulling enormous books from her shelves and laying on the floor with me, pouring through the battered pages, running her fingers around the images of the paintings within, talking about them as if each great work of art was as precious to her as family.

When the mood took her, she and I would make love for what seemed like hours at a time. Abebi led, instructing me, telling me to change positions, speeds, and rhythms. She liked it best on ecstasy when our bodies were heightened to every sensation of pleasure. She would leave me exhausted, bruised, and sore, and return immediately to work. When she painted, it did not matter if it was day or night outside her studio, she worked for eight, ten, twelve hours at a time—sometimes longer still. She produced at a rate of one large canvas around every three weeks. When she showed me the finished works, I saw that they were painted in all the colours of her happy heart: bold yellows, daring oranges, deep teal, and fine mists of blushing pink. She claimed that artists can draw great emotional power from colour alone.

"Yellow is Van Gogh's," she said. "He defied his melancholy in bold and vibrant shades. Picasso turned grief a shade of cold blue. Francis Bacon covered his shame with black panels."

Abebi rarely left the flat. On the rare occasions she did venture out into the city it was usually to attend the exhibition openings and the shows of her friends. On those evenings, I was her plus one. My tickets would read: Abebi Oladele Isah (+1).

Her friends were a parade of intellectuals and artists, exhibitors, and tastemakers, none of whom saw me as someone with anything to offer them. Some would talk about me casually to Abebi, asking—*and who's this on your arm tonight?* Or they would raise the pitch of their voices, and say—*well, you are a handsome one, aren't you?* That was about all that anyone ever engaged with me. Abebi would then talk with the other artists about their creations and ideas with an intensity that excluded all others.

In truth, I was quite content to be excluded. I found most of those people instantly unbearable and saw little to like in their art. I would take flutes of champagne and walk around London's minor galleries, trying to find the merit in such works as the ripped red canvas titled *Spatial Illusion*; the blank canvas titled *This is Not a Painting VII*; or the enormous work that resembled TV static by the name of *An Ophthalmic Discourse, in Greys*.

During one such evening, Abebi almost left without me. Another man had interested her—a Japanese man with lilac irises. I caught them standing on the street outside the gallery, hailing a taxi. In the car, I learned that Abebi spoke some Japanese and they both seemed greatly amused by whatever scant phrases they were exchanging. She said that she wanted to capture the pigment of his eyes and then let him—a total stranger!—into her studio.

I could not believe it. I was left to drink alone in the kitchen and haunt her hallway, listening to the muffled voices emanating from behind the shut door. I seethed and felt sick with envy as every bump and rustle transfigured into the sound of bodies writhing and rutting against the hardwood floor.

The Japanese man finally left in the early hours of morning. I remember trying to talk to Abebi then, insisting that the man was not capable of understanding her art the way I do—but she was uninterested in the conversation and took herself to bed.

At the time, it seemed only fair to enter her studio myself. I found a mounted canvas painted with pale purple shades and covered it with wild strokes of my own. When my rage subsided, I was petrified. My actions could neither be hidden nor retracted. I confessed all in the morning, fully expecting a response of pure brimstone that never came.

"Your handling of the paint was actually quite interesting," she said after going to inspect the canvas. "I haven't seen anything quite like it before. The image I was exploring probably was too literal—I think you've given me something far more interesting to work with."

She based a full-sized canvas around my sabotage, a work that looked almost like peacock feathers. She titled it *Purple Eyes, Green Eyes*, and sold it for 1.1 million. I was ecstatic—I always knew that the connection between us ran deep, and now I had helped Britain's greatest living artist create a masterpiece.

Helping felt so good that I started looking for other ways to gain her attention and approval. The floors of the flat were grey with dust and almost every surface was covered in paperwork, used kitchenware, and discarded rotting food. I started to clean our flat, to pay the utilities bills, and wash our clothes. She never acknowledged these efforts. Indeed, I don't believe she even noticed them—Isah barely noticed anything sometimes, so lost was she in thoughts of hues, gradients, and the bulging contours of paint.

I witnessed her going without food or drink for entire days at times, despite me knocking on her door with offerings of water, coffee, breakfasts, and lunches that were left to congeal and harden in the corridor outside. Often when I spoke, I knew that she was not listening. I threw nonsense phrases into the conversation sometimes, phrases such as "Lord Trampoline for tea," or, "everyone's sheen is wood, isn't it?" just to watch her agree politely—her gaze fixed somewhere past my face.

I struggled before her growing apathy and I drank more and more. When I realised she did not care about expenditure, I began purchasing rare and aged wines on her credit card and drank them with an increasing dark cynicism, pounding back expensive glass after expensive glass without savouring them at all. I spent my days watching cartoons and documentaries, stoned or drunk, in her bed, sulking and eating junk food, letting my hair and beard grow wild. I stopped going to the gym and put on weight. I felt drained and empty, so much so that replying to the few texts or calls I still received began to feel arduous and revealing. I began seeing red ants crawling on my arms and chest, little red ants that disappeared whenever I focused on them. In the living room, I found an old canvas with the words: *painting is not a picture of an experience; it is the experience,* written many times over on both sides in a loping drunken hand. I dreamt that Abebi had taken me for a sacrifice. That she had extracted everything good from my heart and soul for use in her art leaving nothing but an empty husk in her wake.

Her paintings lost their light tones during the winter, and my nonsense expressions followed suit. She would nod, disengaged completely as I would say, "I might as well not be here," or, "tomorrow I will buy a gallon of petrol, so I can set fire to it all."

Her block returned and Abebi became almost unbearable to be around. Any time that she was not trying to paint through it, she would sit opposite me, sneering over the rim of a wine glass, attempting to provoke fights—asking me exactly what I had done that day or how she was ever supposed to respect a man who clearly doesn't even respect himself. I tried to fix her block again. I went back into her studio while she slept and painted all over her current work-in-progress. When she woke that time, she did not compliment me on my handling of the paint.

"You have defaced the painting," she hissed, "you have betrayed the trust I placed in you, and you have defaced my art."

It wasn't fair.

It wasn't consistent.

I tried to explain myself, but she did not care.

"I have sacrificed friends and lovers for my work before, I will not hesitate to do so again," she warned as she took an armful of wine bottles with her into the studio and locked the door.

Sometime in the spring of 2003 we attended an exhibition opening of one of Abebi's friends—a photographer. Abebi invited me in a tone that made me feel quite unwelcome.

I attended and supported her out of pure spite. The taxi ride lasted for over forty frosty minutes. We sat the whole time in silence, our hands no longer seeking each other out across the back seat, both of us looking out of windows. When we arrived, Abebi began circulating immediately, leaving me alone without a backwards glance.

I hated the pretentious photographs on display as much as I hated everyone there. I stood boorishly by the young girls holding the trays, tipping back flute after flute of cheap fizz. I wanted to embarrass Abebi, I wanted to cause a scene. I wanted to find the so-called artist responsible for the exhibition and tell them that anyone with a camera could do what they do, and that filter lenses were no substitute for depth. I wanted to unzip my fly and take a piss over everything and everyone. I wanted Abebi to notice me. I wanted to take the smiling girl holding the tray of champagne flutes, rip open her cheap white shirt and fuck her like our lives depended upon it—just to see if Abebi would care. I wanted to go back in time, or else smash my glass against the wall, tear open my throat in front of everyone and laugh wildly as their pleasant bourgeois evening was forever ruined.

My memory of that night blacks out. The next day, however, Abebi informed me coldly that I had gotten paralytic, that I had insulted many people and fallen over. The security guards had felt it necessary to eject me from their gallery. I had swung a fist at them, missed, and fallen face-first on the floor. She had been forced to leave with me, assisting the guards as they bundled me into a taxi, she said I told everyone present to fuck themselves, over and over and over again.

My growing bitterness consumed me one day as I went out walking. I used a public phone box to contact the police, informing them anonymously that I had witnessed someone selling drugs in my building. I gave them Abebi's address and a full description of her assistant, along with the colour and registration of her Mercedes Benz.

The police must have smelt a scandal the moment I gave them the postcode. I could barely stop myself laughing as I watched Abebi's assistant being intercepted by several police officers and half a dozen journalists from a window. Her head hung as she was searched and photographed, though she happened to be clean that day. My snide joy ebbed away to nothing as I watched the girl shaking and crying as she told Abebi everything she knew about the incident. Neither woman suspected a thing, thankfully enough. They blamed their cavalier behaviour and predictable routines before they went looking for betrayal. The matter merely festered privately, gnawing at my conscience, making me hate myself—not just for what I had done, but because I realised that I had grown too afraid of my lover to ever clear my conscience with a confession.

I was a cowardly parasite.

I was an ugly shade, cast by the bright brilliance of my lover.

I was a wounded moth, beating against the embers of a dying affection.

I gathered some things and, taking the credit card she had given me, I booked myself into a nearby hotel and stared at the dark window of my phone screen. When she failed to call in the morning, I extended my stay by another night. I drank Whiskey Sours alone at the bar and vowed to stay at the Tartufo until she noticed my absence. In the restaurant that evening I took a table in ragged jeans and a stained tee shirt and washed down steak and oysters with a bottle of Dom Pérignon. I pushed a wad of notes into the jacket of the maître d' for keeping her disdain down to a mere flicker. Each night I drank the minibar in my room dry, bathed in the cold blue light of the screen. I talked drunkenly aloud to the characters on the television and laughed along when they made jokes. When the credits rolled on the final programmes, I purchased pornographic films and revelled in those baroque depictions of total sex in all its sordid screaming melodrama, stewing in my morbid malaise.

I stayed at the Tartufo for five nights, I think, in total. When I left, I paid a bill of over eight thousand pounds in defeat. The great spree had proven as unfulfilling as it had been futile, Abebi had not called or messaged me once and yet I could not exorcise her from my thoughts. Dark fantasies had played out constantly in mind—fantasies that oscillated between genuine concern and petty jealousy. I thought she might have already thrown my things out into her hallway and changed her locks. I pictured her somehow dead from a slip or an overdose, alone and abandoned in her studio. In lucid moments between sleep and waking I imagined scenes in which I returned to find her beneath another lover, her face twisted and mocking as she caught my gaze.

*

My belongings were not in the hallway when I returned. My key still worked in the lock. Inside the stale and dusty flat, glasses, bottles, and clothes were strewn everywhere. I saw the answerphone was heavily queued with unheard messages and I knew that she had not checked the phone the entire time I had been away.

I knocked on Abebi's studio door and announced my return. She shouted the word *ok* from the inside and that was that. Or at least, it would have been if I had let it. I knocked again and insisted that we have a conversation in the kitchen, repeating the words until she agreed. When Abebi emerged, she looked thin and twitchy, her pupils larger and more dilated than I had ever seen them. She looked like she had been bingeing for days, her lips purple with dried red wine.

"I was out for the day," I said.

"Cool," she replied, in a wary and guarded tone.

"Except it's not been a day. I've been away a bit longer."

"Yeah?" she replied, her relief obvious. "I thought so."

"How long do you think I've been gone?"

"I don't know. A few days?"

"Do you care where I've been?"

"I certainly don't care for this kind of bullshit guilt-trip," Abebi replied quietly but firmly. She seemed agitated, her body language suggesting that she was keen to conclude our conversation and return quickly to her work.

"You don't give a shit about anything," I said, flushing with fury. "Did you even notice I was gone?"

"I've been working," she snapped. "Go find a dictionary sometime and look the word up. I was on the verge of something interesting, and this…this is not the time to have this conversation."

She turned heel and made for her studio door.

"You know, I used to enjoy your work. And I used to imagine you as a much nicer person," I said, moving swiftly to catch her up.

"Isn't life the great disappointment?"

"But everything that's good about you is left on the canvas," I found myself saying, ignoring her terse and cynical interjection. "Abebi's art has a soul, but Abebi does not. The woman holding the paintbrush depicts emotions that she does not experience. She is a monster, a monster who invites humans into her life for observation so she can then paint them into exhaustion and make herself millions. You aren't an artist, Abebi, you're a fucking parasite."

"And what do you do that's so interesting?" she replied, turning to face me. "You sit in your stupid dressing gown, in my flat, drinking and eating at my expense, sleeping in until the afternoon—and now you have the audacity to feel sorry for yourself? Do you really want this conversation? Fine. You have to leave—leave *my* flat today."

The suit of armour I had fashioned out of resentment and self-righteousness dissolved into nothing before her words.

"But... I love you" was all I could find to say, my voice suddenly the voice of a child.

"And I do not feel emotions," she replied.

She was closed to me then in ways that I had never seen before, her face was a mask of cold indifference. I knew that any appeal I could make would be cruelly smashed against the jagged rocks of her folded arms and her steely gaze. I wondered how she could be so lacking in compassion, so able to rid herself of her lover and her biggest fan?

"Those are your words," Abebi continued, filling the silence. "And they aren't true by the way. I'm not a psychopath, I just don't love you. I never lied to you either. I told you; nothing matters but the painting. You helped me overcome a block and now it's over. That's all. Do you understand? It really is best for us both that you leave."

"I understand," I said eventually. "I understand something that perhaps you do not. You're blocked again, aren't you?" She did not reply. "You need new feelings to explore, and I can still give you them—me alone."

I beckoned her through the flat, uncertain of myself as I stepped out onto the balcony. Abebi followed me outside, her expression one of deep curiosity. The air was neither warm nor cold that day, it had a grey and empty quality. I recall thinking it would be a drab day to die.

"I don't think there can be anyone else for me," I continued, forcing myself to step onto the railing. I held myself steady against the wall as I turned my attention back to her. "You once told me that artists can draw great emotional power from colour alone. Maybe Picasso blue, or black like Bacon."

I held myself steady, though my stomach seemed to be lurching and sliding erratically and my knees were water. I looked down to the street below where people scurried busily. I considered the fall, of how terrifying and exhilarating it would feel to see the ground rushing up to obliterate my body, and how a primal scream would tear itself involuntarily from spirit and flesh and blend with the howling air as it was torn asunder by the hurtling mass. I tore my eyes back from the street to look at Abebi and, for as long as I live, I will never forget the ghoulish face she wore in that moment. She seemed to have stopped breathing entirely. Her mouth was open in anticipation and her eyes were alight with excitement. Her unfolded arms seemed to be reaching shakily out towards me, moving of their own silent volition as if she had fallen deep within a trance. She took a step forwards, her hands reaching up towards her balcony, though to what purpose only she could say.

"We must all suffer for our dreams and passions," I said, repeating her words back to her. "I promise you; you won't be blocked again for years. You might even become iconic. Don't you want all that?"

She stared silently at me for what seemed like an eternity. When she finally moved, she did so with the slightest of nods.

With that small gesture Abebi proved to us both that she is an artist before she is anything else, and that I was only ever material to her—discardable material. I was hurting in ways that I did not even know were possible. I was furious too when I stepped off from the railing.

*

Life felt a little muted after all that. I slept on a sequence of sofas provided by the smattering of friends that still answered my phone calls. I landed a quiet job in a dull office and started over.

Abebi was quiet for around a year after our relationship. When she returned, she did so in triumph with a solo exhibition at London's Serpentine Gallery advertised in four- and five-star reviews on posters all throughout the city. The culture sections of major papers vivaciously acclaimed her new work. "*The greatest colourist working in Britain today has scaled dramatic new heights,*" claimed the Telegraph. "*Important, breathless, and captivatingly human,*" read the headline in the Observer.

In the accompanying photographs Abebi reclined proudly and did not smile. She stared out with a defiant gaze that seemed to me almost a challenge to do my worst and assassinate her character in the press, to leak details about her lifestyle and frequent drug use, or to even talk about the incident on the balcony.

Not that I had any intention of doing any of that. No—when I looked at her face, I felt only guilt and shame. I found my own actions around the time quite disturbing. When I asked if I should jump, Abebi nodded—or at least, I think she nodded—but she never put me on that railing. I regretted putting the only person I have ever loved in that situation, just as I regretted calling her revolting as I stepped backwards onto her balcony, leaving her standing transfixed and agape while I gathered my things and left.

I visited the Serpentine of course. The exhibition was filled with gorgeous and radiant visions, set starkly against sterile white walls. No other painter could hope to breathe more life and humanity into abstract art. It was indeed as if each work was not an inanimate object at all, but a living, breathing thing created from pure and urgent feeling.

One painting caught my eye in particular—a large piece titled, *Composition #5*. The colours of the composition were uncharacteristic for Abebi—shades of cold blue and black—and there seemed to be some strange form painted with unusual sharpness in the foreground of the piece, a shape that to my eyes looked very much like the railing of her balcony. I found myself returning several times, picking out quiet moments to visit the gallery. I would stand breathless before the painting, feeling my skin prickle and my heart soaring from that deep sensation of connectivity. I still don't know for certain—perhaps I was imagining things again—but perhaps Abebi Oladele Isah paints for me, and me alone.

At The Gare Saint-Lazare

The newly-weds ate their breakfast in near silence, still smarting from the first wounds they had inflicted upon each other. They apportioned their fruit, toast, and coffee with a courtesy that felt almost hostile in its coolness, while the few words spoken seemed to hang awkwardly in the stifling air.

The discordance between them had begun the previous afternoon, following their visit to a small exhibition by the infamous Édouard Manet—that salacious champion of wild outcasts and artistic outlaws across the city. Felix had been somewhat amused by what he saw as rough and provocative works that bit a grubby thumb at convention. Yet Marie's interest had run much deeper. She had lingered for a long time beneath an image of a bare-breasted woman, reclining on a chaise-longue and staring out of the canvas with a defiant air. However, when, on their walk back home, she had expressed her desire to paint a female portrait of her own, she had been astonished to hear that her new husband forbade the notion, saying: *I feared this would happen, Marie. No—absolutely no. And that will be the end of the matter.*

Marriage, she supposed, leaves nowhere to hide. Throughout their brief courtship they had presented ideal versions of themselves, ideals that would now erode until their true selves were revealed. She watched as Felix took hold of an enamelled spoon, its hilt painted in the Japanese style, and ran it through the sugar pot. He raised the spoon for inspection and sliced away the superfluous grains with the edge of his knife before lowering it into his coffee. He stirred his drink with five precise revolutions, all without spilling a single drop. In this new morning light Marie could not help but wonder if this behaviour would prove somehow portentous—if she would perhaps learn that a scrupulous dictator lurked beneath his bohemian guise.

"Your berry compote is a masterpiece," said Felix, his eyes darting up to meet hers as he served himself a second slice of toast. "I love its rough texture and sour notes." He smiled as he spoke; a fraught expression that seemed to lack the conviction of genuine feeling—as if deep-down he recognised that compliments so obviously deflective in intention would be incapable of bandaging the sore moment. Marie acknowledged his words with hollow thanks, and he reached over the kitchen table to pat the back of her hand.

Was this an attempt to direct her? Was her husband suggesting that she frequent herself less with the easel and more with the kitchen, until all her masterpieces were compotes and pastries? The man she had married did not look like some fusty conventionalist. Felix Bracquemond resembled a haughty feral creature, one whose face was framed by shaggy tufts and wild ringlets of dark hair. His eyes peeked out from beneath thick eyebrows with a reflective quality that made him appear quite pensive, as if he spent every waking moment lost to contemplation. Most days he wore white linen shirts, musty, and discoloured by time and washing until they were all various shades of greys and beiges and each of them stained in the folds with his engraver's dust. Felix was a proud artist, an intellectual, and progressively minded—surely. And yet, even as she thought back to their first meetings—when they had chattered side-by-side through the hallowed corridors of the Louvre—she recalled that even his praise and passions had often expressed sour notes of their own. For instance, his heartfelt acclamation of Rousseau had turned swiftly into derision of the artist's British imitators who, according to Felix, simply had no business making ceramics in the Parisian style. Then Marie had taken his words as jests and had laughed along with him. Now she could not help but wonder if he held such thoughts with real conviction, and if he believed that other kinds of people were also unworthy of making art.

"This morning I would like to take a stroll," suggested Felix. "Perhaps we should walk the Seine along to the Tuileries."

Marie found his suggestion quite unreadable. Was she simply supposed to accept her husband's invitation—or had he extended a hollow courtesy, designed to mask a secret desire to spend some time away from her and their cramped apartment, filled as it was with books and boxes and the many things left unsaid? She looked to the quivering branches outside her window for guidance before looking back to the orange that she had picked at for almost half an hour.

"My dear," Felix continued at last, "you will find a morning walk most invigorating. It will surely clear your head of all maladies and melancholies."

"And you would like me to accompany you?"

"Of course."

"Then, my love," Marie replied, managing to inject jovial tones into her voice, "then nothing in this world could make me happier."

Marie excused herself from the dining table and made her way to their bedroom. She closed her eyes as she removed her nightclothes. She hoped that when she would open them her husband would be standing in the doorway, waiting for her with ardent apologies and an impassioned heart. She would have him say that he loved her, that their quarrels were silly, and that his preclusion was nothing but a misspoken moment. She would have forgiven all. She would ask him to take her in his arms, push her slowly back onto the bed and everything could be made right once again—if only her husband would be there.

But Felix was not with her when she opened her eyes. The faint clattering of crockery coming from the kitchen suggested that he had instead chosen to occupy himself by scrubbing the dishes. Marie dressed quickly and returned to the living room. She declared herself ready for their walk in a voice that annoyed her in its uncertain haltingness. He replied with a curt nod of his head and went to dress himself alone.

*

A forlorn quality not felt in Paris all throughout the long summer months had taken residence in the air. The cold hit Marie immediately in the back of her throat, chilling her blood down to her fingertips. Felix pulled his fraying greatcoat close around his frame and exhaled shudderingly as he rubbed his hands together. He closed the door of their building behind them and wordlessly beckoned her forwards with his palm outstretched.

How strange each forward step felt that morning! Where once the couple had skipped forwards in erratic bursts—turning often to gaze at one another, or nudging shoulders with cute, fortuitous missteps—they now seemed to march briskly from their home, as if all their faults and troubles dwelled in the dull bricks behind them. Marie felt her husband's hand drifting towards her own as they walked. She allowed him to find her and for one austere moment they gripped each other before they pulled apart again.

"I heard them talking about the painting you liked yesterday," said Felix as they walked along the bank of the great shimmering river, "One man was saying that the artist should have travelled to Venice and pissed directly onto Titian's grave if he wished to defile him so badly—that way at least he would have spared the innocent paint and canvas. They were all *laughing*, Marie, everyone all over the city is laughing at him."

Marie had heard the scepticism of the crowd. Their scorn and outrage had not interested her, and she had found their jests deeply tiresome.

"Have you heard of his followers?" Felix continued, "those lunatic painters that sit outdoors in the freezing wind, painting the pelting rain? They have not a week's tuition or training between them. The academies refused them as students and would sooner close their doors forever than let them show their work. I hear that they will exhibit anyway—not in the Salon of course, they will exhibit in some dingy coffee shop, or some barn, or somewhere else equally as undignified—that is if they do not all die of pneumonia first!" Felix turned fully to look at her, his eyes almost pleading. "They are *not* to be admired, Marie. They are ridiculous. They are a spectacle."

"He calls you a friend," Marie retorted. "How do you think he would feel to hear you talking of him in such a way?"

"Manet is Manet," Felix replied with an indifferent shrug. "But you are intelligent and so talented. You have exhibited in the Salon for God's sake! I only want what is best for you. Do you understand? I cannot—and will not—stand idly by and watch a woman of your calibre join the circus."

Marie found that she had no reply beyond a contemptuous and futile snort. She found that no better answer was waiting for her among the immaculate lawns and expansive walkways of the Tuileries either. The couple endured their beautiful surroundings in a stiff and moribund silence until Felix finally pointed north-west.

"Do you know, Luca has just moved into a house on the Rue de Rome—by the Gare Saint-Lazare" he said, "it is perhaps only fifteen minutes from here. Would you like to see his new home?"

Luca, her husband's friend, was a playwright of modest success. His stories—mostly thwarted romances, comic farces, and tales of piracy and adventure in the far-flung corners of the world—were often performed in small theatres and public gardens where a family could enjoy an afternoon's entertainment for as little as fifty cents. In truth Marie cared little for the man and cared even less about seeing whatever place he now called home, yet that morning she would have welcomed anything that might alleviate the tension between herself and her husband.

As they left the Tuileries the names of the streets surrounding the Gare Saint-Lazare called to Marie's spirit like the songs of the sirens. France had delayed its railway construction. When the station had finally been built, it had connected Paris with stations and cities around the continent. The architect, Baron Haussmann, had emphasised this new connectivity by situating his station between six grand boulevards that he had named after the newly possible destinations: the Rue de Londres, the Rue de Madrid, the Rue de Constantinople, the Rue d'Édimbourg, the Rue de Rome, and the Rue de Saint Petersbourg. For a fleeting moment as they walked across Le Pont de l'Europe, Marie found herself indulging in fantasies of happier lifetimes that might perhaps have happened if only she had the fortune of being born elsewhere.

"The streets around the station are named for other capital cities of Europe," said Felix as they descended from Le Pont de l'Europe. "You see, there is Madrid, Rome, London, and the others. I would suppose that the trains leaving here can take you to them all." He sniggered derisively. "Though for my life, I cannot understand why we ever agreed to make it easier for the British to visit our great city."

They walked through the streets below where their mutual diffidence was swallowed amidst the clamour of people, horse carts, and bicycles that streamed in all directions beneath torpid gas lamp sentinels. Felix misremembered Luca's number in the first instance and, knocking on the wrong door, was greeted by an old man in a grubby vest who coughed an oyster into his hands before sending the couple on their way. When Felix did locate the correct address, he embraced his friend in his hallway with such warmth that it seemed almost like gratitude.

Luca took them both through to the kitchen and sat Felix at the table opposite him. As the two men leaned in close to talk, Marie filled the percolator on the side with tap water and listened vaguely to their conversation as she searched Luca's cupboards for clean china cups.

"My friend, I believe that the last time I saw you, you were struggling to finish a play."

"I finished it last night, thank the muses."

"And how did you resolve…"

"Oh, yes—*that* problem. She succumbs to temptation, of course."

"You mean she is unfaithful?"

"The solution was obvious when I thought of it."

"Of course, quite obvious—her death is too much like tragedy otherwise."

"Indeed, my friend… No Sophocles am I; I am merely a humble writer of lightness and farce."

"Would you like more coffee?" queried Felix as Marie placed two cups before them.

"Well, I suppose ten is a little too early for Brandy," Luca replied with a mischievous wink.

The men laughed. Marie excused herself, informing the disinterested room that she wished to take in the air at the back garden. She stepped out of the kitchen door into a long rectangular garden grown wild and littered with rusted tools, smashed crockery, and a sodden rug streaked with snail slime. She found a flagstone path amidst the long grass and hopped languidly from one to another, away from the house and towards a tall black railing at the end of the garden. As she approached, Marie could hear the distant hissing and whistling bells of an oncoming train and the ground beneath her feet began to tremble. She pressed her face close against the shuddering bars to witness a modern marvel in action.

It seemed as if the very air around her ripped apart when the great billowing mass of metal and smoke hurtled past—the wheels on the tracks blurring and the crankshaft pedalling furiously. She cast her gaze upwards and caught glimpses of happy passengers in the windows, laughing together and wearing their finest on their way to whatever glad occasions awaited them. Between them a woman as pale and as incorporeal as a ghost stared directly back at her. And then, just as quickly as it had come, the train passed out of sight leaving the world eerily still and quiet in its wake.

Marie stood, rooted to the ground, still staring at the space that had been briefly occupied by her flickering reflection—to where she had seen herself as some sad and pitiful creature, staring out mournfully from behind bars.

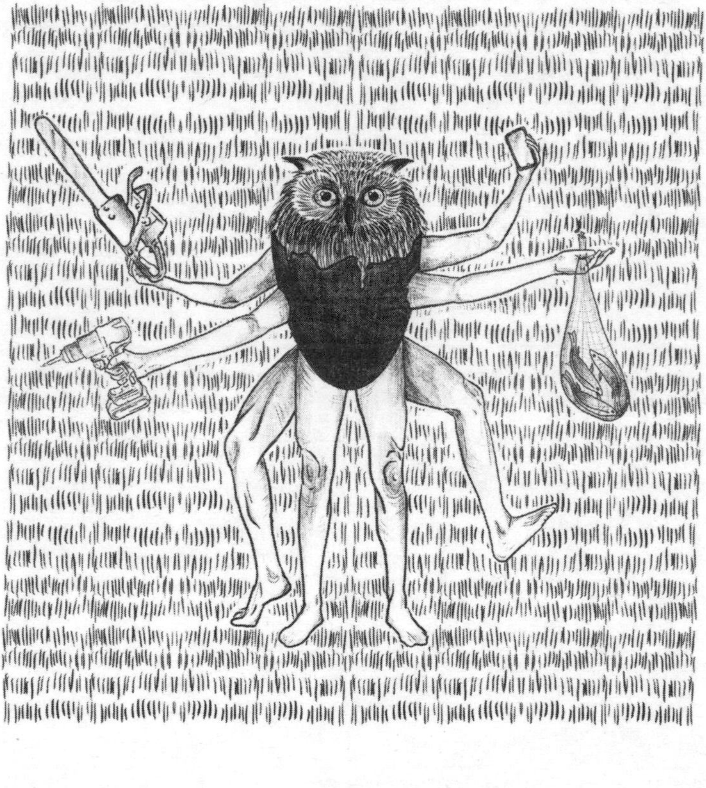

Earthly Delights

When all was new the first clouds assembled above the terrestrial globe in light and formless delineations. Gently they released the rains upon the land below. The sun warmed the soil, which became profoundly invigorated by this symphony of light and moisture. The earth pulsated and hummed with germination until the first sprouting life tore its way out from the dark to stand beneath the call of the sun.

The lands stretched like clay. Unseen forces slowly pushed up great formations of rock and earth until mountains towered in majestic surveyance of the landscape, and ranges of hills arched and curved in playful meandering tracts. The tallest of these formations met the clouds. They gathered cold air and moisture as ice and snow and sent it back in torrents to the earth creating great waterfalls and lakes.

The globe was then luscious and bountiful. It was endless in its fecundity, producing an astonishing variety of plants that emerged from the mud to thrive. Proud trees strove for status in canopies. The flowers flirted, vying for attention through a thousand expressions of beauty. Other blossoms provided still more pleasures, the globe making itself a banquet of scents and flavours and inviting all of life to partake in the great miracle.

From primordial waters came the first creatures. They were slithering and crawling oddities; eyeless and scale-ridden things, compelled seemingly by a search for warmth and food. They enjoyed a brief and harmonious age before the first predators turned to flesh.

A great lake occupied the centre of the globe. It seemed to respond to the dynamic land around it. Over time it pushed forth a mighty fountain, in appearance like a vast pink flower. The waters that cascaded from the tip of the fountain appeared different. The creatures flocked to the great lake and drank greedily from it, becoming ever larger, and ever more diverse.

Soon the quiet was shattered by a million different voices. The skies were suffused by the cawing and screeching of winged and feathered creatures. The waters filled with frolicking fish. Large creatures covered in fur, or covered in scales, engaged in duels of strength with the trees, forcing their branches down towards the ground so that life might consume everything.

Yet everything was not enough. Life could never be sated. Desire had infiltrated the globe, and the seeds of carnality were sewn. Many creatures mutated into new and violent forms. They turned on other living beings, devouring the bodies of the weak for sustenance, and battled each other both for meat and for mating rights.

The most curious of all new creatures walked upright on two legs. They were only medium-sized and not gifted with great strength or speed. Their bodies were soft and pliable things, more suited for the sensuous than for survival. Yet they possessed an intelligence like nothing else living. Using all their cunning they ascended to a position unrivalled among the other creatures and quickly declared themselves the masters of the globe.

*

These new masters explored their diverse world with curious fascination and revelled in an endless age of plenty. They pulled handfuls of sweet and juicy fruits from the trees and bushes, eating only the prettiest specimens, they discarded the ugly and misshapen fruits, or else threw them at each other in play.

They discovered that the consumption of some plants and grains lead to pleasing and unexpected reactions. Fermented fruit sent its drinkers into frenzies of a most enjoyable kind. They made wild music and danced without inhibitions. When heated into smoke, many kinds of leaves would make the masters grow giggly and tingling. Some plants had stronger effects yet—mushrooms and cacti seemed to offer glimpses of other worlds entirely, and the masters brave enough to eat them would walk around in wonder, observing lights, patterns, and forces visible only to them. They tried everything eventually, coughing and spluttering from smoke and heaving under many failed experiments. Many of the masters died during these trials, while others expired slowly through over-consumption. Their deaths did nothing to deter the others.

The flame was conquered and weaponised. The masters sharpened spears and created traps to catch the other beasts, slitting their throats and peeling back the skins, hacking flesh from bone. They learned that their ability to craft tools and manipulate matter allowed them to reshape the globe to better suit their tastes. They tore down trees, carved boulders, and used bones and hides to construct large ramshackle temples and houses. They extracted burnable fuels from the ground, as well as pretty stones and precious metals to adorn themselves. They grew to love the water, for they became as vain as they were curious, and found few things more enjoyable than gazing lovingly at their reflections.

Beneath waterfalls and in the shallows of the lakes, the females took to bathing together. The ecstatic males would clamber onto the backs of the beasts and ride them in great looping formations around these waters, whooping and cheering with joy at the sight of so much alluring flesh in one place. They created a raucous din in these moments, bashing out rhythms on the shells of arthropods, and whipping their hogs and mules in a screeching, braying, orchestration. They rode in overlapping circles, each revolution, consciously or unconsciously, recalling the act of copulation, for the masters remained driven by the same base instincts as the lesser beasts under their domain, and they loved everything connected with the sexual act. They erected phallic shrines and cloistered sanctuaries. They pleasured each other and themselves constantly and rutted on the globe's grass plains. They discovered every means and method of gratification available to them. And when, at last, it all grew dull, they pioneered new ways to merge pleasure with pain, finding fresh new thrills in humiliation and degradation.

At first, the masters worshipped the great pink fountain. They prayed to it and blessed their offspring in its sacred waters. When they swam the lake to touch it for themselves and enter its petals, they found it hollow inside. Some of the masters declared themselves spiritual leaders among their species and took up residence within. Daily they drank its waters and bathed beneath it. They drove away the other creatures to keep its waters for themselves. Around the lake, the masters built their own shrines and towers higher and higher, eventually hoping to eclipse even the great fountain. Some less restrained masters were seen urinating and spitting into the sacred water or fornicating within the sanctity of the fountain's pink seclusion, until, at last, the great fountain seemed to crack and wither, it's purple tip visibly drooping back within itself above the shrinking waters.

The masters found many other uses for their fellow animals, beyond food. They staged combat between the fiercer creatures, betting and joking among themselves as the great beasts tore each other apart. They stole gigantic eggs from the nests of mammoth birds and lizards, cracked them open and evicted the embryonic forms within. They would climb inside the eggs themselves then, and float atop the flowing waters for leisure; or else, they would drag nets beneath them as they drifted, ensnaring fish and other amphibious beings, laughing as they observed the irony of water creatures flapping vainly and drowning in dry air.

They ripped the heads, shells, and horns from captive animals and paraded throughout the land in the garb of abominations and perversions, wearing wild and bizarre combinations of beaks and claws, manes, and feathers. They took all that they could from their fellow creatures—their silk, their milk, their hides. They cut the horns and tusks from the beasts that they thought most virile and ingested them in futile hope of gaining their strength and prowess.

The once pure air became infected by the putrid scents of smoke and smog, of rot and decay. The green grasslands of the globe became heavily scarred and littered with shells and husks, with dwellings constructed and abandoned, with the bones and bodies of the abundant dead. The forests were cut back, leaving acres of stumps where once there had been splendid trees. The ground became pockmarked and scarred from the many digs. The avarice of the masters saw that everything was taken from their globe, until the great forests were no more, until many other species had been hunted to extinction, until their waters ran dry, and their world warmed around them.

Still the land was dominated by the joyful voices of the masters. They grew to love themselves more and more, dedicating their shrines to the earthly delights of beauty and pleasure. Their dance was a maniacal one. It was a dance of fornication and fighting, consumption and killing, abuse and waste, and of taking without restraint. On and on they danced, filling the globe with their festivities, and making music destined to echo throughout time itself, a song of pleasure in perpetuity and a celebration of their eternal mastery.

*

The mountaintops exploded in fire and dust, belching forth red-hot streams that incinerated all in their path and swept away the proud edifices of the masters, the stones smouldering and sinking into smoking ruins.

The masters that survived the first eruptions fled towards the safety and protection of the great lake. The diminished fountain shook and trembled and seemed to shrink down into the boiling sacred waters. As the fountain disappeared many of the masters—driven wild by fear and remorse—dived into the waters after it. They received nothing but a screaming, thrashing, agonised death. The rest fled to the hilltops, clinging desperately to their lives.

When the fires finally burned out, the few survivors were able to descend once again. They found a world very different to the one they had left. Where once they had enjoyed a light and temperate globe, they now lived in darkness, shivering in thin air choked by dust. No vegetation could live on this scorched earth. Most animals had perished. Those remaining were desperate and hungry. The lakes and seas now contained only luminous clusters of sinister and inedible jellyfish that rendered the waters useless. The birds had also changed: scared and ravenous they attacked and harried from above, overwhelming the weak and the malnourished masters, feasting on their eyes and tongues as they called for help. Even the insects seemed to endlessly bite and sting, as if they too had nothing else to consume, or else that the impetuous masters had enraged all that had ever lived.

The age of the last masters was brief and wretched, a time of innumerable sad atrocities. The starving survivors quickly turned on each other amid flame and fear, ripping trophies from the slain, wearing skulls, bones, and ears of the weaker members of their own kind. The special creatures who had once worshipped themselves as Gods came to resemble demons more closely. They filled the air with a degenerate music of rib cages played like war drums and stomachs blown like bagpipes. Deformed and insane, they ripped babies from their mothers' arms and cooked them squealing. They fed unwilling victims to the beasts, or else drowned them, or gave them to the flames, hoping vainly to appease the heavens once more.

Yet this broken world was no longer theirs. The final masters were hollow and sad creatures, their faces etched with incalculable regrets as they came to understand the paradox of their fate. Free will had been forced upon beings too flawed to choose restraint, and it had made them most unworthy stewards.

The masters were long gone when the clouds finally released clean rain once again. Over time, this water came to purify the lands of the globe. Daylight pierced through the dust clouds to invigorate the soil in a symphony of light and moisture. The earth pulsated and hummed with germinations, until the first sprouting life tore its way from the dark once again to stand beneath the call of the sun.

THE VANITAS

Chapter One: Assumption

I.

The sky was torn asunder, the clement blue rupturing to reveal the golden splendour beyond this mortal plane. Flights of precious cherubs had descended on felicitous wings, and lo! they had taken the blessed virgin and raised her above her former companions—their grief turned to wonderment and joy as they waved her onwards towards eternity.

"Do you see how her arms are outstretched?" asked Sandro, the marvel of the sight leaving him quite short of breath. "Most assuredly, her pose obliges her elevation. But also, does it not remind you of the crucifixion? Can you not help but recall that salvation itself sprang from that miraculous womb?"

"How could we ever forget?" replied the young man standing beside him.

"Look to her eyes! Can you see where she gazes?"

The youth did not reply.

"Where is she looking, Tommaso?" Sandro insisted.

"It is beyond what we can see," drawled the youth, failing to conceal his boredom.

"My boy. Well said! Indeed, it is beyond our comprehension. But in which direction?"

The young man shrugged. "Above?" he tentatively replied.

Sandro could not prevent a slight chuckle from escaping his lips—he did not truly expect his apprentice to understand every profound didactic conclusion that should be inferred from this deceptively simple act of staging.

The Assumption of the Virgin was a favourite scene painted by the small army of artists that occupied Rome. Indeed, the scene stood proudly in hundreds of churches across the city, and, like so many of the essential expressions of faith, the subject had been painted almost to exhaustion. Yet Sandro Signorelli was a well-versed singer of optical hymns. He had come to realise that only one fluent fully in the vocabulary of the aesthetic could deviate from it with purpose, and that only the seasoned master—with comprehension attained and experience hard-earned—was capable of transcending convention, of finding novel significance in symbolism, and renewing the waning interest of the masses.

"Precisely so!" Sandro declared. "Our Mary looks *above*. Others have depicted her otherwise. I have seen a multitude of Marys shown in prayer, their eyes cast downwards as if they are bidding farewell to the Earth. Yet consider this: if the eyes do not look upwards, Tommaso, how can they receive their judgement? Our Mary is experiencing the celestial rapture, the divine ecstasy of the Assumption. Her eyes must be fixed upwards: up towards the light, towards a destiny fulfilled, towards the promise of paradise that rewards all whose faith is true!"

The apprentice did not seem to share his master's excitement. The boy's stomach had been growling for some time now. Sandro supposed that his mind was perhaps not in the heavens, but in the kitchen already. They had worked together on the altarpiece for nearly six months, all the while discussing composition, colour choices, paints and glazes, and the glorious history of iconography. Now that Sandro thought back on it, those discussions had been a little imbalanced and, perhaps, on occasion, a little self-indulgent. Nevertheless, he would allow himself one further point before permitting the boy to leave.

"Tommaso, understand this: I am thirty-three years of age. I am well-acquainted with poverty and hardships. My purpose is to serve God through art, and yet He does not make life easy for his servants. I have served Him faithfully throughout my whole life. Still, success eludes me, and my income is meagre. What does that tell us?" The boy opened his mouth, as if to answer the question, however his master was merely sermonising and hurried to provide the correct interpretation. "It tells us that the Lord wishes us to be tested. He would see a demonstration of faith and diligence before he would dispense His reward. But—do you not see what we have created here? This is a remarkable thing: dead materials, wood and oil, have been imbued with divine purpose—praise be!" Sandro found himself ruffling the boy's hair. The physical contact seemed to surprise them both. "I believe you are hungry, child. Please, feel welcome to visit my kitchen on your way home. Fernanda has promised a feast of dumplings this evening!"

"Thank you, master," Tommaso replied, taking his leave.

"One last thing," Sandro shouted at his back. "I have been lost to creation. Which date is it today?"

"Today is May fifth, sir."

Sandro searched his mind for great significance in the date. He found none.

"May fifth, in the sixteen-hundredth year of our Lord. This will be a day we shall remember for the rest of our lives,

Tommaso. Truly, I believe this work will prove the making of us both."

Tommaso smiled weakly before hurrying from the studio. Amused, Sandro watched him from the window. He expected the boy to break right, towards Sandro's house and the promise of dumplings. Instead, the boy turned left and raced towards his family home. Sandro shrugged and turned back to his painting. Truly this was the accomplishment of a lifetime. He pulled up his stool and sat before it, taking in the perfect...the *near*-perfect, he corrected himself...rendering of the subject. Those great problems that beset the artist: proportion, composition, palette, animation, had all been solved, gloriously—at last! And how fitting the subject matter!

Indeed, this was a painting worthy of a Roman Church. He might get his chance to move the residents and pilgrims of the Great City; to position the voice of Sandro Signorelli, lowly and insignificant as it may be, within the same divine and eternal chorus as *Raphael*, and *Michelangelo*. The notion excited him beyond all feeling. He stood quickly and scratched his address onto a spare scrap of parchment, for dalliance today might transform into cowardice tomorrow.

II.

Sandro raced through the narrow backstreets, over uneven cobbles, through the crowds of people and their livestock. Rome was filled with chatter and song as cool breezes washed over the city—like the first whispered suggestions of the night.

His business was at the Basilica Santa Maria. Among the Carmelites there was one Father Donato Salamena, a childhood acquaintance whose friendship had been lost to the currents of time. A chance encounter two years previously had briefly rekindled something of their friendship—a rekindling they had since neglected as their respective professional and domestic duties had re-absorbed them both.

The streets parted, opening out into the grand Piazza del Popolo, dominated as it was by the towering Obelisk. Sandro tarried in the shade to catch his breath. A nearby clock told him it was quarter to six, giving him a little time to find Donato before the commencement of evening Mass. He had hoped for a peaceful moment to mentally draft his request, but it was no good. The noise of the Piazza was most intrusive. The widows wailed piteously before the gallows as the day's executions were hacked down and carted off.

Sandro hastened to Santa Maria, which was so dark inside that his eyes required several moments to adjust. Eventually, he spied Donato, wearing the dark robes of the Carmelite Order and lighting candles beside an altar. Sandro approached him quickly, though his nerve deserted him at the last. It was no small favour that he would be asking of the man. He wished now dearly that he had made the effort to cross town after their last meeting—just once!—without his cap in hand.

Sandro lingered silently behind the monk, watching his fingers moving with deft purpose. He found himself thinking that, in another life, Donato might have made quite the promising sculptor.

"Can I help you, my son?" the Carmelite asked softly.

"My friend, it is me—Sandro."

"Sandro Signorelli!" Donato remarked, his cheery tone diluted by palpable confusion, "why, this is a welcome surprise!"

"Indeed, my friend—my *dearest* friend! I have come to you with a matter of some urgency. May I please have your ear?"

"Of course. After Mass, you may even have both. Stay if you will and pray with us."

"That would be a great pleasure, friend," Sandro declared, aware that these repeated affirmations of friendship sounded artificial, even to him, almost as if they were obvious overtures for favour sought.

As Father Donato took the lectern Sandro looked for space among the pews. His lips soon became automatons, responding appropriately to rite and ritual. His mind, however, raced along private tracts, imagining every probable path of the conversation to come.

Contemplative and somewhat enigmatic, even as a youth, Donato always seemed to regard humanity as a rather inadequate reflection of the sublime. Always he demonstrated wry amusement whenever confronted by the more harmless foibles and failings of God's creatures. Yet Donato could also bare his temper in the face of more serious transgressions. In this grand temple of solemnity and moral judgement, Sandro could all too clearly imagine the Carmelite taking grievous offence, accusing him of abusing the residue of a once-sincere relationship in service of delusional self-gratification before casting him out from the Basilica and publicly revoking his right to call him 'friend' henceforth.

Sandro took Communion and prayed to God for the chance to give his painting immortality. An immortality, he promised, that glorified not himself, but *Himself*.

At the close of service, the congregation filed duly back onto the streets. Sandro took a deep breath and approached the font.

"Sandro Signorelli, my good friend," started Donato. Sandro was unsure if he detected a note of mockery in the way Donato had said the word *friend*, or if that was merely a manifestation of his private guilt. "And what purpose do you have with me?"

"My friend," Sandro started, almost blushing as he said the word once more—and there it was, Donato's familiar pinched smile—Sandro forced himself onwards nonetheless.

"My friend, in November of last year, I was commissioned to paint an altarpiece depicting the Assumption for a church being built in the town of Villanova. I was paid an advance instalment by the town priest and began the work. I had neared completion when I received word of tragedy. The town was beset by bandits! During the melee, the Church was looted and burned." The Carmelite sighed and made the sign of the cross. Sandro found himself copying the action and, doing so,

119

realised that his next words would cast him in a rather grasping light. "This incident has left the town unable to purchase the painting. And, while gifting them the piece without taking payment would surely be the divine recourse, alas, the needs of my family leave me in no position to do so."

"You are asking for forgiveness?" the Carmelite asked, sincerely perhaps.

Sandro dithered, unsure of the correct reply.

Donato sighed. "I believe that I understand. You are asking for my help in purchasing the painting. My friend, I am afraid we cannot purchase the work. We have just commissioned a piece for ourselves. An Assumption, as fate would have it, by a painter named Annibale Carracci. Do you know him?" Sandro did not. "No matter," Donato continued, "the work should be delivered later this year."

"Father, I must..."

"*Father*? And only moments ago, Sandro, we were such good friends," Donato chided playfully.

"Father, when last we met, you told me you had the ear of Cardinal Borghese. Is that still so?"

"Scipione? Of course. He visits Santa Maria often. Indeed, he is due here at six tomorrow morning."

"Father, please, time is running out for me. You know that the cardinal can make an artist with a single word. There is not a church in Rome in which he holds no sway! Even the Pope is said to solicit his opinions when it comes to aesthetic matters. My friend, despite the tragic events in Villanova, my Assumption was a success."

The Carmelite raised a thick eyebrow, pushing Sandro to quantify his boast.

Sandro knew then that he must choose his next words wisely. For a work by an unknown to be presented to the Cardinal Borghese it must be truly exceptional. If Sandro tempered his enthusiasm, he might see this favour gently declined. To overstate the matter and declare his work a masterpiece would be unseemly at best, and offensive at the worst. Sandro elected to perform his own minor act of transubstantiation: he would turn his desperation into pride. Holding his tongue, he pushed forth his scrap of parchment.

"Find enclosed the address of my workshop. My Assumption is housed there. Father, I wish only to serve the Lord by whatever means and talents He has bestowed upon me. Please, entreat the good cardinal. He must come by and see the work at once."

"Must he indeed?" replied Donato, as he tucked the parchment into his robes.

"Without delay!" Sandro declared. He left the Basilica with his head held high, though his hands shook with every step.

III.

"If the eyes do not look upwards, Tommaso, how can they receive their judgement?" Sandro's own words were the devil's instruments, demons dispatched by his memory to punish his pride.

His family had eaten their evening meal without him. Fernanda, Sandro's wife, had reserved some dumplings and kept them warm for his return. Sandro apologised for his unanticipated absence as he tore up the remaining bread crusts and searched for the courage to meet his wife's inexorably silent gaze amongst the melted butter and shredded mentuccia that had pooled at the bottom of his bowl.

His inability to look his wife in the eyes was not borne from a belief that his brief absence had angered his wife. No, Sandro's reticence emanated from feelings elsewhere. Fernanda's eyes had once been bright and shiny. They had once brimmed with respect, enthusiasm, and belief in his work. As time passed, Sandro felt as if he had watched that light dim until, slowly, they had transformed into soft and mournful things. In the eyes of his wife, Sandro believed that he could see a silent story of regret and remorse for ever marrying her life to his.

A prolonged silence had followed his account of events at the Basilica Santa Maria.

"Darling," Fernanda said eventually to fill it, "your time and your efforts must be employed fruitfully. Now that the Villanova painting is finally finished, we need it to be sold—and quickly."

"My darling," Sandro insisted, forcing himself to lift his head, "that was precisely what I was doing. He shall be the buyer—Borghese will be the buyer."

"Cardinal Borghese, *the* Cardinal Borghese, will cross Rome tomorrow morning, visit your workshop and purchase your painting?" Fernanda replied in a tone that was neither scornful nor hostile but something else. Sandro had heard his wife speaking in such a tone on many occasions before. It was the same tone of voice she used when explaining to their children how Eve was created from the rib of Adam and how the two had populated every far-flung corner of the Earth. Or why miracles occurred exclusively in days of the unobservable past. Or how the rules of judgement in the afterlife could be fairly applied to heathen ancestors and dead infants alike. It was the tone of the bewildered believer, straining with sincerity against incredulous manacles.

"I have a good friend within the priesthood," Sandro insisted, "a friend who knows Cardinal Borghese personally. Don't you see? Fate is God's canvas—He paints what He ordains. With this work, and with this chance, I believe that He has finally chosen to paint victory!"

Fernanda exhaled slowly. She looked as if she might be about to say something. No doubt she was moments away from one of her daily musings on the nature of should: Sandro should, for instance, spend his days scouring every address in the city for a new buyer of the Assumption, even before it was finished. He should also spend less time fretting about the minor details of his paintings, and more time worrying about his family's financial situation. It was, he reflected in petulant silence, almost as if Fernanda supposed that he was feverish and plagued by visions of false success. As if he thought himself rich as a Medici. As if the sight of his beloved wife and children skinny and clad all in threadbare rags did not already fill his heart with so much shame and frustration that the feelings invaded his unconscious mind at night and jolted him awake at erratic moments in the darkness. No, Fernanda did not seem at all disposed to see God's victory. But then, Sandro realised, how could she when she had not yet seen the finished painting?

"The work is complete," Sandro said, taking to his feet. "The Assumption is the greatest thing I have painted in my entire lifetime. My darling, please believe in me. Tomorrow the matter shall be placed in His hands, but tonight I would put it in yours. Will you come with me now?"

She nodded and took the hand he offered. Sandro led her out of their home and down the street. He unlocked the door to the room he rented for a workshop, and they stepped inside. Fernanda wrinkled her nose when confronted by the smell of the space. Sandro understood that the building had been used recently to store and age cheeses. He suspected that this might still be the case. Although he never saw anyone coming into or going from the cellar below, a potent musk wafted perpetually upwards, a commingling of sweet and sweaty odours that could prove quite sickly to an uninitiated nose. The workshop faced eastwards, by evening time it was dark and gloomy. Sandro requested that Fernanda close her eyes while he placed candles around his Assumption. He smiled slightly as he did so, the thought occurring to him that this arrangement and lighting would conspire to create something like the atmosphere of a chapel—the stench notwithstanding.

"Please now, open your eyes," he said once the final candle was lit.

The gold glimmered by the slight flames. It had been a procurement of near-crippling expense, and yet no other material was fit to depict the heavens. Sandro drew Fernanda's attention to his depiction of the Virgin's face, and towards the faces in the crowd below. Coyly, she asked if the cherubs had been painted with anyone in mind. They had.

"This one looks like Sophia!" laughed Fernanda. Just as in life, this version of their middle child had a slight air of mischief written across her face. "And this one is Matteo!" Fernanda continued, pointing to a second cherub. Matteo was their youngest child, just five years old. He was their only son and, by far, the quietest and sweetest of their children. "And so…" Fernanda looked for the likeness of their third. When she found it, the faintest of frowns shot across her face.

Sandro had also included Ilaria, their eldest, born shortly after their marriage nine years before. However, he had chosen to improve upon their daughter's appearance in one small and relatively minor way—Ilaria had a deep pink scar running from her chin and beneath her lip on the left-hand side. In life, the scar ran up towards her ear. In the painting, it was omitted altogether. Neither of them liked to talk about Ilaria's scar or the circumstances around it and so Sandro thought it best not to let the moment linger. Instead, he shepherded Fernanda's attention towards the other two cherubs included within the group of five. The fourth, he confessed, was an imagined likeness of the younger Tommaso. The fifth was an imagining of the child they had lost at birth.

"It is very beautiful, my darling," Fernanda conceded quietly as she took his hand.

"The best I have ever achieved." Sandro's words were caught halfway between question and statement. Fernanda agreed. She put her head on his shoulder, and they lingered a long time before the painting in the flickering silence.

IV.

At breakfast the next morning Ilaria recounted her bedtime story, Orpheus visiting the underworld in search of Eurydice and his violent death at the hands of crazed Bacchante revellers. Ilaria declared that the old myths were far superior to Bible stories, especially as many of them involved the city of Rome.

In truth, his daughter's chatter was muffled and distant to Sandro on the morning in which he might present his greatest work to a prospective patron of such wealth and influence. He had awoken to find a great battle being fought in the very pit of his stomach, a battle between a small deputation of staunchly defiant hopes and a vast host of apprehensions. The conflict seemed to gnaw at him all morning, putting him in a terse and quivering stupor. He excused himself from the dining table at the first opportunity and rushed to open his workshop.

Memories of the day before had flooded through him, washed now not in triumph, but in doubt. The expression on Father Donato's face had filled his dreams. Had the Carmelite been laughing at him? Had he such little regard for Sandro's talents that the very notion of soliciting the attention of the Cardinal Borghese seemed ridiculous to him?

Perhaps it *was* ridiculous.

Sandro wondered if he was making a complete farce of himself. When he looked at his work it morphed before his eyes until he could see nothing in it but magnified imperfections. Was one of the Virgin's arms ever so slightly longer than the other? The Tommaso cherub had never looked quite right. The more he examined it, the less the cherub resembled a divine being, and the more it seemed to resemble a shrunken old man in a gold-limned wig. Sandro could not even bring himself to look at the crowd below. There were four further figures amassed there— surely, they would present a catalogue of further flaws.

His Assumption needed correction. It needed work. He recalled his insistence only twelve hours ago that the cardinal must see the painting. Without delay, no less!

"Oh, Sandro," he muttered aloud, *"what an excitable fool you are!"*

Sandro was well-acquainted with indifference. He knew it as a heavy blanket, readily capable of smothering even the hottest fires of passion. Donato might well have, unwittingly or otherwise, neglected to extend his invitation. And, even supposing Donato remembered, the cardinal would most likely decline it. Perhaps on this occasion, the world's indifference towards Sandro and the paintings he made might just work to his advantage.

Tommaso arrived, as usual, at nine in the morning. They used the time between commissions to develop the boy's skill as a draughtsman and colourist—though lately there had been far more of this time than was healthy for business. Sandro took some old scraps of parchment from their drawer and laid several out across his desk.

"Today you will work further on cherubs," he declared, absent-minded, as he passed Tommaso the drawing chalks.

"Master, could you perhaps demonstrate something of another figure? I feel quite accomplished drawing cherubs by now, for you have me practising them in every slow moment."

"Indeed, you are accomplished," Sandro replied, irritably. "Very accomplished. This, my child, is because of practice. There is never too much improvement. There is no such thing as too good. Keep drawing cherubs Tommaso, one day you might become the finest practitioner in the entire city of Rome. What an accolade that would be! Your skills would be in *constant* demand," Sandro added in afterthought as he walked towards the doorway.

"Unless, of course, the city discovers a sense of good taste," Tommaso muttered.

Sandro decided that he had not heard this last statement. He opened the door and leaned against the frame. He was just contemplating the possibility of leaving Tommaso in his workshop and returning to Santa Maria to retract his request when he saw Donato turning into his street and walking purposefully toward his workshop. He was accompanied by a portly man in the red and white dress of a cardinal that could only be Borghese.

The sight of one of the city's most influential cardinals drained all the liquid from Sandro's throat and sent it, rather unhelpfully, to his knees, which began to buckle. He darted back inside his workshop and slammed the door behind him.

"What is the matter master?" asked Tommaso.

"No matter at all," replied Sandro, hoping that his tone of voice matched the lightness of sentiment.

They held one another's gaze, allied in uneasy silence that lasted until it was broken by the sound of brisk knocking from outside.

"Is someone there?" asked Tommaso.

"No, I think not," Sandro found himself saying, just before the knock sounded for a second time.

"Master, there is someone there. I am quite sure."

"Rome can be quite a dangerous town. Fair prudence would advise always against opening our doors when we know not who is outside."

"Signore Signorelli," an unfamiliar voice shouted through the doorway. "Are you in there?"

"Sandro," added Donato's, "we have come as requested."

Tommaso put down his chalk and leaned back on his stool in expectation. There could be no hiding. Sandro smiled weakly back at the boy before turning back to open the door.

"Sandro Signorelli," Donato began warmly. "It is my eternal pleasure to introduce you to his eminence, Cardinal Scipione Borghese."

The cardinal wafted a regal hand. Sandro bowed, kissing the soft and pale skin. When he pulled back, he noted the fine-wrought jewellery, rubies set in gold that, even in a passing glance, spoke of the cardinal's vigorous love of the arts. Borghese had a slight beard and a moustache, immaculately trimmed and stylised, like some dark triangular frame around his mouth. Sandro was barely able to form words. He heard himself saying *honour* and *pleasure*, repeatedly as he shook the cardinal's hand for a while too long.

"We came without delay," the cardinal informed when he finally liberated himself from Sandro's grip. "Father Donato was most insistent. He claims that the ebbs and flows of fortune have left you with, so he tells me, a minor masterpiece in desperate need of a home."

Sandro stuttered further, emphasising that he had never used the word "masterpiece", and that really, he must clarify… when Donato placed a hand upon Sandro's shoulder.

"My friend," he said gently. "Do you intend on leaving a *cardinal* standing in the street?"

Sandro apologised for the cheese smell as he showed them inside his workshop and towards his Assumption. He could not bring himself to watch Borghese's inspection of the work. He stood back, his eyes closed, as he offered God a silent prayer. The matter was now firmly in His hands.

All was possible. Validation and ridicule both were mere moments away.

But which would it be?

Donato stood beside him. Sensing Sandro's nerves, he patted him reassuringly on the shoulder. Sandro opened his eyes and looked at his friend. The Carmelite quietly suggested he might wish to release his breath. After several long and silent minutes, the cardinal straightened and walked back toward them with the inscrutable countenance of a seasoned cardsharp.

"The work is of a good standard," decreed Borghese. "It is truly a shame that Santa Maria has already commissioned this very same scene. Have you seen the Carracci?" he asked of Donato.

"No, your eminence, I have not."

"I had recent cause to visit his studio. In many aspects the works are similar. Carracci's brushwork is a little more sophisticated, naturally, and yet I enjoyed the use of gold in your depiction of Heaven," he informed Sandro. "It is an old-fashioned technique, but one that I retain a personal affection for. Should I see Carracci again I think I shall suggest he do the same."

That was all the Cardinal seemed inclined to say. As he made for the doorway. Donato looked quizzically at Sandro as if willing him to break his rigid silence. Sandro found himself quite unable to speak. If it were at all possible, he would have happily fled the room himself.

"Your eminence…" Donato ventured as Borghese touched the door handle. The cardinal turned back. "Your eminence, having made the journey across town and seen this work, might you perhaps consider purchasing it for yourself?"

"Oh, I am no longer interested in the acquisition of church-paintings," replied the cardinal, physically waving the suggestion aside. He looked back and seemed to notice Sandro's profound disappointment. The cardinal walked back to him, gently retaking Sandro's hand.

"My child, your work is good," Borghese remarked. "There is a talent for painting within you. Had you come to me just two weeks ago, perhaps I may have even purchased such a work. However, we have all seen this very scene presented many, many times before. I do not wish to flatter or deceive you, works such as this no longer move me."

Sandro wanted to question whether the Cardinal Borghese had noticed the positioning of the Virgin's eyes. Surely an innovation of such subtle sapience should be perceived and acclaimed by one as learned in aesthetics and theology as the Cardinal Borghese? Sandro's thoughts were coherent, but without the courage to verbalise them they dissolved like rain on hard dry land.

"Tell me, are you familiar with San Luigi dei Francesi?" the cardinal continued, "Last week, I attended a chapel consecration there. The pomp and ceremony were customary enough. And yet, then... then I saw paintings unveiled, paintings such as Rome has never seen! Oh, mere words cannot describe every feeling that they stirred within my spirit—such boldness! Such vision! The artist is named Michelangelo, I believe, and, like his namesake, he appears to be a true master. And so, alas, today I cannot help you, beyond insisting that you must visit San Luigi for yourself at your earliest opportunity. I am envious, to tell you the truth, of how such works shall surely thrill your artist's soul!"

Sandro offered his forlorn gratitude for the cardinal's time and words.

Donato looked between them. "Your eminence," he said to the cardinal, "you say that you cannot help the signore today. What of tomorrow? I am happy to visit this workshop once again should you encounter a prospective patron."

"Very well," said Borghese, "I will keep this work in mind. If anyone suitable presents themselves, I shall inform Father Donato here at once. I can do no more."

And with that, the cardinal left. Donato soon followed him out the door, but not before Sandro took the opportunity to give his friend an appreciative embrace.

Tommaso continued drawing until Sandro declared the faint scratching and rubbing of the chalks to be a nuisance and brought his apprentice's working day to a premature conclusion. He then spent the afternoon alone in his workshop, without food or drink. He found himself quite unable to complete any further work that day. His fingertips contained neither joy nor conviction.

Had you come to me just two weeks sooner I might have even bought the work, the cardinal had said! Sandro reflected with black and self-recriminatory amusement that Fernanda had been quite right—he should have prioritised the search for a buyer over the finishing of the work. He decided that he would withhold this part of the story in his recounting of it later.

Now and then, Sandro cast glances back at his Assumption. Mary's joyful and enraptured expression seemed now to be mocking its creator. Indeed, the entire canvas that only one day before had flooded Sandro's soul with deep pride and an acute sense of accomplishment felt almost painful to look at. If he could, Sandro might have taken a hammer or a knife to the work there and then, he might have thrashed out every ounce of the frustration and humiliation coursing through his being. However, he was unable to even countenance the idea. His very livelihood depended on it. His family depended utterly upon his labours.

He would need to sell it soon, this amorphous success, this dubious achievement of his lifetime, damned now by faint praise. Sandro sat smouldering in contemplation for so long that the shadows of the evening crept through his windows and soon returned his workshop to darkness.

Chapter Two: Vocation

I.

Sunday mornings were always reserved for Mass, the remainder of the day was for rest and leisure. The first leisurely afternoon that followed the visit of Borghese, Sandro took leave of his home for a stroll. He walked across Rome, telling himself he had no destination in mind even as he manoeuvred himself closer to San Luigi dei Francesi with every choice of direction. As he neared the church, Sandro finally resolved to end this self-charade.

He was astonished to see that a large crowd had gathered outside, and that members of the city watch had been stationed at the doors to restrict access to the church. As Sandro came closer, he saw that the line continued until it curled all the way around into Via del Salvatore. A small group of people exited San Luigi and the guards waved through a few of those waiting at the front. Sandro studied the faces of the leaving. They were solemn and silent, their heads bowed. The cheeks of an older woman glistened as the sunlight caught them—a silent affirmation of recent tears. Sandro reflected that never had his work moved an observer in this way. He had once, several years back, thought that a Madonna and Child painted by his hand had caused a nun to cry. However, when he approached the woman to console her passions, she had told him she had wept for some other mundane matter—she had been grieving a recent death, if Sandro's recollections were correct.

He began to follow the line, all the way down Via del Salvatore, into the Piazza Navona where it snaked back and forth to blend amidst the general bustle. Sandro waded through the press, ignoring the attentions of street performers and courtesans, and pushing past the beggars and loafers until, at last, he found the line's end. The Piazza was utter madness! Never had Sandro seen the place so crowded that only the tips of the twin fountains were visible above the crowd.

The line inched forwards. All the while Sandro listened to the words of those around him. He heard one woman declaring that she had heard that the San Luigi works had the power to convert heathens and heretics, and that they could heal the ailments of the sick. A man said that he had heard that bandits, rapists, and murderers had been permitted to model—and as *saints* no less! Another declared that he had seen the paintings already once before, that they were things of pure darkness, and must have been painted by Satan in a mockery of faith.

A young boy stood apart from the crowd. He wore a dark hat adorned with a bouquet of leaves and flowers along with a loose white tunic.

"Come Rome!" declared the youth, his eyes alight with mischievous glee. "This once-great city has grown old and tired! Behold the calling! Behold the new vision! Behold the new visionary!" The shoulders and neck of the youth, Sandro noticed, were covered in bite marks and bruises. "Michelangelo Merisi!" the boy continued, "Michelangelo da Caravaggio! Remember the name, for he is the chiaroscuro sledgehammer, here to shatter the Mannerist veneer, along with all its stale tropes!"

By the time Sandro was finally permitted inside, he found that the wait had turned his knees to liquid once again. San Luigi itself was a sumptuous symphony of marble and gold. It was a majestic and august church. A space worthy of representing the kingdom of God. The crowd inside had congregated before a chapel on the right-hand side. Sandro could see some had taken to praying on their knees. The voices inside were loud, their opinions clamouring over one another, threatening to escalate beyond debate and into argument. As Sandro stepped closer to the chapel they came into focus, the three panels that had kept Cardinal Borghese's purse strings closed to him. From a distance, all he saw was darkness. Standing directly before them, Sandro's mind shut itself off from all other considerations.

The painter—this Michelangelo Merisi—had distilled the life of St Matthew into three scenes, all of which were enveloped in complete blackness, the figures emerging starkly from obscurity into the light.

On the left-hand side, Matthew, not yet an apostle, sat among peacocking sinners in a gloomy den of vice and impropriety. Jesus called from the shadows, pointing to him, and demanding his faith. A shaft of light broke from a window above, matching the trajectory of Christ's finger to illuminate Matthew's shocked expression.

The central painting showed Matthew alone, except for a visiting angel. He seemed to be receiving instruction, writing notes onto parchment. The face was a masterful depiction of sombre contemplation; the nobility and sadness of the evangelist hinted at almost without force. The angel unfurled from the left-hand top corner. The mass of white that, in haste, Sandro's mind had read as wings seemed under closer inspection to be a white tunic. He saw that the angel looked very much like the youth who had stood outside proclaiming the genius of Michelangelo Merisi. Had this youth modelled for the angel? If so, this Merisi had transposed a convincing air of grace to the figure. The bruising and bite marks had also been expunged. Sandro began to see in the angelic robes a tangle of bedsheets. He recalled Fernanda at the start of their marriage, how they once had the time and disposition to lie next to each other, sometimes lost in looks of mutual adoration, sometimes talking for hours when all was new. Sandro shuddered at this strange association he had made with the angelic boy and turned his eyes to the final painting.

There he beheld a monstrosity. A vivid study of hatred and violence. St Matthew, about to receive his Martyrdom, lay prostrate on the floor, surrounded by a crowd of cowardly and apathetic onlookers. A twisted face, an expression of pure hatred, dominated the centre. It belonged to an assassin, one moment away from plunging his blade into the saint; the chiaroscuro illuminating his face with such dramatic clarity that it made Sandro feel almost faint. He saw the angel had reappeared, reaching down from the top left corner. Matthew raised his hand to meet him. The assassin was depicted seizing Matthew's wrist, subduing what he perceived as the apostle's resistance. And thus, the three hands met to complete the trinity of martyrdom: bestial wrath, noble self-sacrifice, and the celestial redemption of man.

Sandro was some time before the paintings of San Luigi while many others came and went. Borghese had been correct. These paintings were simply unlike any that Rome had ever seen before. The inky effect of such an oppressive use of chiaroscuro was so complete that really, it should seem ridiculous. Instead, the effect was a totality that served only to emphasise the strange virtuosity of Michelangelo Merisi's painting. Sandro could not help but jealously admire the fine details: individual strands of hair, the eyelashes, and the vanes and barbs of St Matthew's quill were all painted with the showiest of delicacy. To achieve such tonal effects, Merisi must have used some intensive technique of shading unknown to Sandro.

He stood on his tiptoes, straining to observe evidence of drafting or repainting, yet few clues as to Merisi's process were apparent beyond the unconventional use of a dark primer. Certainly, these innovations were far more radical than a mere repositioning of the Virgin's gaze, Sandro's innovation which, before Merisi's, seemed now pathetically quaint and laughably insignificant.

Never had human figures seemed so real in a painting—Merisi's figures were almost living, breathing, speaking things! Sandro could imagine the sensations and smells of their skin, their hair, and their clothing. He then allowed himself a wry smile. For all that these works of Michelangelo Merisi had proved annoyingly impressive under scrutiny, he, humble Sandro Signorelli, had deduced the flaw in this odd naturalistic style—a flaw that the artist himself had perhaps not foreseen. The figures painted by Michelangelo Merisi simply could not be sacred beings! His figures were dirty and defective, and were, therefore, unable to represent the great prophets and noble apostles touched by divinity. Merisi's figures more closely resembled the people gathered directly before them, those that stood outside waiting their turn, and those that hustled at the outskirts of the Piazza Navona, selling their wares, their tricks and flesh. How could such theologically irreverent paintings claim to represent the faith? How could painting ever divorce itself from didactics without being reduced to some dingy form of apostasy?

No, Sandro told himself silently, the good people of Rome would never, ever, tolerate paintings such as these. He then extricated himself from the enraptured crowd and left the church absorbed so deeply in thought and feeling that he forgot to thank the watchmen at the doors.

He was about to walk home when he spied Tommaso waiting a little way back in the line and marched over immediately. "Tommaso, my child, no," he said. "You do not want to see these paintings."

The youth did not seem at all pleased to see him, though Sandro stood firm.

"I am not your child, Sandro," Tommaso replied, speaking to the ground. "You do not command me here."

"You do not wish to see these paintings," Sandro repeated, "they are quite confusing and... and they are upsetting."

"But I *do* wish to see them, master. They are said to be compelling and new. Look how many other people wish to see them also! Have you ever seen anything like these crowds?"

Sandro seized the boy's shoulders in reply and tugged frantically, trying to force Tommaso from the line. The boy resisted.

"Take your hands off me!" Tommaso shouted in anger. Other men standing in the line were looking at Sandro then, curious as cattle. "This man is *not* my father. I do not know him. He is trying to abduct me against my will."

Immediately a stranger accused Sandro of perverse intentions. Others told him to leave the boy alone and venture hellwards. A chunk of bread hit Sandro's face, wet with saliva. The waiting people were bored and hostile and Sandro had made himself an outlet. His spirit wilted in the face of their collective antagonism, his grip loosening sufficiently for the boy to break free. Thwarted, Sandro withdrew.

Tommaso regained his place in the line and refused his master a second glance. Sandro walked briskly away from the San Luigi and its jeering crowd. A man ran up from behind, calling to his back. Fearing the worst, Sandro quickened his pace and tried ignoring the man. The stranger persisted, overtaking him, and blocking his path. Sandro winced, half-dreading, and half-expecting an attack that did not come.

"Signore!" began the man. "I am glad to find another capable of seeing those paintings for what they truly are—they are but a tempest in a water glass! I watched you a long while back inside. I am speaking to a fellow artist, am I not?"

Sandro regarded the man. He was a little younger, perhaps in his mid-twenties. He had long blonde hair and a perfectly shaven chin. He wore a bright red doublet and matching breeches, while a yellow sash completed a roguish appearance that suggested that this other artist was doing significantly better for himself than Sandro was. Or, at the very least, that this other man had not yet consigned himself to parenthood. The other artist arched his back listlessly and spoke without receiving Sandro's reply.

"Oh, Michelangelo Merisi the *brilliant*. Michelangelo Merisi the *great*. Michelangelo Merisi the *genius*. He is the toast of the city. Veni, vidi, vici!—hail Caesar indeed! Though…naturally, you might speculate how it could be that such a glorious commission as San Luigi could possibly have been awarded to a slovenly mongrel, born beneath some obscure Lombardian privy? If so, address your concerns to the Cardinal Del Monte, and, when he offers you his reasons, look to his teeth—I believe a good number of Merisi's pubic hairs reside there still."

"Signore," Sandro stuttered, casting nervous eyes around the street, "you cannot talk about a *cardinal* in such a way!"

"Hah," the artist exclaimed, "there is not a single soul in all of Rome who does not know that Del Monte spied heaven with his first glimpse of the male anus! They say the bloated old voluptuary found the young Merisi some years ago at market and purchased him like a prime cut of veal." If Sandro's face betrayed his distaste, it did not seem to bother the other artist much. "I am possibly a little bitter," the artist conceded. "Merisi has cost me, not a commission, but my favourite model. Those works back there seduced her soul. She believes that Merisi will make her the most famous face in Rome! I told her, they say he has little appetite for female flesh…though in her *great*, baseless wisdom, she knows these rumours to be nothing more than slander. Models…they are deluded moths, doomed to destroy themselves in pursuit of vanity's flame—are they not, my friend?"

Sandro nodded sagely, though he had little experience of the matter. He painted from his imagination, the time-honoured approach that would ensure that the glory of names such as Giovanni Bizzelli, Marco Pino, and Orazio Samacchini, would never dim.

"I suppose it is no real matter," the artist continued, "new girls are readily found. Nevertheless, I thought it best to come and observe these modern miracles for myself. Really, there is nothing to them but an imitation of Giorgione…" It was as if saying another's name brought his own to mind; the artist placed his hand lightly upon his chest, "Taddeo Zuccari," he finished, drawling as if his name might be already familiar.

"A pleasure to meet you, signore Zuccari. I am called Sandro Signorelli. Though I have not seen Giorgione and can therefore neither agree nor argue."

"You've not visited Venice? Or even Florence?"

"I was born in Rome and have lived my life here."

"Well, my friend, a man may encounter far worse fates than that. I am glad to have met you, however. You and I are among the brave. Let the sheep bleat."

Zuccari spoke with the air of a man whose opinions had been met with accordance. He turned to walk away before seeming to remember something.

"Signore…signore…before we depart—I hope you do not mind the observation, but you look somewhat starved of success. I know a man who is looking to exhibit works of, shall we say, a more *traditional* aesthetic than those aberrations back there. My patron is also a man of significant influence—yes, perhaps even more so than Cardinal Del Monte. With a snap of his fingers, my patron can place art works anywhere that he pleases in this city, and he always ensures his friends and allies are well remunerated too. We shall meet this coming Saturday. At three. Shall I give you his address?"

II.

Sandro opened his workshop early on Monday morning. He covered his Assumption with a protective cloth and positioned it out of sight at the back of the room. When Tommaso arrived, Sandro announced that they would commence working on a panel together, a large panel, a group scene, in fact, painted in landscape orientation.

"Oh?" Tommaso queried, seemingly intrigued by this sudden insinuation of employment. "What are we painting? And for who?"

"I think we shall paint the Nativity," Sandro remarked, initially answering only half of his apprentice's questions. "Yes, I believe that you might enjoy the subject. You could assume the responsibility of creating the likenesses of the animals and spend these summer months learning how to draw the fowl and the goats, the donkeys and sheep." Sandro noticed that he was excited once again. His ideas had agitated his hands and, imbued with wild self-accord, they seemed to be composing an imagined menagerie in the air between them. "Indeed!" he insisted, "we shall paint every humble creature that greeted the birth of our Lord. The work, once complete, shall be quite considerable. Perhaps as large as thirty inches tall, and sixty inches wide—perhaps even larger!"

"Forgive me master," Tommaso remarked, "but this commission seems almost irregular."

The boy's lilting intonation made a question of the observation. Issues such as subject matter and dimensionality were for the patron to decide, leaving the artist with little licence for creative liberty. Sandro and Tommaso were hired craftsmen, paid for their time, efforts, and materials. This was how things had always worked.

"We will be working without a commission," Sandro conceded, his hands faltering in the air, "which is to say, we will, at least, begin the work without a commission. I am sure we shall locate ourselves a buyer in good time."

A multitude of emotions—astonishment, consternation, and something that almost resembled disdain—appeared to chase each other across the boy's face.

"Our choice of subject shall mitigate the risk of wasted labour and materials," Sandro insisted, sensing that his apprentice would benefit from further persuasion. "A Nativity scene of good quality shall surely find a buyer in the months before Christmas."

"Indeed," Tommaso replied, in a voice thin and rancorous, "and if it does not, we can always store it back there, alongside the other one." He pointed to the back of the workshop where Sandro's Assumption now rested.

The boy's impulsive goading seemed to surprise them both. Sandro felt his face flushing red. "Of course, our Nativity scene *shall* be garlanded by cherubs," he snapped, his earlier munificence spoiling in an instant, "and so you will be pleased to return yourself to your work. Immediately, if you would, Tommaso."

Tommaso shook his head and took his seat. As they commenced their work, Sandro noticed that for the first time it felt almost as if there were now three artists present in his workshop. He was stationed at his desk, tracing rough figures around a manger, and trying to discover the general composition of his work. Tommaso sketched cherubs on the other side of the room. The third filled the space between them, though his name remained unspoken throughout the entire day; Sandro could not bring himself to ask for Tommaso's thoughts on Michelangelo Merisi da Caravaggio, and neither did Tommaso offer them—their altercation outside the church was left unmentioned.

At Tuesday's close of business, Tommaso handed in his day's work. Sandro looked at the cartoons. Two of them were sketched in grey-black chalk, the cherubs emerging from the negative space at the centre of this improvised chiaroscuro.

On Wednesday morning Sandro told him, at length, that this was not the established aesthetic vocabulary. That the world existed in a thousand hues, that gold and lapis were infinitely more brilliant than black could ever hope to be, and that a skilled artist should be capable of furnishing a scene *properly*, with backgrounds of buildings, trees, and hills. Aloud, Tommaso agreed, asking what indeed was wrong with painting the same nativity scene as everyone who had ever painted it before them, and then the same Annunciation, and the same Madonna and child—over and over, until the end of days. Those flat and disingenuous words were the only ones he spoke all day.

The Thursday of that week, they travelled together to visit a nearby church in possession of a classic Nativity scene. They sat on the floor, copying the cows and horses. After perhaps an hour, the church priest brought them each a cup of water and a stool. He asked if they, as artists themselves, had seen the paintings of

San Luigi. Tommaso kept his tongue still and his mind focussed on drawing cows. Sandro said that he had seen the works.

"They are the talk of the city," the priest said. "I intend to see them just as soon as I am able."

"They are a curiosity," shrugged Sandro, speaking indirectly to Tommaso as much as to the priest. "This artist—Merisi—rids the world of all its luminosity, impoverishing it until it is entombed entirely in darkness. Though the effect is certainly striking, I cannot imagine it will endure."

Sandro realised as he spoke that it was not truly the darkness that he found so bothersome. He recalled the martyrdom of St Matthew in stark clarity. He recalled the saint dying without a Halo, and, therefore, without the promise of deliverance offered to all those of faith. What indeed was art if it was not this very promise? It was not the place of art, he reflected, to revel in the *suffering* of martyrs, but instead in their dignity and defiance when faced with the worst instincts of man.

"I hear talk of crowds outside," continued the priest, pulling Sandro from his thoughts. "Is it true that guards are stationed there to quell the fever?"

"I think *fever* overstates the matter a little," replied Sandro irritably. "But yes, the Piazza was crowded. And there were guards at the church door."

The priest walked away, shaking his head at such a strange notion. Sandro did not look at his apprentice for some time after that exchange. If anything, *fever* was a perfectly accurate description of the clamour and effusion of the crowd—onlookers weeping before these strange, nigh-heretical, visions!

Tommaso spent all Friday drawing cows. Sandro inspected his progress. The drawings were excellent for an unfamiliar subject. He told the boy so, earnest in intention. Tommaso thanked him, with no great enthusiasm, before returning to the workshop to silence. As the bells sounded at four, Tommaso stood to leave.

"There is no need to come into the workshop tomorrow," Sandro declared.

He had waited all week for this moment. Such a break in routine would surely be queried. Sandro could then enjoy informing his sceptical apprentice that he had been invited to the house of another cardinal. That he had found a prospective buyer for their Assumption. And that, despite their recent frustrations of circumstance, and despite being forced into working without a patron, he was not some ill-fated wretch, forever fettered to fiasco and failure. But Tommaso did not query the command, he simply nodded and made straight for the door.

III.

The strange new cardinal gave forth a cry of great delight as he clapped his hands rapturously together.

"The Assumption of the Virgin!" declared the cardinal in a voice not dissimilar to that of Cardinal Borghese, "The triumph of the faith! And painted with such grace and feeling too!"

Sandro tried to repay the man's praise with his gratitude but found that the new cardinal was far too immersed in the details of his masterpiece to indulge in any such pleasant trifles.

"My child, your use of symbolism is supreme! The virgin's pose as she rises is exactly like that of Jesus on the cross. And are her eyes positioned upwards, and not down? Beautiful! Brilliant! A composition worthy of the great Raphael himself! Together these details—the pose, the eyes—shall serve as a most joyful proclamation indeed! Armed with renewed faith, the true followers of Christ shall indeed vanquish adversity, emerge victorious from tribulations, and defy even death!"

Sandro admitted to his moment of genius with as much modesty and propriety as he could possibly muster.

"And you, my child, have you experienced hardships yourself?" the new cardinal asked, turning to reveal a face devoid of colour or detail, like an unpainted oval canvas.

"I have, your eminence," Sandro replied, managing somehow to prevent himself from physically recoiling from the faceless cardinal.

The cardinal reached out to touch him with a hand that did not exist beneath his billowing robes. "Then it is time for you, Sandro Signorelli, to finally receive your just rewards! I shall ensure your patronage—for life—with immediate effect—and you shall be granted the chance to make your own indelible mark upon this great city!"

The thoughtless exuberance of several children playing in the streets collided with Sandro's reverie. The children apologised and continued their running and laughing. Sandro did not mind the interruption though; the remainder of this fantasy had forever eluded him anyway. As a young painter, he had walked beneath great frescoes and altarpieces painted by the immortals and had dreamed of adding his name to theirs. Now, he could barely imagine what even a modest degree of success would feel like. And yet—just ten days ago Sandro had never met a cardinal. That afternoon he was making his way across town to meet his second. His experience of meeting the first had done nothing to soothe his apprehensions. All was possible once more.

Surely, hope was the greatest torment ever devised by the devil.

He checked the parchment bearing the cardinal's address given to him by Zuccari. The route took him over Sant'Angelo Bridge, towards Saint Peter's Basilica, and through grand and leafy boulevards flanked by the gated villas of great and powerful men. Never had Sandro felt so acutely aware of his ragged clothing and scuffed shoes. He passed patrols of armed city guards who shot suspicious glances at him. He found the cardinal's address on a small, though immodest, side street. He dragged himself, step by step, up a grand marble staircase that led up to an ornately carved oak door and knocked upon the door using the face of a snarling wolf, sculpted in brass. It soon opened to reveal one of the cardinal's manservants, a tiny older man with squint and mistrusting eyes. Sandro was forced then to admit that he could not quite recall the name of the cardinal that he had called upon, for the name was a rather unfamiliar one to him. The manservant looked him up and down and made blunt assurances that the household had not heard the name of Sandro Signorelli either.

"Signore, please. I understand there is a meeting of artists here this afternoon," Sandro pleaded, "I am here on the invitation of Taddeo Zuccari."

"Are you indeed?" the manservant sneered. "It is quite strange how no one felt compelled to inform me of signore Zuccari's ascension to the rank of master of this house!" He paused. "Very well," he added breathily, as if eager to convey his reluctance, "I will ask his eminence."

The manservant retreated, leaving Sandro outside to contemplate how a person might linger gracefully.

When the door eventually re-opened, the manservant beckoned Sandro forward. "Your friend Zuccari vouched for you," he remarked, "he said you were no friend of this *Michelangelo Merisi* that has his eminence so worked up."

"And what is his eminence's name?" Sandro asked as he stepped inside.

"Friends and peers are permitted to call his eminence Cardinal Gabriele Gentile. You shall address him only as Your eminence."

The manservant ushered Sandro down the hall and into a room filled with the low hum of conversation. The cardinal was sitting, side-on, at a table at the head of the room. He was positioned a little apart from the other four men inside. As Sandro entered the room, the cardinal took shakily to his feet, welcoming Sandro as *a good and gracious servant of the Lord*, into his home.

Cardinal Gabrielle Gentile was a significantly older man than Borghese, perhaps as old as sixty. Sandro kissed the proffered hand with deference, yet as he leaned in Sandro noticed that Cardinal Gentile's hand was quite unlike any other that he had ever seen; blotchy and swollen, the knuckle as round and red as a large tomato. He noticed too that the cardinal wore only one slipper—the other had been removed and lay nearby. The foot protruding from his robes was likewise red and bulbous. Gentile seemed to notice Sandro's gaze and swiftly retracted the strange foot back beneath his robes.

As the manservant went to fetch a chair, Sandro took in the room. They were in some form of study, the shelves filled with hundreds of books while several cabinets were topped with maps and globes. Among the several paintings mounted on the walls a portrait of Cardinal Gentile was positioned above the central fireplace. His hair and figure appeared to be rendered incorrectly by the artist; the former was far thinner and the latter considerably thicker in his person than they appeared in oils.

The four other men gathered before the cardinal must be the artists. Among them was Taddeo Zuccari, that day wearing a doublet as bright and as yellow as mimosa blossom. Zuccari beamed at Sandro and bowed his head briefly in recognition.

"Signores, for the sake of our newcomer, I hope you will not mind the slight indulgence of retrogress?" If anyone did mind, they minded silently. "Very good. Signores, Rome is no stranger to suffering. The Eternal City has been plagued by cataclysms enough to shame the heathen Pharaohs themselves. We have endured the baleful intentions of every single heretic who would have torn us down: from Atilla to that most audacious German whose very name recalls the devil—I am talking, of course, of *Luther.* And all that is without considering threats from within—the weak-minded Popes for instance. Indeed, our enemies are legion. So copious are they that I could quite easily sit here all afternoon enumerating."

The old cardinal broke for water, and Sandro hoped surreptitiously that his proposition would remain notional. He felt his smile sagging somewhat and fortified it by force of conscious will.

"However," the cardinal continued, "we are gathered here today to address one discrete and distinct matter. He answers to the name of Michelangelo Merisi, though this malady of a man is known also as Michelangelo da Caravaggio. Signores, whatever we call this imprecation, it has come to Rome with only one purpose in its black heart—corruption. His paintings are a foul poison in the heart of God's kingdom. He terrorises our streets, the head wolf in a pack of venereal vandals who whore and brawl and drink and murder and gamble day and night. I hear you thinking now: *why not simply gather these iniquitous creatures, line them up in that accursed Piazza Navona and relieve them of their heads?*" the cardinal continued. "Well, I cannot. Not quite yet. You see, the devil's powers of seduction are consummate. Through Michelangelo Merisi, he has ensnared the hearts of many men, many of them great men, who have, in turn, proven to be great disappointments. Indeed—Merisi is now quite *protected.*" The last word seemed to agitate the old cardinal's spirit, like an allergy, he spat it out in disgust. "These allies are the very same who plucked his rotting body from the Della Consolazione sick house," Gentile continued. "They pay his damned bail each time he feels the warm breath of justice

153

on his neck! Yet, by granting Merisi commissions they overplay their hand. They permit the devil to laugh at us! No doubt he wakes each morning cackling as the Holy Roman Church *pays* him wages! You hear me correctly signores—we are paying him! Paying him to fill Roman churches with the malign expressions of a soul which lies in darkness—that is far removed from God—and from all that is good and pure!"

The old cardinal was getting furious, his face was reddening, his eyes and nostrils flaring, and the corners of his mouth were gathering vermillion-tinged spittle. Gentile wiped a sleeve across his face and took a drink of water.

"Also, I have it on good authority," Gentile whispered theatrically as if he feared the Lord might interpret volume for implication, "that this lascivious creature is, above all else, a sodomite! Indeed, it seems that while just about anything warm and willing can service the insatiable lust of this grotesque faun, his penchant is for young boys. Young boys with faces so very pretty they may just as well be girls. Yes, drunken, sinful, girl-boys wearing loose tunics. With ringed hair, wet lips, supple thighs and *hairless* little penises."

The cardinal's tirade stuttered to a halt. No one in the room spoke for many heartbeats afterwards.

"Your eminence," ventured Zuccari, "do I understand your purpose with us correctly? That you wish us to provide artworks that do not debase the faith but instead glorify it?"

"Oh yes," replied the cardinal, "I have made several enquiries and there is no way to have the Merisi works removed from San Luigi. The Pope, in his *wisdom*," at this, the cardinal rolled his eyes, "has not granted my request to prevent other churches from commissioning further works either. Therefore, we will find another means to skin the devil... It is no exaggeration

154

to state that this is nothing less than a battle—a war for the soul of Rome. The Eternal City is itself a monument to Christian endurance. We are the righteous of heart. We are noble Horatius, defending our bridge. We shall make our stand directly across the Piazza Navona, in the church of Santa Maria dell'Anima. Together, signores, we will edify the straying flock. We will offer a riposte to the arrogance of Merisi and his odious patrons. We shall demonstrate the lost virtues of piety and humility!"

Sitting in this palatial study filled with the opulent, the bejewelled, and the exotic, Sandro silently observed that almost anything could be lost in this room alone.

"How many works do you require?" asked one of the other painters, just as soon as he was sure that the cardinal had finally finished speaking once again.

Cardinal Gentile had clearly not given much thought to the matter. "Oh…I suppose twelve should suffice," he replied blithely as he stood, "after all, there were twelve apostles, twelve months, and so forth."

Sandro began thinking of how he might advocate for his Assumption. He longed for the opportunity to explain his compositional choices and to describe the sensitivity of his Virgin's face, but the cardinal pre-empted him. "I think we require a title. We shall call the exhibition: *Sacred Images*. I care not one bit how you make up the twelve, decide this amongst yourselves."

"Your eminence," Zuccari interjected, "forgive me for raising such a base issue, but we are poor souls and we cannot afford to work for free."

"Of course, of course," replied Gentile, waving aside the concern. "I can almost certainly sanction the use of, say, five hundred Scudo for these purposes. What is that? Around fifty

Scudo per completed work?" The cardinal opened his door, tacitly inviting them all to leave his study. "We must move swiftly here, signores. If you have suitable works—give your addresses to my manservant on your way out and I shall have the paintings collected."

The artists filed out of the room offering thanks to the old cardinal as he blessed them one by one. In turn, each of them wrote their names and addresses into a ledger book by the door. Sandro did not share the obvious joy and enthusiasm of his fellow artists—was he the only one who had found the meeting somewhat bothersome? And, although his private observation was an ungracious one to make about a senior member of the clergy, an observation that he apologised silently to God for, the old cardinal had seemed almost fanatical to him.

When it was time to add his own name and address, Sandro hesitated.

"Signore, really," exclaimed Zuccari, "have you ever been paid so handsomely in your life?"

Sandro had not. A disciple's share of five hundred Scudo was forty-two—more than ample compensation for Sandro's time. Indeed, the amount was twelve Scudo more than Villanova church had offered in his original commission. The sale would be more than enough money to keep his family fed and housed for the rest of the year. Yet still, he found himself dithering.

Zuccari put his hand on his shoulder, "I have had dealings with Cardinal Gentile before. I invited you along because he can afford to pay his artists so lavishly that you could, if you desired, concert your efforts towards dying some spectacular and syphilitic death. And I expect that no painting of yours has ever sat in such a fine church as Santa Maria dell'Anima! My friend, think of life as a masquerade ball. Fair lady fortune might disguise herself behind a thousand unlikely faces, when just one prosperous spark from her may ignite a raging inferno, we must flirt with every possibility."

"If he does not want to participate, I will have his space," one of the other artists interjected.

"I have three pieces waiting in my studio," another clamoured, "and I am sure I will find some way to use one hundred and twenty Scudo!"

Zuccari offered Sandro the ledger book one final time with an indifferent shrug. Sandro exhaled deeply and made the sign of the cross before adding his name and address to the list.

Later, at the dinner table, Sandro chafed against the exultant manner in which Fernanda welcomed his news. As his wife rushed to her feet and threw her arms around him, Sandro reflected that he must have poured much sugar into his recounting for his tidings to sound so sweet.

"Forty-two Scudo!" she declared breathlessly, "and the good cardinal shall display your masterpiece in the heart of the city! My darling, this news could hardly be better—he has given all of Rome the chance to finally see your talent!"

So, he had slanted his story so fulsomely that he had made Cardinal Gentile the "good cardinal." And with this ready provision of artifice, Sandro had made an unwitting ally of whoever had painted the obsequious portrait displayed in the cardinal's study—both were now outcasts from the noble profession of artistry, their practice had become base idolatry and insidious propagation.

"Something is bothering you," Fernanda said in the silence that followed. She broke free of the embrace and looked her husband in the eyes.

"I am assured that the cardinal will purchase the work in full," Sandro began tentatively. "He offers twelve Scudo more than we had been originally promised by Villanova. The sale is enough to renew the workshop tenancy for another six months, with twenty Scudo remaining to provide for the family."

"Then the offer is a good one," Fernanda shrugged, "I can feed us for months on half of that." If anything, this was an understatement. Fernanda had grown depressingly adept at wringing everything possible from the scant sums of money Sandro's art brought into the house. "And my darling, as you know, the timing is a minor miracle, our purse is almost exhausted."

"Mother was saying, only yesterday, that soon we will have to accompany her at the markets," Ilaria chimed, giggling. "She said we will have to stare into the eyes of the butchers and tell them how poor and hungry we are."

"I can cry whenever I want to," Sophia boasted. She tried demonstrating the fact, wobbling her lips and shaking slightly— though actual tears themselves were not forthcoming.

Fernanda's cheeks flushed a shade of rose pink. She excused the children from chores and sent them to play in their bedroom. She took the seat opposite Sandro at the table as they both chose to disregard the jests of their children.

"My darling, I am yet to hear them," she started.

"Hear what?"

"You have made the best sale of your career and will have your work displayed in the city. Still, your face is darker than I have ever seen it," Fernanda continued gently. "And so, I am yet to hear the things that you are keeping from me."

"I have never met a man like the cardinal before," Sandro admitted. "He spent much of the afternoon talking only of his hatred of Michelangelo Merisi and accusing everybody around the man of corruption—other cardinals and even the Pope himself! And he did not even request a viewing of my Assumption before purchasing it. He will buy all twelve of our works without even seeing them."

"What do you know of this cardinal?" Fernanda asked. "What is his name?"

"He is called Cardinal Gabriele Gentile. I know little about him, though he appears to be wealthy and well-established. And, of course, he is a cardinal of the faith."

She nodded slowly. "God forgive me for saying so, but men of all kinds have worn the vestments and recited the scriptures. You have a friend among the Carmelites, do you not? You sought his advice some weeks back at Piazza del Popolo. Why not go back and speak with him again? He may know something more about this cardinal of yours."

"Pride is a luxury," Sandro said, his head drooping a little, "a luxury that our current situation does not allow. Besides, it is too late. There was no time to consider the offer. I have agreed to the sale already. The Assumption will be collected this week."

Fernanda reached across the table and stroked Sandro's outstretched hand until he lifted his face to her once more. "You are mistaken, my darling. We always have our pride, even if we have nothing else. No one can ever take your pride from you. Do not cast it aside for anyone."

Chapter Three: Sacred Images

I.

The young man standing outside the door of the Signorelli workshop wore billowing crimson robes. His eyes were unblinking blue. His chin and upper lip were as smooth and hairless as a child's. Wisps of sandy blonde hair protruded from beneath a wide-brimmed hat of matching crimson while a black iron crucifix weighted his neck.

"Signore, we are here at the wise and benevolent behest of the cardinal Gabrielle Gentile," the young man explained with a ready smile. "We have been dispatched by him to complete the purchase of a painting."

Though Sandro stepped aside, the young man in crimson did not enter the studio. He turned back instead and beckoned towards a retinue of four armed men standing beside a horse cart in the street. Two of the four stepped forth, filing silently into the workshop. Sandro pointed to his Assumption and was duly handed a weighty cloth pouch by a soldier whose face bore the scars of some past altercation. He emptied its contents onto his desk and began counting out the coins.

Sandro felt eyes upon him. He glanced to the back of the room and found that Tommaso was staring at the money with keen intent. Sandro shirked from the boy's gaze and returned to the count.

He discovered that the cardinal's man had given him forty-five Scudo—three Scudo more than he had been expecting. Sandro authorised the sale with a tentative nod. His Assumption was then lifted carefully by the two guards and taken out to the street where it was placed into the back of the cart and covered with a dust sheet. The young man in crimson thanked Sandro curtly for his time and assistance before turning heel and ushering his men onwards.

Sandro lent against his doorway and watched the cart as it departed. He watched until it appeared to be no bigger than his thumb, after which it became lost among the distant crowd. He looked at the ground and slowly drew a line with the toe of his boot to expose the darker and healthier dirt beneath the surface level. If he were inclined towards further whimsy that morning, he might have stood and stared at his line until the dirt dried and bleached beneath the sun, until the breeze and commotion of the street covered it in dust, and time consumed the trifling mark that he had made. He found himself curiously tempted to do exactly this, though he suspected that he might find a better use for his morning than observing ephemerality winding its leisurely course.

"You see Tommaso," Sandro declared with inflated conviction as he re-entered his workshop, "with perseverance and a little enterprise we can always find buyers for our work. We need only to exercise a little faith!"

Tommaso did not reply, he was still staring at the stack of Scudo. Sandro felt almost ashamed to have left such a substantial sum of money sitting before him. Tommaso had, after all, contributed much to the painting of the Assumption, and had worked at the Signorelli workshop for almost two years without receiving one single lira for his time and efforts. The boy's apprenticeship had been proposed to Sandro by his father, Luca, who had touted his talented son around the city two years ago, hoping desperately to secure tuition. The free exchange of labour for learning was then an agreement, and not an injustice, however much it felt like one that morning.

Sandro swept the money back into the cloth bag and placed it inside the draw of his desk before locking it shut. He flashed his apprentice a false and ungainly smile before bowing his head to focus on the task at hand, his continued experiments with the positioning of Joseph and Mary within the Nativity.

He sat motionless until the pealing bells of a nearby church informed Sandro that he had been inactive for almost an hour. Joseph and Mary still existed only as the outlines of torsos and heads on his parchment. He had wanted to try positioning their arms in different ways: reaching down to touch their divine child, or interlocking in support of one another, but had he truly done the right thing selling his work to Cardinal Gentile? The money was real. It was there inside his desk. It was a heavy stack of silver disks, each one almost as big as his palm. It was more money than anyone had ever paid him for his work. He recalled the insistence of Zuccari—that just one prosperous spark of fortune could become a raging inferno—so why could he still not envision his success? Perhaps, he speculated, the best way to see his success might just be to draw it.

And so, Sandro elected to abandon Mary and Joseph that day, to begin working on a portrait of himself, garbed in the more ostentatious style of clothing worn by Taddeo Zuccari. He was quite relieved to be interrupted soon after by a knocking at the door and to find Father Donato waiting outside.

"Father," Sandro declared gladly, "it is so good to see you again! Step inside if you will."

"Of course," Donato replied, his thin lips almost forming a smile. "Today, nothing would please me more than a visit with my good friend Sandro. I…" the Carmelite tailed off, his nose wrinkling at the punchy aroma of the workshop.

"The smell emanates from the cellar below," Sandro explained apologetically, "I believe it is the previous occupant."

"Good lord," Donato replied, "do you think we should go and check on the man?"

"Oh no, nothing like that," Sandro laughed, his face flushing red. "This used to be a shop. The man was a maker of cheeses; I suspect the cellar is still filled with ageing Parmigianino wheels."

"I see," Donato said with a slight chuckle, "In truth, I had half-a mind to enquire about the odour the last time I visited. The occasion, however, did not seem quite right. We were both rather preoccupied that day—so preoccupied, in fact, that you neglected to introduce me to this young man here."

"The boy is named Tommaso Marelli," Sandro replied. "He is my apprentice. Tommaso, this is Father Donato, an old friend of mine, and a member of the Carmelite order at Santa Maria del Popolo."

Tommaso stood to greet the monk. He lifted his stool and carried it across the room to position it before Sandro's desk. Tommaso then bowed his head reverentially and intimated that Father Donato should use his seat. Sandro watched on, quietly astonished by this novel display of good manners from the boy. Father Donato accepted the offer, conferring his blessings and giving thanks for this small act of apparent kindness.

"Father—are the rumours true? Is Michelangelo Merisi painting works for Santa Maria del Popolo?" Tommaso asked, betraying his true purpose.

"Why yes, it is," Donato answered. "A subject I was coming to in time," he assured Sandro.

"Have you seen Michelangelo Merisi for yourself, Father? I hear that he dresses only in black, that he wears a black beard, and has black hair and black eyes too?" Tommaso pushed on, ignoring the discouraging looks that Sandro shot at him.

"Even the children talk of him!" laughed Donato, visibly taken aback.

Sandro excused his apprentice, but Donato protested.

"Oh, I don't mind a little natural curiosity. Michelangelo Merisi lives on the tongues of half the city, why should we be any different? Let the boy stay."

Sandro nodded permission to Tommaso who clasped his hands behind his back in anticipation.

"It is true, Cardinal Borghese is quite taken by Michelangelo Merisi. He has commissioned two large paintings for Santa Maria. Notionally, Merisi should be painting them as we speak, though if even half the stories told to us by the concerned citizens of Rome prove true it is truly a wonder that he finds the time to even wet his brushes between all the fornicating and fighting. Perhaps you have also heard of his other great debacle?"

Sandro had not. He rolled his eyes while Tommaso leaned against the desk on his elbows, enraptured.

"An altarpiece of his was rejected only last week. The scene requested was the death of Mary. Merisi elected to use a *courtesan* to stand for the Virgin. Moreover, he used a courtesan who, I am assured, is rather renowned among men that find even the scantiest occasion to acquaint themselves with the fair courtesans of this great city… Suffice to say, there were one or two among the priesthood who recognised his *virgin*. Some might have also found her position—horizontal between bedsheets—somewhat familiar to them."

Donato paused, allowing Tommaso a moment's grace to suppress a sudden bout of snickering.

"Doubtless, Merisi had his fun," the Carmelite continued dryly, "though blasphemy was added to his already substantial charge sheet and a decree was issued for his arrest and imprisonment. I believe he went into hiding for three days and two nights before Borghese was able to intervene… The decree was invalidated by Pope Clement himself. Of course, one might be forgiven for thinking that such a circus might have bothered Borghese. However, the cardinal is seemingly ecstatic to have secured the services of the artist. He tells anyone who demands justification for his support that it has been eighty years since Raphael passed, forty since Michelangelo Buonarroti, and that Rome has stagnated ever since. He claims that these paintings will prove capable of filling Santa Maria with voices, debate, and fresh faces for the rest of the year and beyond."

Sandro recalled the scenes at San Luigi. Cardinal Borghese's prediction was likely to be correct. He did not voice his agreement aloud, however, as the door to his workshop opened once more and Fernanda entered.

"Ah yes," Donato added, "as fashionable as it may be to idle away the hours talking of the great and terrible Michelangelo Merisi da Caravaggio, it is not the true purpose of my visit today."

"Tommaso," Fernanda started softly, "I need to speak with my husband. Would you mind sitting with the children in our kitchen for a few minutes? I have left some food on the table for you if you are hungry."

Tommaso looked back and forth for a moment and seemed to conclude that refusal was no option. He smiled and thanked Fernanda and exited the studio quickly, shooting a puzzled look back to Sandro from the doorway.

Sandro looked at his wife's ashen face and then to Donato and back again. "Well," he murmured, feeling inexplicably abashed, "what is this about?"

"Tell him, Father," Fernanda urged.

"Your wife, Fernanda, came to me this morning, Sandro. She told me that you are considering selling your work to a cardinal by the name of Cardinal Gentile. She asked me if I knew anything of this man. As it happens, I do. She also tells me that you only listen to her when you like what she is saying. I suggested therefore that we meet all together to appeal to your better judgement."

"This information is too important for you to disregard," said Fernanda. "Please father, tell him everything, just as you told me."

"Very well," Donato stated, his eyes flickering downwards as if his next words caused him pain. "Gabriele Gentile was not born to such a grand name and station. He was born Giovanni Locatelli, the third son of an army captain. Severity was his father and discipline his mother. His zeal impressed Sixtus so sufficiently that the Pope personally made him a cardinal. Gentile's commitment to the principles and practices of the Iron Pope enabled him to become a pivotal cog within that regrettable administration."

"These are the men who threw open the gates of Rome to the Inquisition," Fernanda emphasised, "they are responsible for that long reign of terror. Do not pretend that you have forgotten how things were back then, Sandro."

Pope Sixtus V, The Iron Pope, had presided over Sandro's young adult life and Fernanda's teenage years. It had been commonly said that the Iron Pope ensured that more heads were mounted on spikes within the city of Rome than there were melons for sale in the marketplaces. Sandro had witnessed it as a time ruled by savage and suspicious hearts, a time in which thieves, prostitutes, and sinners were executed in their thousands, and when the screams of heretics filled the piazzas from beneath red Capirote hoods as they were punished by the flames.

Fernanda and Father Donato were both looking directly at Sandro. He knew that they were both willing him to demonstrate something like moral fortitude. He dithered, acutely aware that a heavy cloth bag filled with money was locked in his desk adjacent to his knee and found himself quite uncertain of what he could possibly say.

"Things are never simple," he found himself venturing in a voice wavering and small. "The past is a contentious thing, laced with innumerable intricacies. Surely the Iron Pope did some good. He drained the marshes, for one, and improved the air. And, if we are honest, the practice of banditry has risen once again since his passing—simply consider my unfortunate church of Villanova!" he added the last with a nervous giggle.

"Do not attempt to excuse the inexcusable, Sandro," said Donato, "I entered the Carmelite order during those years. I was a young man who wanted only to serve God and the people. No man can take from me my faith in God, but Sixtus diminished the purity of my faith. I witnessed friends accused of sexual relations crying out for mercy from the breaking wheel, and receiving none. You and I both know that if there were fewer bandits back then it is only because the Church felt duty-bound to kill them all."

"My friend, I defer to your better understanding of those years," Sandro replied, taking up a different shield. "My understanding of the Inquisition is furnished principally on hearsay and rumours. However, the Iron Pope is long gone and those days with him."

Donato shook his head. "The Inquisition might have fallen out of favour, but they have not left. After Sixtus passed, they backed his right hand. Your new *good friend*, Cardinal Gentile, is certainly not some cadaverous relic of an execrable era. His convictions are unwavering, and his appetite for righteous purpose remains insatiable. The Spanish pay for his operations, they have armed him with soldiers, informers, and divine vindication. Pope Clement does not like him, he does not favour him, he is able to limit and impede his mission, but even he cannot remove his influence and presence in the city."

"Sharp daggers lurk beneath his cardinal's cape," Fernanda observed bitterly, "regardless of his station and however deep his pockets, we should have no dealings with him."

"It is just a painting," Sandro insisted, "and paintings exist only to enable the faith of the viewer."

"The Iron Pope would disagree," Donato said. "He tore down buildings that had stood since the days of Caesar for little benefit. And poor Trajan was removed so that his column might be repurposed for Saint Peter."

"I would have thought you, as a man of the priesthood, would have approved of that much at least," Sandro muttered, his tone churlish and slight.

Donato shook his head. "Rome is a remarkable city," he replied, "its story is a great tapestry woven by a thousand generations. Yet some among the priesthood would cheerfully obliterate all of that, if they could, and make it only one story. Those people no longer wish to enable the faith of the viewer, they seek to conquer and to dominate. Do not mistake the interests of Cardinal Gabriele Gentile. These works by Michelangelo Merisi, and their popularity among the citizens of his city, are an affront to him. He has already spent months crusading for their removal and destruction. His lack of success in the endeavour will feel like a battle lost in a holy war. That will surely serve only to goad his pride and fuel his outrage."

"Sandro, we do not stand with fanatics and murderers," Fernanda interjected. "It is not just paintings that awful man would burn; Father Donato tells me that only this year your cardinal sent a philosopher by the name of Giordano Bruno to the stake for heresy."

"I do not *stand with fanatics*," Sandro replied, just a little defensively. "I work for the money we sorely need, my darling."

"He has the money of the Inquisition," Fernanda emphasised, "he offers us blood money. Please, cancel the sale. We will manage somehow until we find a different buyer."

"It is too late," Sandro said, pointing to the empty space at the back of his workshop, "they came this morning. Darling, we had no choice. You said it yourself; our purse was almost exhausted."

Fernanda said nothing at first. "You are as reckless and as heedless as a lunatic," she snapped eventually. "Once you stood before me, weeping over the bleeding daughter that I had foolishly placed in your negligent care, swearing to God that you would change your ways. Now you have chosen to align us, your family, with murderers and zealots in search of vainglorious renown. No—choice is no excuse. For you, there is always a choice. It is us who have no choice—me and your children—we are forced to endure the currents of your rabid passions and capricious ambitions. One day, you will drown us all."

With that, Fernanda exited the workshop, leaving Sandro and Donato in a contemplative silence. The monk did not to excuse himself, nor speak any asinine pleasantries that might have excused Sandro from acknowledging his wife's words.

"She speaks the truth, does she not?" Sandro asked. "My situation is lamentable; it has made me a wretched and impetuous creature. One determined to degrade and distress myself by multitudes. I even had you summon the great Cardinal Borghese here, to this malodorous hovel of a workshop—probably he is still laughing to his friends about me today!"

"My friend," Donato said, standing to leave the workshop "strike the memory of Borghese at least from your great list of regrets. As we left here, the cardinal expressed only sorrow that he was unable to help you personally. What is done is done, my friend," he added with a shrug. "You have the money that your family needs. I will entreat upon you, however, to make that the end of the matter."

"I shall involve myself no further with Cardinal Gentile. The rest I leave in God's hands," Sandro replied, bowing his head.

"And I shall pray nightly for your protection," the monk said, opening the door to the street outside.

"That is surely unnecessary," Sandro laughed nervously. "I cannot imagine the cardinal or his soldiers pausing to give me a second thought!"

"They shan't need to if your wife throttles you in your sleep," Donato said with a smile. "From time to time, my good friend, you should consider listening to her when she speaks."

II.

As May passed into June the daylight hours advanced on two fronts until the night was a feeble and fleeting thing. Rome became a city bathed in an endless sticky sultriness, punctuated by bursts of pelting rain and waspish summer storms. Fernanda seemed intent on remedying the heat outside with her icy demeanour. She took the money that Sandro had made from his sale, but she did not thank him for it. As she frequently observed, the only other recourse would be to inflict homelessness and starvation upon herself and their children. Her mood during these weeks oscillated between outraged accusations of moral subjugation and bouts of deep melancholia that Sandro had never witnessed in his wife before. She cooked and ate meals without conversing. She withheld her affection from him, enduring his embraces with a cold rigidity. In bed she showed him only her back, falling quickly asleep whenever he climbed into the sheets beside her, or else feigned to do so.

Sandro was happy to work all the while in his workshop on his Nativity—at least, in theory he was happy. In practice, Sandro was frustrated by his inability to generate either ideas or enthusiasm for his painting. In a traditional Nativity scene, the artist places the Christ-child in his manger at the centre. Mary,

Joseph, the adoring shepherds, and all the animals spread out on either side and the cherubs fly above. And yet, as Sandro sketched versions of the image, he was plagued by the subtle suggestions of Borghese, and the less than subtle suggestions of Tommaso, that his work lacked originality—yet, how else could a Nativity scene make sense?

Sandro wondered if he could find some new angle or technique to breathe new life to the subject. He drew a close image of the Christ Child held proudly aloft by his mother in profile. He then rejected the idea. Their dramatic occupation of the foreground denied any space for the shepherds and the animals, and without shepherds and animals there could be no Nativity. His second drawing was perhaps more radical still, imagining the scene from a position almost above as if seen from the perspective of a descending angel. The effect seemed profoundly imbalanced and odd to him. Besides which, he found it difficult to draw the figures from such an angle, and more difficult still to show anything of their faces. He was almost tempted to ask Tommaso if he had any ideas of his own, though a stubborn streak of pride prevented him from doing so. After all, he reasoned, it was important for them both to remember which of them was the master of the studio, and who was only an apprentice.

Sandro soon abandoned his visionary experiments and reverted to the traditional composition: Christ's manger at the centre, the other figures surrounding him in a measured and balanced manner and with a flock of cherubs flying above—how else could a Nativity scene make sense?

On the afternoon of June 21, a little over a month since the sale of Sandro's Assumption, a young boy came to the Signorelli workshop with news that Cardinal Gentile had finished collecting the Sacred Images and had them installed within Santa Maria dell'Anima. Sandro thanked him and shut the door quickly before the boy had the chance to outstretch a grubby hand for payment.

Sandro spent the rest of that day fretting about how Fernanda would greet this news and wondering whether she would even agree to accompany him to see his exhibited work. He was content to listen to his children talking while they ate their evening meal—a vegetable stew cooked in lemon juice and garnished with sliced garlic, capers, and olives. He sat beside Matteo, wiping away the seeds of the stewed tomatoes that coated his son's chin and fingers. When they were all finished, he asked Ilaria if she would look after her younger siblings in their bedroom for a moment while he spoke with their mother.

For the first time in nine years, Sandro felt nervous when left alone with his wife. He understood that she had closed parts of herself to him only because he had hurt her, though he did not know how he was supposed to reach her once again. He was then gripped rather unexpectedly by some strange species of courage and the dread question that had long festered beneath the surface of his thoughts effectuated itself unexpectedly onto his tongue.

"Do you…do you find yourself regretting it?" Sandro asked his wife.

"Regret what?"

"Accepting my proposal all those years ago. Choosing to marry your life with mine."

Fernanda hesitated. "There were several other suitors," she admitted, her voice as quiet as it was emotionally inscrutable.

Sandro had been painfully aware of these other men at the time, not because she had ever once before spoken of these other prospects to him but because her father had made sure

173

that Sandro understood that he was far from his favoured suitor. On the day before the wedding Fernanda's father had described Sandro's ring as fool's gold and had said that he wished that his daughter had been born with enough sense to discern a good investment from a bad one.

"I knew and was not in the least bit surprised to learn it," Sandro finally replied. "I was only surprised that you returned my affections. Your father informed me that some of your other suitors had already found their success in stable professions such as banking and trade."

"They had. And yet I chose the artist." Fernanda declared softly. She looked deep into his eyes and said nothing further for several long moments. "Banking and trade never excited me—they never once moved me," she continued with a slight and mournful shrug. "I remember one suitor appeared at my parent's villa very drunk and received a gift of a broken nose from my father when his hands began to wander. Another was a young Florentine banker whose self-love would put Narcissus to shame. A third was a merchant—from Perugia I believe—afflicted with a most unfortunately dull disposition. That man spent the entire time it took to traverse the Albano Lake explaining, in exhausting detail, the financial realities and demerits of dealing in silks and wools. To this day, when unable to sleep, I find my mind straining to recall that flat voice of his, droning on and on about tariffs and tax rates."

For the first time in weeks the two of them shared a smile. Sandro found himself laughing then, just as much from relief as from amusement.

"You will not be too surprised to learn that my father championed that Umbrian merchant." Fernanda continued. "I would be marrying money, he said. I would become the mistress of a country villa on the outskirts of the city, I would eat meat and fish every day and wear Venetian jewellery and silken gowns. It sounded like a fine life, but it was not the life that I wanted—not enough to pretend that I could ever love that man. No, I liked the polite and nervous man who came alive when he spoke—with such intensity and passion—about the wondrous skills and superlative techniques of the many painters and sculptors whose talents had made Rome the greatest city in the world. When I told you that I would see you a second time, you returned with an exquisite little drawing of my face."

"Oh yes!" Sandro breathed, "I had quite forgotten that drawing! Do you still have it?"

"Of course. It lives with everything else dear to me, under key, inside my jewellery box. I liked you from the moment we met. I admired your ardour and your abilities as an artist. I believed sincerely, as I told my father, that you would be a great success one day. And so, to answer your question, even though our lives have followed a different path, I cannot regret my choice, for our love was true, and true love is no choice at all."

Sandro stood and crossed the kitchen floor. He held his wife close and kissed her lips. "I would like to see that drawing again," he said softly. "I would like to see it as a memento of the happiest day of my life."

Every moment of that magical wet morning in March had been etched into his memory in vivid detail. Sandro Signorelli, then aged just twenty-two, had accompanied the young Fernanda on a stroll through the grounds of her parent's villa. They had found it easy to talk and laugh together. They had found their gazes lingering, their shoulders bumping nervously against each other. The hour that they had been permitted passed so quickly that the movement of the clock hands seemed like some cruel trick. When Fernanda had told Sandro that she was due back inside shortly, he had found himself beset by a fever of the heart and had fallen to his knee. The proposal had been so instantaneous that Sandro had landed in a mud puddle and was forced to maintain a façade of soggy stoicism as he awaited her reply. He had been overjoyed, if a little astonished, when she told him that she intended to accept.

Securing permission from her parents had taken months of considerable persuasion from Fernanda. Yet eventually her parents had relented—her mother had always admired the paintings she saw in churches, and her father had often dreamed of placing a large portrait of himself hanging in his hallway, a portrait that Sandro had made and gifted with a glad heart as the wedding was arranged.

"However different we find the path of life to be, we can only walk it," Sandro said in the contemplative silence they had found themselves in. "We do not know what waits for us in the future, yet I believe that everything we dreamed of could still happen. My Assumption has been placed in view of multitudes. It hangs there right now! An erudite fellow of my recent acquaintance told me that it takes just one prosperous spark from fair lady fortune to ignite into a raging inferno… perhaps, just perhaps, we shall finally be free from these blighted years and thwarted hopes."

Fernanda exhaled slowly and seemed to ponder her words. "Time and time again I have tried to offer you counsel. Time and time again you have chosen to ignore it," she observed. "Your actions and your pride have made us poorer than we ought to be, and far more desperate. You have now made us share a common cause with cruel and barbaric men. Yet, our fates and fortunes were entwined the moment we exchanged rings. I have little choice now but to forgive your mistakes. However, my forgiveness does not come without condition. Nothing like this can happen again. Due consideration must be given to every and any patron. In the future, you must agree to consult with me on every decision that could affect the family."

"I would consider that a great honour," Sandro said grandly. "My blood runs too warm at times. Yet, for your forgiveness I shall swear that any commission or any patron that you do not approve of shall be politely declined."

Fernanda nodded curtly. "Very well. Then we shall go with pride to see your work, finally displayed for all of Rome to see. We shall go first thing tomorrow, all five of us as a family."

III.

Marshalling all five members of the Signorelli family was not a trivial undertaking, however. The process began after dinner, with Fernanda sitting each of them down in turn to trim their hair towards something respectable. She then sent them all to bed early, for Fernanda and the girls would need to wake with the dawn to begin the arduous ritual of dressing fully for a public outing.

Sandro woke with them. He selected his least-worn white shirt, a pair of black breeches and white stockings, along with his black waistcoat. He took a large kitchen knife and held it aloft to catch sight of his reflection in the lustrous flat of the blade. That morning, he quite liked what he could see: his poverty was still somewhat apparent, and yet he also felt that he might also look something like an artist.

Matteo waited with him, mercifully content to sit quietly in the corner and play with the wooden dogs that Sandro had carved and painted for his fourth birthday. Sandro considered his son as he wiped his boots clean with an old rag. From the moment he had finally been blessed with a son, Sandro had hoped that Matteo would one day join him in the workshop. The thought of turning his practice into a family business used to move Sandro to happy tears; now he wondered if his son would have a better life learning a different trade. Besides which, the experience of teaching and working with Tommaso had somewhat soured his fantasy—Sandro could hardly bear the thought of his son growing similarly disenchanted with him and developing his current apprentice's propensities to sulk and snipe.

At last, the girls came through the kitchen door. They were a radiant vision. Fernanda was always beautiful to him, of course. Yet still these rare moments of full attire reminded him sharply of the fact. Fernanda had braided and plaited her hair; her best skirt had been constructed and padded; her eyelashes had been darkened and her lips painted a deep red; and her bodice and her dazzling range of rings and hoops had made their way out from their dusty boxes. She looked like some prized beauty from one of Ilaria's old myths.

His girls wore blouses, with skirts and petticoats. Sandro thought that they resembled little angels. Though, even as the thought occurred to him, Sophia shoved a heavenly fingertip deep within a nostril. Ilaria noticed too and disciplined her younger sister by punching her hard in the neck. Demons dressed as angels—Sandro corrected himself as Fernanda brokered the ensuing fight.

When Tommaso arrived at the workshop later that morning, he found the whole Signorelli family waiting outside for him. Sandro cordially informed his apprentice that the moment had come for them to return to the Piazza Navona; only this time, they would travel there together, concerted in triumph. The crowds had reduced a little since Sandro's last visit. Both fountains were now fully visible through the thinning throng.

Still, the line at San Luigi proved enticing, far more so than the empty space at the other end of the Piazza.

"Look children," Fernanda exclaimed, quite astonished, "all of these people have come to see your father's painting!"

Tommaso could not contain a snort of laughter as Sandro hastened to correct her. He pointed across the Piazza, towards Santa Maria dell'Anima.

Fernanda looked between the churches. Understanding the situation, she began to quietly usher the children away from the long line they had instinctively made towards.

Sandro did not mind the confusion. As his family crossed the Piazza, he felt the summer sun flood his whole being with warmth. He felt a lightness to his gait and a pleasing sense of hollowness, as if not knowing what was waiting for him inside the church had somehow made him another person entirely. True, he told himself, Santa Maria dell'Anima would probably not inspire quite as much curiosity among the public as the Michelangelo Merisi works, but curiosity is a base instinct, befitting of children. Art, he reminded himself, should not seek to sate the salacious appetite, it should call like a beacon to all of those who would remember that faith is a matter of spirit, not flesh, and for those who choose to worship hope instead of despair.

A boy stood before dell'Anima, entreating the public to visit the exhibition. "People of Rome!" he cried out, "Jesus Christ refused the solicitations of the devil! Cardinal Gabriele Gentile invites you to do the same. The benign cardinal has provided for the city and for the people he loves so dearly. Walk this way—away from the darkness, towards God's artworks, towards the Sacred Images, towards the light!"

Sandro smiled at the youth as he passed.

"Another form of copying! Michelangelo Merisi did that first," Tommaso scoffed.

"Oh, you are jealous!" Sandro replied dismissively. "Perhaps I am training you in the wrong vocation after all—young Tommaso is no painter, he is a *seamstress*, who does so love to prick and needle with his words!"

The boy had no response. His silent concession pleased Sandro greatly. Today was a day for victories after all.

Taddeo Zuccari lounged in the doorway of Santa Maria dell'Anima, dressed that day in a quilted azure doublet and a black cap adorned with emerald feathers. Sandro noticed that Zuccari wore peculiar black leather shoes that twirled upwards at the toes. He had not realised that men would ever wear such things.

"Signore Sandro!"

Zuccari was beaming. Sandro felt himself returning the smile. He stopped before the doorway and widened his arms in an invitation of embrace.

"Signore, the sun is ferocious today," Zuccari laughed. Even in the shade, the quilted doublet was surely a triumph of style over practicality. A few drops of perspiration on Zuccari's forehead betrayed the extent of the discomfort he was clearly attempting to mask.

"And what do the good citizens of the great city make of us then?" asked Sandro. "Have we many admirers?"

Zuccari glanced back within. "We have some."

"Then, my friend, this is a truly glorious day! I hear luxuriating is good for the soul, whether one chooses to do so in sunshine, or indeed, in admiration!"

"Be my guest signore. Myself, I await a lady friend."

181

Zuccari flattened himself against the doorframe to let them pass through.

Inside the church, the Sacred Images were unguarded and mounted unnaturally on the walls. The twelve works were too crowded, immediately the competition seemed to Sandro to diminish their individual and collective impact. Only a handful of the semi-curious public had accepted Cardinal Gabriele Gentile's invitation of salvation. They strolled past the paintings within and talked to each other of matters completely unrelated to the arts.

Sandro and his family walked to the first painting, a Madonna and Child of poor quality. Tommaso gave the work a derisive snort and moved quickly onto the next canvas. This was a respectable St Jerome, whose acceptability as a figure was undermined by the adjacent lion, stodgy and toothless, as if the artist had used some flea-bitten old dog as a model. Then there was a Passion of the Christ, in which Jesus looked more drunk than agonised. And so on through mediocrities, until, at last, they reached the familiar Assumption.

The painting was tucked into a dark corner, near the chapel. A family was nearby. Their children were snickering as one of the boys imitated the Virgin's pose and facial expression, pushing his nose up and biting his bottom lip slightly to exaggerate her rapture. The impression provoked a great response from the other children, who laughed uproariously until their father noticed their amusement and almost lazily slapped the boy across his face. Sandro looked at the laughing children. He looked at his own and saw plainly that they were underwhelmed. He looked back at the near-empty church, and at the poor artworks on the walls. He heard sparse notes of laughter and disdainful words echoing loudly around the space and felt his cheeks flushing with blood.

Fernanda smiled and squeezed his shoulder lightly. Sandro could not return the smile.

"Master, are you well?" asked Tommaso.

"Thank you, Tommaso, yes I am quite alright," Sandro replied, covering his face with his hands so that neither his apprentice nor his children might witness the tears that were welling in his eyes.

"Would you…would you like a moment alone?"

"Thank you Tommaso. Yes. That would be quite decent of you."

Sandro heard Tommaso leading his children away. Fernanda stayed by his side, stroking his shoulder and the back of his neck until he managed to compose himself.

"It's not so bad," she said, her voice stretched and conflicted, "perhaps next week this church will be busier. It takes time for word to spread, after all."

In the long quiet that followed her statement, Sandro could hear the paintings being laughed at once more. He found that he had looked up from his hands to look skywards, as if on some unconscious level he felt everything might just be God's fault.

"Perhaps next week the church will indeed be busier," he repeated softly. "I shall never know, my darling, for I will never set foot inside again. Here is the place where a mad cardinal has constructed a stock, and where I thrust myself within for all of Rome to see!"

Sandro was so absorbed by his grief that he could barely focus on Fernanda as she told him not to give so much credence to the laughter of children, and that Sandro was surely overstating the consequences of Gentile's exhibition on his reputation. She did not seem to understand that the only words that could spread from this would be derisory. That far from making his name, this exhibition might force him to change his now, or else be laughed out of any and every commission that might have once come his way. Still, he did not argue aloud. He let her lead him to where Tommaso and their children waited.

"Master, your painting stands head and shoulders above the others here," Tommaso stated with a touch of quiet indignation to his voice.

Sandro was caught a little by surprise.

"Thank you, Tommaso. That is kind of you to say," he replied. "Though I think it is best that we leave now."

Zuccari was still waiting in the doorway. Sandro instructed his family to wait in the Piazza while he spoke to his fellow exhibitor.

"I thought we might have a few more admirers than that," Sandro snapped. "If fair lady fortune is hiding in that church, she is well-hidden indeed."

Zuccari did not seem to like Sandro's tone. "What were you expecting," he asked, "a crown of laurels and a four-horse chariot ride to the Capitoline?"

"I expected something a little better than that. I heard people laughing inside! They should have been rounded up immediately and…and stopped. Where was Cardinal Gentile? I do not think he would allow such disrespect in his exhibition. Why would he not attend his own exhibition?"

"Because this is not truly his exhibition," Zuccari drawled, his eyes fixed on the streets to the north, "It is mine. I knew of a man who has Gentile's ear and so I had the notion placed there. Cardinal Gentile has ready access to vast sums of money, and this seemed like a good way to take something back from the popularity of Michelangelo Merisi. The arts are only something of a minor interest to the Cardinal. His true vocation is the extermination of evil. Daily he searches the city for heretics, and then interrogates said heretics for the whereabouts of further heretics. He has confessed to me on more than one occasion that he will die a happy man if he can hold Michelangelo Merisi in one of his cells for even just a day." Zuccari looked back at Sandro and seemed to hesitate for a moment. "Of course, I believe that both of us would benefit from such an outcome," he continued softly. "Those who visit Gentile's cells tend to return with fewer eyes, fewer fingers, or perhaps even fewer hands than they entered with. That is, those who return at all... You are something of an artist yourself. Perhaps you could imagine how such interrogation might impair your talents."

"Signore, please," Sandro said, recoiling from the statement. "Do not say that has been your purpose all along!"

Zuccari gazed into the distance and broke into a broad toothy smile aimed elsewhere. He then focussed on Sandro once more, his friendly façade dissipating in an instant. "Come now, you do see that Michelangelo Merisi needs only break wind for all of Rome to run sniffing? Surely you can see that we cannot hope to seriously compete against him. No...I do not work towards his destruction, signore, but neither shall I be saddened on the day it inevitably comes. You and I may not get our chance to talk to eternity; but I assure you, quilted doublets and fair lady friends do not come cheaply either." Zuccari smoothed his hand through his hair and checked his breath on the palm of his hand. "Signore, when I saw you for the first time outside the San Luigi, I pitied the sight of you. I saw a luckless, penurious wretch in sore need of charity. To my mind, I did you a favour. You got paid at the least, did you not?"

Zuccari then strode away from the church without giving Sandro another glance. Sandro stepped out into the Piazza and watched him greet a beautiful fair-haired young girl. The two embraced and walked away talking and laughing loudly enough for the whole of Rome to hear.

Chapter Four: Martyrdom

I.

The morning after viewing the Sacred Images, Sandro woke and found himself quite immobile. Fernanda promptly left their bed to greet their stirring children in their room down the hall. His family chattered away contently as they made their collective way down the stairs and to the kitchen to begin their breakfast.

Sandro lay completely still against the padded straw of his mattress. He tried to muster himself but found that his spirit was like a drained vessel. It was almost as if he was being pinned beneath a great invisible weight, or else that mischievous sprites and imps had visited in the night and chained him to the bed.

One of his daughters came thundering back up the stairs to rouse him. It was Sophia who peeked her face around the door, laughing, for some inexplicable and irritatingly happy reason, as she informed her father that some melon had been sliced for him and was waiting on the table. Sandro smiled an enfeebled smile, thanked his daughter, and informed her that he had no appetite that day.

Fernanda came back up the stairs some moments later. She sat at the end of the bed and took his temperature with the back of her hand.

"There is nothing that suggests a fever," she observed. "No obvious signs of sickness."

"My darling, I believe you are wrong," he muttered in reply. "Though it is imperceptible to the eye, a sickness dwells deep within me. The soul of a poor artist is a calloused thing—yet it remains gravely susceptible to hope. I allowed mine to rise again and, like Icarus before it, it has plummeted down beneath an indifferent sea."

"Sandro," she started softly, "you have longed for that moment for as long as I have known you. True, it was perhaps not the grand victory you once envisioned, yet your work hangs in a Roman church—that is some victory nonetheless."

Her words did little to alleviate the profound despondency within him.

"Any victory that tastes so foul can only be described as a hollow one, at best," Sandro snorted. He would have said more but his words shrivelled beneath the intensity of Fernanda's chagrin. He pulled his bedsheets over his head instead. "Longing for things, hard work, keeping faith," he mused, "I ask you, what purpose is there to any of it at all?"

Fernanda said nothing. He heard her exhaling slowly and felt her take her weight from the bed. She stood for several heartbeats before ripping the bedsheet away from him, seizing his wrists and extracting him forcibly from his bed. Sandro cried out in shock as he tumbled gracelessly out onto the floor to land beside his wife's feet.

"There, above your head, that ceiling is your purpose," she snapped, "it keeps the elements from our heads. Down in the kitchen is also your purpose—three of them waiting for their father to join them. And I—I am your purpose. Once again you have a choice before you—work, and provide for your family, or sulk and gripe because the streets are not filled with proclamations of your brilliance. Whichever you choose, remember that I have forgiven one poor decision of yours already this year. Another might test my patience."

Fernanda turned and left him pressed against the floorboards. Sandro dragged himself to his feet, put on his clothing and faced the world with all the lightness and cheer of a man sentenced to an immediate execution. He struggled to retain focus on anything all day, and during the days that followed. The voices of other people seemed distant and muffled. Food and drink lost all flavour, while chewing and swallowing was an arduous and joyless ritual. Sleep came to him reluctantly and was quick to desert him in the darkness. He found that his limbs were leaden and slow, that his vision swam, and his head ached.

Progress on the Nativity painting was beyond slow. Often, Sandro would find himself staring into the distance for hours at a time. He found that his hands were devoid of skill, so much so that he could barely bring himself to despoil perfectly good parchment with his prosaic talents. He found that he was instructing Tommaso less and less, and that even when he made the effort to delegate tasks and responsibilities, he could barely think of anything to tell the boy.

One day, he found that Tommaso did not appear for work at all. Sandro did not know what to do. He looked to the ceiling and found no answer waiting for him there. He located a sizable section of blank parchment and without hesitating to question why, he began working on a portrait of Tommaso.

He sketched out the eyes first: bright blue and piercing, almost like those of a wolf. In fact, it had been those eyes that Sandro had first noticed, two years ago, when Tommaso's father first brought the boy to his workshop. Tommaso had been twelve years old then. In addition to being of sharp mind, the boy was enthusiastic, and then, rather respectful. At the time, everyone had been happy with the arrangement of labour for learning— and all of them blissfully unaware of just how desultory and mutually unavailing the arrangement would prove to be.

Sandro continued to draw. He drew the mouth that so rarely smiled anymore. Those pursed lips. That hurtful instrument of youthful impudence and perfunctory ridicule. He then drew the nose. That nose which…which… Well, Sandro supposed— after much consideration—the nose was perhaps one appendage that he could not hang a hurt upon. Tommaso had a long and pointed nose, beneath it though was the first sprouting of a moustache, a sign that his apprentice was leaving youth behind and embracing all the trappings of manhood.

Sandro spent that entire afternoon working with a peculiar, though very real, purpose on this portrait of Tommaso. When it was finished, Sandro cleared his throat and, increasingly aware that his behaviour was a little strange that day, he asked the drawing when did their relationship begin to deteriorate so? And had not Sandro tried his best to do right by them both?

He was just on the cusp of tears, yet the sound of a man shouting Sandro's name on the street outside spared him any further mawkishness. He made cautiously towards the door and saw that outside a man was running up and down the street that connected Sandro's home and workshop. When Sandro caught sight of the man's face, he saw an expression of wild-eyed panic. It was a man that Sandro knew. It was Luca Marelli, the father of Tommaso.

"Signore, please, what is the matter?" shouted Sandro as he stepped out into the street waving his hands high.

"Signore Signorelli, please," pleaded Luca racing back towards him. "Tell me my son is with you?"

"I have not seen Tommaso since he left here yesterday."

"This morning, my son tells me he is coming here to work. Then his cousin comes by our house telling tales of Tommaso among a gang of armed thugs, insulting the passers-by, waving a sword, and drinking from a flagon in the street. I said this must be some other man's child, for my Tommaso is surely where he is supposed to be. He will be here, at his master's workshop."

"And where did this cousin say he saw Tommaso?" asked Sandro.

"The Piazza della Rotonda."

"Then we go there at once," declared Sandro with such force and instantaneousness that they both seemed quite convinced of his courage.

*

The Piazza della Rotonda was near deserted in the quiet dusk. Tommaso was nowhere to be seen, neither was any gang of drunken youths. Sandro and Luca agreed to split up: Luca headed south to search the Pantheon and the surrounding area while Sandro began combing the northern backstreets.

Sandro heard no disturbances. He searched desperately without a single clue to guide him forward. All the while he blamed the paintings at San Luigi. He blamed Michelangelo Merisi da Caravaggio for turning his sweet young boy's head towards darkness. Then he began to realise his own faults. He had lapsed badly into melancholy. He had neglected his responsibilities to the boy and done nothing to address his growing disillusionment—and he did not simply mean in

the days following the accursed Sacred Images exhibition—
he had been vain, conceited, and selfish once again.

Sandro stopped everyone he saw, pleading for any
information about a gang of troublemakers and a drunk
young boy. He got nowhere at first, though eventually one
man exiting a taverna, looking somewhat the worse for wear
himself, squinted at the question before declaring that there
was a group inside matching that description. Sandro thanked
the man and made for the door.

Inside, the taverna was bustling and boisterous, the
atmosphere thick with sour alcoholic fumes and dozens of
people, each one vigorously engaged in the art of intoxication.
Long seated tables crowded the sides, in the centre were
upturned barrels where many of the taverna patrons gambled
with cards. Michelangelo Merisi da Caravaggio infiltrated
his mind, the taverna transfiguring into something like the
scene from the Vocation of St Matthew. Sandro wondered if,
by this unwelcome act of surreptitious allusion, he had cast
himself in the role of Jesus searching for souls to save amidst
this demonstration of indecorum, the loud slurring voices, and
discordant notes of song.

A waiter emerged from the kitchen, holding aloft a plate of
artichoke hearts. Sandro stopped the man to ask if he had seen
a drunk young boy with blue eyes and dark hair. The waiter
nodded slightly and flicked his eyes over to a table at the far
end of the room. The group stationed there was the wildest
of all. A man, dressed in a striking yellow and black doublet,
stood on top of the table, drinking red wine directly from the
carafe as his companions clapped and cheered him on. Among
those companions were two women, likely unmarried, and
possibly even courtesans, who were drinking as unscrupulously

and laughing as maniacally as the crazed Bacchantes of Ilaria's old stories. Tommaso though was not obviously among their number. Sandro looked through them several times over and turned back to the waiter with a shrug. The waiter nodded at the floor below the table. There, writhing and rolling, face down near a congealing mess of vomit and straw, was Tommaso.

Sandro approached the table quietly, hoping to snatch the boy away unheeded. He ducked to the floor and crouched above the boy. Tommaso's chin and cheeks were coated extensively in the thick bile of drinker's remorse. He seemed unable to speak, his eyes white and rolling and showing no sign of recognition. Sandro managed to pull Tommaso from halfway under the table and lift him to his knees before his new companions noticed.

"Lazarus rises!" exclaimed the man on the tabletop, pointing to Tommaso.

"He has been touched by a holy man," sneered another, turning around to regard Sandro through puffy and unfocused eyes. Sandro recognised this man as the youth who had stood wearing a tunic and garland in the Piazza Navona, declaring the genius of Michelangelo Merisi.

"We are visited by a wandering vagrant," one of the Bacchante women laughed, leaning back to pull at Sandro's hem, "a holy man dressed all in tattered rags!"

"Signore holy man," asked the other woman, her hands clasped in a pantomime of prayer, "does the man who cured Lazarus also possess the power to restore a woman's honour?"

The group descended into giggling and shrieking, some of among their number collapsing fully onto the tabletop.

"Shame upon you all," replied Sandro, unable to swallow his indignant eruption.

"Shame does not live here," shouted the man on the tabletop, outstretching his arms wide in a gesture of celestial defiance. "Shame is a falsehood. It is a trap, invented by hypocrites, designed to ensnare the soul of man and tether it to a meek and petty life!"

"Deplorable, vile carrion!" Sandro continued, pulling Tommaso onto his back. "To take and defile a sweet young boy this way! When that poison has vacated your mind, you should, all of you, kneel before the morning sun and beg God for forgiveness."

"Fuck your forgiveness, and fuck your God too," said the man on the tabletop, so loudly that the entire taverna was shocked into silence.

Sandro shook his head and made for the door.

"Watch him scuttle away to safety," the man on the tabletop shouted at Sandro's back. "A contemptible and cowardly creature! A meek and dirty follower of the pig-god!"

Sandro said nothing as he kicked the door open and stepped into the street. He was smouldering with both fear and fury. The evening light caught Tommaso, his head resting against Sandro's neck, and the atmospheric change seemed to revive him somewhat. Sandro was halfway down the street when Tommaso began to slur, an indecipherable remonstration against changes not yet understood, though nonetheless objected to profoundly.

Sandro placed the boy down and took his head gently in his hands. Red wine had spilt all over his shirt and chin. It had dribbled around his lips, the stains flicking upwards like something resembling a sinister smile. Sandro held Tommaso tightly until the boy's swimming pupils eventually found him and a flicker of recognition crossed the face of his apprentice.

"Tommaso, it is me, Sandro. Can you hear me? Are you poisoned? Are you dying?"

Tommaso laughed, seemingly without reason.

"Sandro...Sandro Signorelli has...has come for me—hooray" his head rolled back as he collapsed under his own slight weight. "Look, master, I cannot be... cannot be, *dying*. They do not come for me! The sky is free of your revolting cherubs," the boy laughed once more. "I despise them, master...flying babies...trumpets and halos and trumpets and cherubs..." Tommaso's voice trailed off as his eyes rolled up into his head and a new stream of refutations bubbled from his lips and trickled down to pool in Sandro's lap.

An onlooker shouted for someone to run back inside the taverna and bring forth a cup of water. Sandro shook the boy and begged him not to die.

"I am so very sorry," murmured Tommaso, snapping suddenly to full alertness.

"All is forgiven child," replied Sandro tearfully.

"Master, no. Hear me. I am sorry...sorry that you have... *squandered* your time on this Earth!" A meanness flashed across his face. "Sandro! Sandro! Sandro!" Tommaso sung in a flat melody. "A good man. A poor man. Whose... Work is trite and...and... vulgar." The drunk Tommaso went limp once more. "I am truly sorry," he finished before lurching sideways to retch into the dirt.

"A good man, a poor man, his work is trite and vulgar..." drawled a voice behind Sandro.

Sandro turned and saw that around a half-dozen of the taverna gang had filed out after them. Among them was the Piazza Navona Youth. Under the evening sun the yellow and black doublets worn by the men resembled the bodies of wasps. They were buzzing accordingly, their aggression clear and terrifying.

"Good friends, I meant no offence to you all back there." Sandro began falteringly. He pointed to Tommaso, "I simply wanted to return this boy back to his..."

"You meant no offence?" one of the women laughed, "You called us *deplorable, vile carrion* in the complementary fashion then?"

"Son of a whore!" snarled the blasphemous man from the tabletop in a voice that dripped with insincere mock offence.

Sandro stood and found himself begging for mercy as he stepped back, away from the boy.

"Now then," The Piazza Navona Youth replied, slowly and deliberately pulling a dagger from its sheath. "How can you ask carrion creatures to relinquish a carcass when they see one? And such a fat and juicy carcass at that!"

The gang broke forwards gleefully to commence their attack. Those seconds seemed to elongate into minutes for Sandro. He cursed his apprentice aloud. Tommaso had insulted him, vomited on his breeches, and had now damned him to die a violent and arbitrary death. Why, oh why had he not simply remained to the safety of his workshop?

The first blow was a jumping kick from one of the men. It sent Sandro reeling back against the wall of a building. It was followed by a swinging fist that, somehow, Sandro managed to catch as he stepped a further step away from Tommaso.

He supposed he could not have stayed in his workshop. The thought of Tommaso in peril had stirred something deep inside him. Something that he knew would have been precisely the same if it were one of his own children in peril.

He caught the second punch too, however a third came from his periphery and landed with such force that his vision flashed white. He felt the long-nailed fingertips of one of the women gauge his face and eyes. Sandro's attackers were too many. They had flanked him, and he could not hope to protect himself on three sides. He did not even see the fourth blow though it landed so hard on his ear that it sent him reeling off-balance.

The fifth punch sent him crashing to the ground. Boots kicked at him then, from every angle. The pain was so encompassing and complete that Sandro felt oddly at peace. He curled inwards instinctively, though his arms could only cover so much. He heard his attackers laughing, mixed with the sound of onlookers screaming for assistance and pleading with the gang to stop their attack.

Perhaps, he thought, the man who would die for another cannot be described as selfish any longer. Perhaps news of his death might even spread through the city. Perhaps the artist who died so that a boy might live might find fame in some other unexpected fashion.

He was pulled round onto his back; his arms wrenched away from the protective cocoon they had formed around his head. He looked up and saw a woman's face, grinning at him with callous amusement, before pulling back to smash the heel of her boot into Sandro's face. A yell of pain seemed to linger oddly in the air—his own yell of pain, Sandro realised, and yet it felt for all the world like it must have emanated from other lips, or from some far-away dream.

Sandro felt his strength fading, his arms were going limp, a strange ringing sounded throughout his skull. He wondered then if he would still have all his teeth tomorrow. That was a vain thought, he corrected himself, the true question was if there would even be a tomorrow. He sank into a new kind of darkness as the blows continued raining down upon him. His final thought before losing consciousness was of Fernanda, and if they would next meet in Heaven.

II.

The painting was almost finished, he simply had to concentrate through the pain. He blended tones of crimson with the pale pink of the lips. He was painting a masterful portrait, quite unlike any painting he had ever made before. The subject was a striking woman in a three-quarter profile, dressed in a flowing gown made from human eyes. The likeness was incredible—his use of sfumato was unparalleled in its sophistication! He had managed to give great depth to his subject. There was something like life lurking in the details. He felt as if he knew this woman—he winced in pain as he reached for a smaller brush. There was someone with him in his studio. A shadowy figure was standing some way in the distant corner of the room wearing the dress of a cardinal, its head bowed. Someone close by called out his name. He started and looked around him. No one was in the room but the shadowy figure who remained immobile and mute. His name was said a second time and he knew that the voice belonged to the woman in the painting. The woman asked, *where was Ilaria?* He did not know. He had to concentrate for the work was almost complete. He took up the finest brush he could find and dabbed it softly in black paint. The woman in the portrait told him that *he should be watching Ilaria.* The woman needed to hold her pose while he finished the work, but she would not stay still. She was pleading and begging and crying as she ducked his brush. He was very tired—his hands would not hold his brush aloft much longer. *Why were you not paying attention to Ilaria?* the woman demanded, tears in her eyes. *Look at what you have done!* she screamed, pointing to the floor. He looked down and saw that he was standing barefooted in several inches of blood. At his feet, a young girl was splayed out, face-down and unconscious. The woman's cries and accusations of neglect and selfishness seemed to fill the workshop and it was as if a great fog was lifted—he knew that the woman from the portrait was Fernanda. He stooped to lift his daughter and took Ilaria's head in his hands. When he turned her face to his he saw that her chin was riven by the impact of her fall, the split so deep that he could see the splintered bone in her jaw. Ilaria's face shattered under his scrutiny and broke into tiny shards. He heard the walls and floorboards around him screaming in fury. The ceiling was screaming too. The room was screaming all around him. He looked around for help and for forgiveness. The shadowy cardinal lifted its head and jumped across the room in a single abrupt motion to stand now directly before him. Sandro's own fearful cries were lost among the disembodied screaming. The shadowy cardinal was a Strix, a bird of ill omen, its face like an owl's but with cruel red eyes. It screeched and flew at his face, slashing and snapping with beak and talons. He felt his face split open and blood bursting. He tumbled backwards, falling right through the floor, and landing on a street outside with such force that his entire body spasmed in pain. He cried out to the Lord to give him the strength to overcome his suffering. The clement blue sky was torn asunder in revelation of the golden splendour beyond this mortal realm. Above him there loomed an assassin, a twisted face, an expression of pure hatred. Wielding a bright blade, the assassin began singing, *Sandro, Sandro, a good man, a poor man, his work is trite and vulgar,* in a flat melody as he kicked him in the stomach and the ribs. He crawled through the mud and straw of the street, begging the cowardly and apathetic onlookers for their assistance. Not one of them came forward. Among them was Fernanda, her voice full of sorrow as she cried out his name. Donato stood with his head bowed as he made the sign of the cross. Tommaso was also among them. The boy shook his head and slipped away. The assassin laughed and kicked him further and further down the street. As he crawled, he noticed that the colours around him began to drain away. He could no longer see the sky, could no longer see buildings, could no longer see the ground. All was dark mist. He called out for God and yet Michelangelo Merisi exists where God could not be found. He saw the silhouette of an enormous figure sitting and waiting for him at the end of the street, perhaps fifteen feet tall, reclining on a great throne. An eerie music seemed to fill the air, shrill and shrieking strings, and the clattering percussive rhythms of beaten tin. He was kicked forwards still, towards the malevolent shadow. He saw the blessed virgin in chains beside the silhouette throne, the bright blue of her mantle emerging starkly from the darkness. Around her danced a multitude of naked Bacchantes, wearing blood and flesh in place of make up as they sang wordless incantations and worked themselves into a state of frenzied abandon. As he was forced onwards, the savage women began to rip at the virgin's mantle, tearing it from her and ripping at her hair. The Madonna's face did not change. She looked impassive and serene as the sparasso intensified and her body was twisted, torn apart, and consumed by those that revel in excess and suffering. The enormous silhouette stood to full height. It had cloven hooves, its shaggy legs were covered in thick black hair, it slapped its bulbous dripping penis impatiently against its thighs. It wore a black doublet, and when it bowed its head in silent greeting, it revealed that long sharp horns protruded out from a mass of black hair. He pulled himself up to his knees and begged the creature for mercy. It said nothing. Its eyes were pitiless black. He felt the assassin take hold of him from behind. He struggled momentarily, trying to break free, before he was flung to the ground again. When the sword was raised above him, he raised his hand to the sky for any sign that salvation might come. He found none. The blade went through his hand and a rib and punctured his heart.

Hell was not a place of flame and scalding rocks. Hell was dark. It was cold and wet. His sodden clothing clung tight against his skin. His entire body screamed in agony. Around him, voices cried out in rage and fear, the strange and hostile echoes of the damned.

A paroxysm of outrage shot through him—momentarily eclipsing even his bodily suffering. He had been subjected to so many indignities back on Earth, and now this! Granted, he was no saint, nor some great man whose place in heaven was assured; but had he not spent his whole life demonstrating contrition and fealty to his creator? Had that not been sufficient? Surely, purgatory would have been a more suitable sentence for a lowly earthworm whose sins amounted to little more than the occasional absences from church and various magnitudes of envy and pride.

As he lay, shivering and listening, he began to place some of the voices of the souls situated beside him in the dank abyss—they were voices of the hateful gang from the taverna. As deserving of perdition as their thuggish souls undoubtedly were, their despair and anguish brought no real joy to his heart. In truth, he would have preferred to endure endless eternal torment alongside almost any other beings from history—even cruel Caligula, remorseless Atilla, and Judas Escargot himself would have been preferable companions.

He forced himself to roll onto his side to see more, gasping as a pain in his ribcage seared through him. He felt a sheet of wet straw covering a hard cobbled floor. Pools of moisture had formed in the cracks and dimples. It smelled strongly of bodily fluids best left unmentioned. He saw the shadows of many people crowded around him, four were crouched with their backs against the walls while three others were standing and shouting out towards the faintest flickering of light which caught dark metal bars. Seven people in total had been crammed into a space so small that four would have filled it.

Emerging from delirium and into lucidity, Sandro was able to deduce that he was not in hell, but within a jail cell. He tried to alert somebody, anybody, that he was alive and should be released immediately as an innocent man—yet he was incapable of forming the words. He moved a hesitant hand over his face and found that his lip was split, that he had bitten his tongue badly and that he was missing one of his front teeth. His face was bumpy and there were enough cuts bleeding out over his body that he could not be certain how much of the cold fluid that covered him was his blood. He found sitting far too painful. His ribs were shot through. The attempt made him gasp aloud, though his voice was lost among the dismay that ran vocally throughout the guardhouse.

Sandro slumped, face-first, back into the straw. He was exhausted. He closed his eyes and imagined himself in his bed at home, with his family positioned around him. He felt then he could hear the fluttering of great wings. He imagined Ilaria casting open his bedroom window and gasping with astonishment and wonder as a great Caladrius flew towards the window ledge to deliver Sandro his fate. The sound of the white-crested bird calling was like holding water between his fingers. Yet even as the glorious bird approached the window it seemed to hang static in the sky. His home, his family, and the flapping Caladrius dimmed back into the darkness as he drifted back out of consciousness.

III.

Sandro owed his next awakening to the pail of cold water that was upended over his face some indeterminable amount of time later. He kicked out instinctively, though the motion surely caused far greater pain to himself than to his captor.

"I told you as much," his shadowy jailor laughed as he wrenched Sandro to his feet, "The dead do not snore."

A bright torch was raised to his face. The man holding it leaned in close to inspect Sandro. He had blue eyes and an easy smile. Sandro recognised him instantly as the same man who had collected his painting a month before on behalf of Cardinal Gentile.

"This one must have fought hard," the Blue-Eyed Man observed without a flicker of recognition, "he's the colour of Caesar's robes."

"I didn't bring them in," the jailor said with a shrug.

"Your men can go too far," the Blue-Eyed Man said, pulling back. Sandro attempted to thank his saviour, but his fat lip and shredded tongue reduced his gratitude into a rasping incoherence. The Blue-Eyed Man silenced his efforts with a frosty look. "Remember the limits of your duties, Gigo. Execution is beyond the jurisdiction of the city guard."

"No, no," the jailor replied, "I understand. The dead do not snore, and neither do they betray conspiracies. Clever men do not murder suspects before they have a chance to torture them first."

The Blue-Eyed Man broke into a slight giggle. Sandro frantically redoubled his efforts to verbalise his innocence but found himself swiftly gagged, his wrists and ankles were shackled, and a cloth sack was hoisted over his head and fastened tightly around his neck. He was then marched through the guardhouse until he felt the warm and clean air of the outside. The taverna gang were ahead of him, their voices coming as a muffled and wordless chorus of discontent. His jailors lifted Sandro up a small flight of wooden steps and pressed him into a mass of tightly packed bodies who did their best to push back against this involuntary intrusion. Sandro was beaten across his back and his legs until he managed somehow to delve deeper within the protesting helpless crush.

The door of the prison wagon cage was fastened and locked behind Sandro and the horses were whipped into action. The ground pulled fast from under their feet and the prisoners began falling in ungainly unison with every twist and turn of the rough and winding streets.

Soon they must have hit the city's thoroughfares. Sandro could hear crowds of people mingling talking. Some observers took to jeering the prison wagon, offering inflated condolences regarding their impending executions. From the braying crowd that he could not see came a bawdy song about eleven murderers gathered at the gallows. As the song hung each murderer, one by one, the crowd gave a cheer. First one stone, or something else small and hard, pelted against the wagon bars. It was soon followed by others. Some of the projectiles must have breached the bars. Sandro could hear his fellow captives crying out in pain and recoiling as best as they could. The prisoner next to him broke then, Sandro heard the young man gasping and sobbing against his gag.

*

The Piazza Navona Youth sat with his head in his hands, rocking backwards and forwards in slight and involuntary motions. He had been shorn of his curls. His scalp was cut and bleeding. He had been stripped to his loincloth and lashed with a barbed whip.

Sandro rubbed his palm against his own scalp and felt the strange and uneven bristles where the razors had been passed forcibly through. He had not the strength to resist his head shaving—and that much had spared him the whip at least. A dryness tickled at his throat, and he exploded into a fit of rasping and coughing. He dragged himself slowly over to the wooden bowl filled with water that had been left by the guards. His hands shook and his thirst was deep, the water splashed his face and cascaded messily down his chin.

Across a narrow corridor were several cells containing the other members of the taverna gang who had beaten him in the street, interned in pairs. They had all been bludgeoned into submission by their new guards. All of them had been shaved completely and stripped to their undergarments—the women included.

The clattering of soldier's boots marching against the flagstone floor brought them from their collective silent reverie. Two guards filed into the corridor then, large men wearing breastplates and grieves, their hands on the hilts of their swords. They stood to attention on either flank of the Blue-Eyed Man wearing long crimson robes.

"These days, it would seem that Roman civilisation is little more than borrowed clothes," began the Blue-Eyed Man as he fingered his iron crucifix. "They are ill-fitting clothes, ill-fitting to the point of vulgarity. This is a city that reeks of shit and sinfulness, its people appear to be uninterested in anything beyond base desires and savagery." The Blue-Eyed Man began to prowl along the corridor as he spoke, addressing each of the taverna gang as he spoke. "Our eyes and ears did not need to be especially attuned to detect your more elementary transgressions—public disorder, drunkenness, and brawling in the street...these are not the most effective shrouds for fugitives to wear."

The Blue-Eyed Man stooped by the cell containing Sandro. He stopped and stared through the bars with an expression that sent shivers down Sandro's spine. The Inquisitor's face seemed almost free of malevolence but filled with something far worse. Sandro could see within it a composed and implacable assurance that this was a man whose true vocation was brutality.

"Yet I have not brought you to this place because of a street fight," the Inquisitor continued, walking on. "You are here because a full taverna will attest that—among many utterances of blasphemous words and unspeakable and licentious insults directed at both God and the Church—you were heard of boasting about a close relationship with an artist of ill-repute working within this city. I am speaking, of course, of that Lutheran agent by the name of Michelangelo Merisi da..."

He got no further in his speech. He stopped before the cell containing the Bacchante woman who had stamped on Sandro's face and called him God's Holy beggar. As the Inquisitor peered through the bars at her, the woman lunged swiftly to her feet, and spat a thick clod of mucus and saliva onto his face.

An uneasy silence lingered in the air.

"Very well," the Inquisitor said quietly, wiping himself clean with the hem of his crimson sleeve. "We begin with her."

Sandro sank back onto the bench and averted his eyes away from the brief and futile struggle taking place across the corridor. He heard the guards tying the Bacchante woman's wrists so tightly by chains that she broke and screamed aloud, and she was dragged away until they could hear her curses no longer. He leaned his back against the wall of his cell and closed his eyes. His stomach was compressing and tying itself in knots. He thought of Fernanda and his children, and whether they stood any chance of finding him in time. Yet— where would they even begin? Not one guard had yet taken his name. Indeed, Sandro would not even match the description of the man arrested by the city watch—he had, after all, been arrested as an acolyte of the accursed Michelangelo Merisi da Caravaggio, and as a thug and a drunk. A hundred such men must be arrested in Rome each day under such a description. Even if he survived for a week, Fernanda would be quite forgiven for failing to locate him before he met his end.

His cause was all but hopeless.

A dread stillness hung over the cells and the scent of death seemed to permeate the air. The guards returned before nightfall with fresh water and stale bread. They ensured that every cell received provisions. Then, when the last of the gang had eaten and drank, the guards seized one of their number unexpectedly, and took the young man screaming.

As the darkness deepened, Sandro did not sleep. He stood upright carefully, the pain shooting through his ribcage once again, and exhaled a slow and rattling breath. He made his way to the corner of the room and emptied his bladder against the stone wall.

"Signore," began a sad and small voice close by in the darkness. "Signore, I am sorry."

No reply presented itself to Sandro. He snorted angrily, pulled up his loincloth and lay back upon his bench.

"We are wild and crazy," the Piazza Navona Youth continued, perhaps more to himself than to Sandro. "We drink, we feud, and we fight. If you had just taken the boy without insulting us in public... We had to ruffle your feathers. That is the way of the street—that is vendetta. We would have left you breathing. But now, they will torture and kill us all. I suppose if anything good has come of today it is only that I have this opportunity to offer my sincere apologies before I die."

Sandro found he had little forgiveness in his heart that night. "What of the boy?" he asked in due time. "The boy I came for?"

"I saw him taken aside by a man who was not a city guard."

Sandro pressed for further details, beginning to describe Tommaso's father to the best of his ability but the Piazza Navona Youth interjected.

"I was hit in the back of the head and was being choked on the ground," he muttered with a dark chuckle. "The details blur a little. Though from the little I saw, your description sounds thereabouts."

Sandro chose to ignore the nagging voice that lived in the doubtful recesses of his mind, the voice that reminded him that there were many reasons why could not entirely trust this account. Tommaso had escaped the taverna and the brawl outside unharmed, he decided. With his suffering, and possibly also his life, Sandro had bought his apprentice this much at least.

His mind was relentless in the long night that followed. He might die in the morning, if not the next day, and he could not decide which thought was worse. He wondered if his body would even find itself returned to his family. In all likelihood the bodies of those declared heretics and bandits by the Inquisition would be buried in mass nameless graves, or else taken to the farmlands and fed to the pigs. He wondered how many days it would be before Fernanda gave up her search and mourned him as a dead man. What would happen to her then? She would surely return to her parent's villa with the children, and her tail between her legs, ready to endure the chiding of a father who had always warned her against the marriage. Yet, with her parents, Fernanda could make something of a life out in the country. It would be hard with so many mouths to feed, a life of penny-pinching and living off the land. The girls would be married off quickly or else put to work. Matteo might grow up without even remembering his poor and disappointing father. As for Fernanda herself, death may separate her from her husband, but she would never be fully liberated from the taint of her union with failure. Should she ever be inclined to look for a second marriage, her prospects would be likely limited to the misfortunate and the deficient. She might be forced to choose a lonely older man of a kind-hearted disposition perhaps—or perhaps a man blighted by his own share in calamitous circumstance who might choose a miserable alliance with a bankrupted widow and mother of three children.

The thought of Fernanda and his children making any life with another man filled Sandro with a new variety of pain.

He felt nauseous and faint. He felt flushed with fury. Life, he reflected, had been so grossly unfair to him. Had Sandro Signorelli been born only one generation before, he might well have tasted the sweet dividends of success. He might have been acclaimed as one of the greatest painters in the city of Rome. He could have bought a spacious townhouse with a studio included in the upper rooms. He might have even toured the great cities, his name and work filling great churches in Tuscany, Naples, and Umbria. He could have used his wealth to make Fernanda the mistress of a country villa on the outskirts of the city and bought her silk dresses from Milan and finely wrought jewellery made by Venetian goldsmiths. They might have eaten their share of meat and fish and drunk wine together as they raised their family in happiness and comfort. Yes, he decided, the Sandro Signorelli of just forty years ago would have been content and successful. That man would have had a fine life indeed.

What hand had the fates dealt him instead? A lifetime of poverty and humiliation, and now a torturous and unjust death. Desperation had made him ignore his dear wife once again, and now he could expect nothing but a brutal clandestine death at the hands of the very fanatics that his wife had warned him against—all in defence of a stranger, a man he despised, and a rival who did not even know his name! Sandro did not know if he should weep or indulge in black laughter.

*

Shortly after daybreak the guards came for another of the taverna gang. They entered the cell of the man who had danced upon the tabletops and who had dared to insult God. The young man did not fight, or plead for his life, he merely outstretched

211

his hands forlornly and allowed himself to be taken while the other members of the gang said their tearful farewells.

Sandro watched and wondered—was this it? Would they be taken, one by one, to be tortured and murdered by these lunatics? When later that day he heard the now-familiar sound of boots starting down the corridor towards his cell he found himself strangely determined to die with the nobility and grandeur that had eluded him in life. Sandro pushed out his chest. The zealots could mutilate and degrade his body and take his life from him, yet their victory could never be complete if he comported himself now with the bravery of a saint.

"Yes," Sandro said softly aloud, "in dignity shall I find redemption."

The Blue-Eyed Inquisitor reappeared at the bars of his cell, flanked by two guards. Sandro found himself staring directly at the man, as if it were he who was conducting interrogations— as if he were questioning telepathically how a man clad in the insignia of the merciful Lord Jesus could ever commit acts so barbarous and unchristian as torture and execution.

Sandro perhaps looked at the Blue-Eyed Man for one moment too long.

"Bring me the bruised apple next," the Inquisitor stated, pointing straight to Sandro.

As the guards began unlocking the cell door Sandro found that his newfound resolve was a thing of gossamer. Indeed, he became a shrieking embodiment of obsequiousness as the guards stepped inside the cell and lifted him from the floor.

Sandro turned his head back as the guards dragged him past the holding cell. He took a last look at his cellmate. He found that the Piazza Navona Youth was staring right back at him, the boy's eyes wide and terrified. They had not spoken a second time and yet if Sandro had just one more moment alone with the youth, he knew then that he would have gladly forgiven him if it helped unburden his troubled soul even slightly before the end.

The guards took Sandro along the corridor and up a narrow and winding staircase. Every step upwards brought him closer to an awful sound. It sounded like a man screaming some primal broken scream over the whirring of chains and cogs and snapping bones. Sandro pleaded his innocence and begged for clemency as best as his thick tongue and swollen lips could manage. His appeals were met only with stony silence. At the top of the staircase was a hall with flagstones that were stained copper red. Sandro could see the sun through a window for the first time since he had gone looking for Tommaso—however long ago that had now been—and that he might never see again. The shaft of light broke through the thick stone walls and iron bars and landed on the body of a man laid out on straw. The man was missing his eyes. His brains were seeping out of the empty sockets. His bloodied mouth showed only the shards of teeth that had not burst from their gums.

Through a large oak door was a chamber dominated by a large rectangular frame made of iron that was raised waist-high above the floor. On the walls were fixed maces and barbed whips, alongside jagged-fanged vices, scolds, and every other clawed, pincered, and sharp-edged implements ever devised to excruciate and humiliate the soft tissues of the human body. Sandro was cast down and tried at once to crawl to safety. The guards suppressed his weak resistance with their boots, one of them stamping his full weight down onto Sandro's hand as it was outstretched against the cobbles. The pain of impact felt like bones splintering. Sandro gasped as his body went limp and what little fight he had left deserted him.

"Once I met a man whose head was full of the most curious notions," began the Blue-Eyed Inquisitor as Sandro's prone form was lifted and placed at the centre of the frame. "Word reached me that God, so they said, had visited the town of Benevento, and imparted a great spiritual revelation to a man living in the town," the Inquisitor continued as Sandro's wrists and ankles were placed inside manacles positioned at each corner of the frame. "I travelled to Benevento myself, curious, as it were, to hear the new gospel. When I arrived, I found that this, so-called, enlightened man was no preacher at all—he was a simple embalmer of bodies. This enlightened man claimed that we are not God's children, we are but His food and drink. God, so he said, lived in the fangs and jaws of the beasts—He is the waves and is the dirt beneath our feet and, in due time, He shall feast upon us all. As he misled crowds of several dozens, this self-declared prophet from Benevento would produce small creatures from jars and pouches and devour them while they lived. On the first occasion I saw this man talk I witnessed him biting the head from a snake. On the second occasion, the legs of a large brown spider writhed and thrashed against his face. When I asked him why he did this, he replied that the idea of sin was a fallacy, that the rabbit is not more innocent than the wolf, merely weaker. He concluded that it is the process of predation and consumption that drives this Earth, life feeding life, and that if he were able to ingest enough of it himself, he would become as God... I investigated the strength of his convictions in these very cells. We spoke for three full days, until finally the heretic confessed that this false revelation was given to him by none other than Lucifer. Before we begin *our* conversation, I feel compelled to remind you that God does not equivocate. Sin is not fallacious. Sin is the prism through which the worth of the soul is weighed. Your transgressions have brought you to me; they shall be examined, and they shall be answered."

The guards tightened the metal manacles until they bit deep into Sandro's flesh. The Blue-Eyed Inquisitor nodded to them as they stepped back.

"Where can we find Michelangelo Merisi?" the Inquisitor asked, winding a handle until the chains holding Sandro were taught enough to suspend him above the frame. "Where can we find him, and who, precisely, protects him? These are my principal questions to you. Lie to me and you lie to God. Lie enough and we shall discover your breaking point. Now...let us begin. Where can we find Michelangelo..."

Before the Inquisitor could finish his question, the chamber door flew open. Cardinal Gabrielle Gentile stormed inside, clad that day not in his cardinal's robes, but in the same billowing crimson as the Blue-Eyed Inquisitor.

"I came as soon as I was able," said the cardinal, rubbing his hands in an anticipatory manner. "I am told you have several of his allies."

"Your Eminence," Sandro rasped, physically shaking under intense and contradictory feelings. "Please, Your Eminence, look at me. It is I, Sandro Signorelli."

The cardinal turned his attention sharply towards the rack. "I am the servant of the light," he barked in reply, "I am the righteous shield, raised by the Lord Himself to oppose the filth and the darkness. I do not care to know your name nor the names of any of your impious kind." Cardinal Gentile then looked back to the Blue-Eyed Inquisitor. "Begin," he demanded with a brisk wave.

The Blue-Eyed Inquisitor nodded and reached for the handle.

"Your Eminence!" Sandro shouted in his clumsy, thick-tongued voice. "You do know me—I am a simple artist! I provided an Assumption of the Virgin for your Sacred Images."

The Blue-Eyed Inquisitor paused with a slight shrug and awaited Gentile's instruction.

Cardinal Gentile seemed somewhat incensed by this development—inconvenienced almost. He walked close to Sandro and stared deep into his face. The old cardinal seemed lost in thought as he leaned over. He furrowed his brow and slapped his lips together in listless contemplation, causing tan-coloured spittle to bubble and leak from the corners of his mouth.

"Oh, yes," Gentile murmured at long last. "I do seem to remember you... That abominable affair... *Sacred Images*! You cannot imagine how mortifying the failure of that exhibition was to a person of my stature." The cardinal's eyes narrowed. He seemed almost as if he might even have been considering the possibility of proceeding with Sandro's torture purely out of spite. Instead, he straightened his back slowly and reluctantly. "This man is nothing," the cardinal declared to the room. "And we shall learn nothing from him. My time is too precious for that. Release him and bring up one of the others. Quickly now."

The cardinal turned his back on Sandro and began conversing in hushed tones with the Blue-Eyed Inquisitor. Sandro was released from his shackles and escorted out of the interrogation chamber by a guard. The unapologetic mute then led Sandro through hallways and corridors and into a sunny quadrant. Sandro breathed deep and gave tacit thanks for his deliverance to the blue sky that just moments before he had presumed to never see again.

He saw a cage suspended above his head. Inside a woman was huddled, her shaved head cradled in her hands and knees. Sandro recognised her as the woman from the taverna who had stamped on his face and spat in the face of Blue-Eyed Inquisitor. She had been stripped naked. Her back and arms were covered in welts and lacerations where extensive whipping and thrashing had completed the taming of the Bacchante.

The guard escorting Sandro pushed him roughly for his dithering. He pushed him onwards across the quadrant, through another room and corridor and back onto the busy streets of Rome. He was told to start walking and to not look back as the door slammed shut behind him.

Sandro hobbled slowly through streets that he did not recognise at first. He held his broken hand tight against his shattered chest, his teeth chattering with every step. The people he passed often turned incredulously to stare at him and he knew that his appearance must be hideous and desperate—a bloodied and broken man with a shaved head, wearing nothing but his loincloth. He stumbled upon a marketplace by the Tiber and deduced that he was on the western bank. His remaining strength seemed to vanish as he realised that his home was two long miles away yet.

Resting against the side of a building, Sandro felt every damage sustained by his body over the preceding days peeling out like the bells of a score of churches. He could barely keep his eyes open. He was not sure if the darkness that wished to cover him was sleep, or if it was death.

Two men approached him in that state, one younger and one older. They asked a dozen questions of him that he possessed neither the strength nor the concentration to answer. Sandro repeated the name of his street over and over until at last, the men brought him to a horse and cart. He muttered his thanks to the men endlessly as they lifted him atop the crates of oranges and lemons in the back and made promises to deliver him safely to his family.

Sandro heard the crack of the whip and the horses whinnying as the cart set off. Above him, the tops of Roman townhouses seemed to come alive through movement. The tall and rickety edifices loomed and swayed hypnotically as the cart creaked and rumbled across the bumpy roads. Above them the clouds in the sky began to streak and swirl. They seemed almost like thick brushstrokes, as if God Himself was making some unbridled painting against his sky of brilliant blue. The delineations began to take shape until they formed themselves into a white-crested bird, a great Caladrius, which stretched out its vast wings above the city to guide Sandro back home.

Chapter Five: Ecce Homo

I.

He would awake next in his bed, in the company of his family, and in more pain than he had ever thought was possible. Fernanda was sitting beside him. She burst into wild tears the moment he had opened his eyes and Sandro cried with her.

"I thought you were…" she stuttered, "that you might not…"

She did not need to finish the thought.

Fernanda cradled his head, and gently chided him for not saying anything to her on the night he had left his workshop to look for Tommaso. She had learned what had happened from Luca, the boy's father, who had sprinted across town late in the evening to inform her of events just as soon as he had returned Tommaso to their family home. That night, every jailhouse in the city that Luca could think of in his state of blind panic turned both him and his story away. He had returned to Fernanda just before dawn with promises that they would resume the search together.

She had not waited for him. Fernanda raised her children from their sleep and marched them out of the city to stay at her parent's villa. With no time to linger in detailed explanation, Fernanda tore back into the city to conduct her own search.

She had encountered several commanders in charge of prison day watches, most of whom had only scant understanding of who had been brought in during the night, or what crimes they were supposed to have committed. Fernanda was not permitted entrance to the jails to inspect the prisoners personally, though some of the more obliging commanders had walked the cells for themselves and none saw a man matching Sandro's description. One sympathetic commander had called out the name of Sandro Signorelli repeatedly to his inmates and a stranger had elected to chance fate. A grizzled and muscular man with a torn ear and a heavily scarred face was presented to Fernanda, his hands manacled and his expression apologetically hopeful. She had the man sent back to his cells with her furious curses ringing in his ears.

Between them, Sandro and Fernanda deduced that it was perfectly possible that she might well have visited the correct jailhouse that day. They would never know however, for that day was the day in which Sandro had been lying unconscious and mute on the floor of a cell crowded with bodies.

Fernanda had spent the second night alone in the house. She had found that there was no preternatural bond or deep instinct in her heart that allowed her to divine her husband's fate. Fear and dread engulfed her uncertain soul and yet the sweet voice of hope remained defiantly persistent. When she had eventually passed into a shallow and fearful sleep, she found that her dreams were plagued by visions of her husband's vacant dead face, sinking beneath the surface of the Tiber, or else covered with dirt in some hastily dug and unmarked grave outside of the city. In the darkness, she had broken for the first time.

As Sandro was being taken on the second morning to the cells of the Inquisition, Fernanda made her way to Santa

221

Maria del Popolo. Father Donato and the Carmelites had heard no news of the incident and could do no more than comfort her before setting out into the city to make their own enquiries. Fernanda had not eaten for more than a day. Father Donato took her to a quiet room and watched as she slowly picked at a bread roll and a clementine. She had found herself shredding the citrus peel into tiny fragments while reflecting on the nature of violence, and just how awful it must be to have life beaten from the body—and how terrified Sandro must have been. By evening, the other Carmelite monks returned to the church with no sign of Sandro and no reports of his whereabouts. They had apologised to her and said that they could do no more.

Fernanda had found her parents and children waiting for her outside her house upon her return. They insisted that she should not be alone, and that they should all stay together on the third night. Her father was the first to pronounce the demise of his son-in-law. Fernanda found that she did not mind hearing the word 'dead' as much as she had presumed to. The dreaded word contained no new power over her, and hearing her fears said aloud did not seem to make her husband's fate feel any more or less certain. She did mind, however, the way he had said the word—verbalised before her gathered family, he had forced Fernanda to locate new reserves of strength to comfort the tears of their children.

After her third awful night without Sandro, Fernanda had woken dizzied and petrified. A fourth search of the city's jailhouses seemed to be a fruitless and exhausting notion, and yet there seemed to be no other action that could be taken. She took her children with her that day, haunting the streets of Rome as if it were, in fact, she who was stuck somewhere between life and death. They walked for hours until her legs seized up and seemed to refuse any further motion. She sat on the sweeping steps of some grand and unfamiliar church and wept ferociously, even on the morning that Sandro was taken and affixed to a rack on the Tiber's western bank.

They had returned to their house drained and despondent. Ilaria, it seemed, had kept hopeful vigil from her bedroom window. After some hours, she had spotted the unusual sight of a market cart being wheeled down their narrow and crooked street and towards their house. As it neared, Ilaria had seen a man stretched out across the back, his body exposed, prone, battered, and bruised, and had felt immediately that the man would prove to be her father.

When Ilaria shouted through down the stairs, Fernanda had rushed outside. Initially, she had remained unsure of his fate, and yet as she had thrown herself at his body she had wept once again—though this time with both joy and relief in her tears—as she heard him breathing.

During those initial days of recovery, sleep would come for Sandro with irresistible force. He would sleep so deeply that his mind was untroubled by dreams. When he was awake, Sandro would come to realise that he had spent over three decades of life taking painlessness quite for granted. Indeed, it seemed that he need only focus his mind upon a body part for it to sing its own song of pain. His right eye was so swollen that he could not see out from it. His mouth hurt so much that speech was difficult and smiling impossible—though fortunately, there was little about his situation to inspire the latter. The bones in his hands felt as if they had splintered beneath the boots of the Inquisition soldier. The worst pain of all though came from his ribs. Even slight movements were agony. Moving his weight from one side to another was slow and difficult. Sitting upright was even worse. The severity of his condition turned even the love of his children—their cuddles and their clambering—into sweet torment.

Fernanda tended to his every injury with great devotion. She spent many hours beside him, rubbing his scalp, talking with him, washing, and dressing his body. She made bowls of broth and peeled his fruit for his ease and comfort. She even insisted upon aiding him in his use of the chamber pot as much as Sandro's pride would allow.

Back in the safety of his own home, Sandro felt his soul slowly flushing with deferred fury and horror. Memories of those days away were almost as foul as the experiences he had felt at the point of occurrence. He recalled the faces of the hateful taverna gang, their spite and contempt as they had kicked him along the ground. He recalled the drunken expressions of the people inside—women included!—mocking and taunting him for performing his Christian duty. He thought of the revolting Cardinal Gentile and the Blue-Eyed Inquisitor who emanated such impassive brutality. He recalled the crushed head of the man he had seen in the hallway and the woman stripped and humiliated in the cage of the courtyard—and all the torture and degradation that was being committed in the name of merciful Christ.

Perhaps a whole week had passed before Fernanda informed Sandro that Tommaso had been visiting their home daily, pleading for the opportunity to apologise for his actions and their dire consequences. When Sandro granted permission, the boy cried at the sight of him.

"No apology is needed," said Sandro, making sure to rasp just a little more than was necessary. "My actions that day were borne from love and duty; those most noble of impulses that eschew all thoughts of self-preservation entirely." He adopted the impression of grace and forgiveness personified. Secretly though, each teardrop and every sorry utterance pleased him immeasurably.

"I did not mean for anyone to get hurt," Tommaso insisted. "I only intended to visit San Luigi again that morning. I went to sketch the paintings within. One of the youths outside approached me—he told me the most bewitching tales of Michelangelo Merisi da Caravaggio! He says that Merisi carries a silver dagger inscribed with his personal motto: "without hope" on one side, "without fear" on the other. Without hope—without fear...do you not think this is *exactly* how he dares to paint? How he seems to live his life? Oh, master, they were all such awful people—it was so much fun!"

The boy's final recollection of the day, it seemed, involved drinking wine from a flagon at the suggestion of one of the boys. He claimed no memory of the taverna, or events outside, and had only been told what had happened to his master when he eventually sobered up. Tommaso produced a bottle of brandy sent to assist Sandro with his healing, a token of heartfelt thanks from his father. He then showed Sandro faint bruises of his own, a token of extreme displeasure from his father the morning afterwards.

"Father reported Michelangelo Merisi to the Papal Police. He accused him of abducting me with sexual intentions!" Tommaso shook his head incredulously. "His story fell on deaf ears. The Papal Police told my father they receive so many stories such as this that I would be perhaps the seventh child that Merisi had abducted or abused that month."

"Was he there?" asked Sandro. "Was Michelangelo Merisi with you in the taverna?"

"Honestly, I cannot be certain of anything. And yet I do not think he was ever present. Even in such a state as I was in, that surely would be a meeting to remember!"

Sandro reached for his water, though through force of habit, he reached erroneously for his beaker with his broken hand. He winced badly as he knocked the vessel clumsily to the floor.

"Your hand!" Tommaso exclaimed as he rushed to assist his master. "Is it badly hurt?" Sandro stared at his hand which was bandaged into a white mitten. "How will you paint now?" Sandro had no reply. Tommaso breathed a soft and guilty breath in the silence that followed. He wrang his hands and began to excuse himself. However, before he left Sandro's company, he was compelled to impart some further bad news. "Master, Cardinal Gentile closed the Sacred Images exhibition. When I heard rumours of this, I went to Santa Maria dell'Anima to investigate the matter and, if possible, recover your Assumption. I spoke with the cardinal's men who were just then removing the works from the church walls. They said that Cardinal Gentile officially declared the exhibition a failed venture and would no longer tolerate having his good name associated with such ignominy. His men told me that the paintings have been sold to some wealthy merchant from a town called Oxford, in England. They are, all of them, to be shipped abroad next week."

Sandro nodded as the boy left. He fell back against his pillow and reflected that he would never see his Assumption ever again. His masterpiece, his achievement of a lifetime, now taken out of his city, out of his country, bought by God only knew who and placed God only knew where... In truth, he found that he did not mind this development so much after all.

II.

At first, Sandro's shaven scalp sprouted sharp grey bristles. As the weeks passed, the follicles softened and darkened. By the time his hair was thick and voluminous once more, Sandro was able to leave his sick bed. He could eat with his family in the kitchen. He could even walk very slowly down the street for fresh air—if indeed any of the hot city air could be described as fresh, thick as it was with bugs, midges, and the wafting scent of human and bestial effluence.

If their circumstances would have allowed it, Fernanda and Sandro would have taken the Scudo given to them by Cardinal Gentile and given them all to the poor and the needy. However, pride had indeed become a luxury—this enforced period of artistic unproductivity was facilitated exclusively by the cardinal and his overpayment for the Assumption. Still, the quotidian prayers and thanks that Sandro and Fernanda offered for their sustenance during this time emerged from pursed lips. They decided that their food and drink tasted bitter, almost rotten to them both—though no such complaints ever came from the children, who were told only half truths regarding their father's condition and his period of absence.

Soon, autumn worked its subtle magic on Rome. Sandro received the temperate season with greater enthusiasm than he had ever done in his life before—every shift in colour and mood are felt more keenly by the artist's soul than by any other. He saluted the newly crisp quality of the evening air, he embraced the muted quality of the daylight, and gave thanks for the cooling air. He appreciated how the days were now bookended with blushing skies of pale pink, how the city gardens began to fill with blossoming roses, and how Fernanda began working her culinary wonders on the new seasonal offerings of arugula, broccoli, zucchini, mushrooms, pumpkins, and chestnuts. Sandro welcomed every mark of seasonal transition as a sign that the most ferocious and tumultuous summer of his life was finally over at last.

He began to spend time in his workshop once again. With his right hand still too damaged to grip a chalk or a brush, Sandro was forced to use his left hand. This, he found, was almost like an alien entity, an entity almost as talentless as his feet. Still, he persevered diligently with his self-tuition, working alone each morning sketching disembodied arms and noses, eyes, and ears, all to varying degrees of incompetence.

On the morning of September's twentieth day, Sandro found Tommaso waiting for him outside his studio to request a moment of his time. Inside the boy's eyes darted bashfully around the deeply familiar space that he had not occupied in almost two months. His gaze lingered a long while on Sandro's rough left-handed sketches left out on his desk.

"Master," he said, his voice small and shaking. "Master, if you had not come looking for me, you would not be in this state. I wish to make amends. With your permission, I would like to draw and paint the work for you, using your composition."

Sandro raised a sceptical eyebrow. Tommaso had not yet attempted anything so large and so complex. He had purchased a large wooden panel, almost six feet by four, to contain the Nativity. If anything went awry, Sandro would struggle to afford a replacement.

"You will not be able to complete the scene by yourself," Tommaso insisted, "not for weeks—perhaps even months—yet. How long can you continue to feed your family without working? I swear to you, master, I have continued work all summer. I have been drawing donkeys, cows, and sheep all these weeks. I will work under your supervision, slowly and carefully, and we will practise the scene to scale, many times over on parchment before we commit it to the panel. There will be no mistakes, I promise."

Sandro looked into the boy's eyes and saw that he was being entirely sincere. With a small nod, Sandro forced himself to swallow his memories of the drunken Tommaso and his taunts regarding his lack of artistic originality and talent, before opening his desk drawer and producing the sketches he had made all those months ago. The two of them examined all their options, discussing all the while the merits of each variation and marking out alternative positions for the figures until, together, they had decided upon a final design for the Nativity scene.

"The composition may not be radical," Sandro proudly conceded, "but it is solid and harmonious, and those qualities were good enough for the great Raphael."

Sandro had positioned Mary and Joseph standing with straight backs, their heads positioned forward to stare out from the drawing. Tommaso tentatively suggested that they should be engaged more, both with each other, and with the Christ Child below. He wondered if Sandro and Fernanda could model the figures in the workshop to enable a more dynamic depiction of posture and expression. In the silence that followed, Sandro heard the words that Tommaso had left unsaid: *as Michelangelo Merisi does.*

Modelling proved to be an arduous and painstaking experience. Sandro and Fernanda found their pose—stooped over an old cradle with one arm around each other and the other pointing down into the foreground—was a difficult one to maintain for four hours straight, though they were granted intermittent breaks to stretch their spines and drink a beaker of water. Tommaso had promised that it would take three sessions to draw the two central figures, and that colouring could be completed later in a more leisurely fashion. He worked with such concentration and seriousness, ignoring every distraction, such as the giggling, chattering, and play fighting of the children crowded into the workshop with them, that Sandro could only feel a touch of pride watching the boy.

"Father, have you heard of the ghost that was sighted near the Castel Sant'Angelo?" Ilaria asked during a long absent-minded silence, "they say it was a woman, a headless woman. They say it was the ghost of a dead woman named Beatrice Cenci. They say she was patrolling the bridge by night... as if she was searching for something."

"Was she looking for her head perhaps?" Fernanda replied with what seemed like listless interest.

"They say she was cradling that in her arms."

"Well then," Sandro interjected testily, "if she has that already, why must she persevere in despoiling the greatest bridge in Rome?"

"I recall the accounts of her execution. It was said to be especially brutal," said Fernanda.

"That night marked the anniversary of her death," Ilaria declared, grandly. "I heard that she intends upon returning to the site of her execution on the evening of September the eleventh, forevermore, to remind all of Rome of the barbarism and injustices she endured."

"Oh, she is to be fixed to the calendar now, is she?" Sandro snapped. "A regular pestilence—like the droppings of starlings beneath the October murmuration? Kindly, remain still and quiet please."

When Tommaso revealed the finished drawing of the central figures, now committed to the wooden panel, Sandro stared lovingly at every perfect detail of the figures Tommaso had drawn. However tedious and awkward Sandro had found the experience of modelling, he had to admit that the finished drawing had enabled Mary and Joseph to come alive at the centre of the composition. The figures felt solid and weighty. Their faces were detailed and expressive. Tommaso had even completed something interesting with perspective—Joseph's hand began at the fingertips and receded into the background in a convincing depiction of perspective and multi-dimensionality. Yet, of everything that Sandro admired about the drawing, his favourite new aspect was this new resemblance between Joseph and himself, and between Fernanda and Mary. It offered him some small measure of private joy to think that, should the work sell, their likenesses might hang for years somewhere small and modest—God willing—for decades after they themselves had passed into the next life.

By the time that the full drawing was complete, Sandro was able to hold a brush once more. The two of them began working together once more, building up their image with colour. Outside, the deepening October mirrored their endeavours, the Roman foliage dying in resplendent shades of crimson and bronze. Their scene became a rich blend of forest green and sky blue, with bestial furs offset against the pure white of the cherubs above. Tommaso focussed his talents upon the animal figures. The quality of his work was quite astonishing. The boy painstakingly painted the texture of feathers, fur, and horns, all with the virtuosity of a Dutchman. Sandro noted how lifelike the creatures appeared, the eyes and mouths of the beasts were rendered without sentiment, without anything to humanise them. Thanks to Tommaso, their Jesus was truly born among beasts, one could almost sense the slop and stench on the ground. Love was arranged above across two stratospheres. The human figures showed the fallible love of mortal man. The cherubs in the skies were emissaries, sent directly from that perfect and eternal love from the heavens; their presence signifying that these humble beginnings were a façade, a gossamer disguise for the most joyous and monumental of all births. Sandro had not used all his gold on his Assumption. He used the little he had retained to put the finishing touch on the panel, crowning their Christ Child with a brilliant halo.

Standing, at last, before the finished work, Sandro felt less excitement than he had before his Assumption; instead, he felt a deep satisfaction. The work was, he felt, a tender masterpiece. He turned to Tommaso to ascertain his feelings about the finished work.

"I believe we have constructed a very fine nativity scene," the apprentice replied. He paused and gave a heavy sigh. "Master Sandro," he began, kicking the floor lightly, as if he was forcing himself to utter his next words. "Master, of late, my father and I were talking my situation through. We wondered if, now that you are almost healed and that this painting is complete, it might be best if I reduce the time spent here with you. If perhaps three, and not six, of my days should be here in the workshop."

Sandro had not expected this response. Indeed, of all the ways that the boy's words had ever pricked and needled, this polite request was somehow the worst. Clearly, it marked the beginning of the end. Tommaso, doubtless, intended to find a new master.

Sandro stared deep into the nativity. The work was even better than the Assumption—he was sure of that—and the improvement had been born from true collaboration.

Contemplation of their painting could, however, provide only a fleeting refuge from making his decision. From the corner of his eye, Sandro could see that Tommaso was unrelenting in his focus. He would be answered.

"Tommaso," Sandro found himself saying, at last, "please do not take my hesitation as anything more than the foul pangs of sentiment. Despite the turbulences we have endured, my fondness for you has flourished greatly, just as your skills as a painter have flourished despite every inadequacy of my tuition."

Tommaso looked to the floor and said nothing.

"Watching you these last weeks, I agree that you have now all-but superseded your paltry master. Moreover, you have done so before you have even celebrated your fifteenth birthday! If you feel you have outgrown our arrangement, I quite agree— and this work shall stand as proof." Sandro pointed at the canvas with an open palm. He could barely speak the last as he reached this painful moment of parting, the lump in his throat was almost insurmountable.

"Master," Tommaso began, "I…"

"No," Sandro interrupted, turning heel to face Tommaso with a smile on his face. A new idea had sprung quite miraculously into his mind—as if God Himself had planted the notion. "No, I am not fit to be called your master any longer, Tommaso. The time has come for me to release you from our former arrangement. Yet there is something still that I can offer you, something that will aid you greatly in your development, something that is perhaps more suitable for us both than this continued pretence of tutelage… Tommaso, I would like to make you a full partner in this workshop. Or at least a partner of sorts. You would be free to develop your own works and painting style, and free to pursue your own commissions, yet if you wish, you can remain situated here, using this workshop without charge from me during the meantime. We could, perhaps, learn from each other, asking for and giving advice as we went along. Once you begin making money of your own, we could perhaps share the costs of materials and perhaps even rent one day—though, of course, whenever the day comes that you can afford a workshop of your own, you would be free to leave whenever you choose to."

The boy stared back at him, the expression on his face deeply quizzical and disbelieving. The offer, Sandro reflected, may well have appeared too good to be true for such a young artist.

"What do you say Tommaso?" Sandro pushed, "I promise you—you need never paint another cherub ever again."

Tommaso remained dumbstruck, yet he was quite unable to restrain himself—he fell onto his former master and embraced him warmly, and for the very first time, physical contact between the two of them felt altogether natural.

Chapter Six: Conversion

I.

Above the door outside the Signorelli workshop hung a small wooden sign that Sandro had once painted his name upon. Together, the former master and apprentice removed it and replaced it with something prouder and considerably more noticeable, a new sign, large enough to display the words "Sandro Signorelli & Tommaso Marelli—artists for hire."

Tommaso seemed almost like another person entirely. Gone were the eye rolls. His jokes had no targets. There was laughter in his voice and in his poise. However, a major problem persisted for them still. They had begun working on their Nativity scene without a commission and had not yet located a buyer. Tommaso volunteered to tour the city personally, offering the work to every church he saw for any fair price around thirty Scudo. Yet a somewhat wilder, somewhat more ambitious notion had occurred to Sandro. He sat at his desk in coy silence as he entertained the thought, occasionally enacting a strange and irritating ritual—opening his mouth to speak, before swallowing his thoughts and quietly reproaching himself by muttering the words *no, no, no*—until Tommaso could stand it no longer.

"What is it?" the boy finally snapped. Sandro dawdled, struggling against his better judgement, wondering if his idea might indeed have merit or if it would make him appear like some desperate and ridiculous figure in the eyes of a person less than half his age. "In about two moments, I will look back down and continue my drawing," Tommaso warned, "I shall not look up again until the work is finished."

"Tommaso... I believe that we can still contact the Cardinal Borghese!" Sandro declared tremulously. "You were here that morning—present in this very room! Did not the great cardinal say that he saw some promise in our work? Tommaso, this painting is better than the Assumption. And Donato told me personally that the cardinal expressed his regret that he could not help us further. Together—does this not imply that Borghese's decision was close? Or that the newness of Michelangelo Merisi's work made his decision a mere consequence of poor timing? Tell me Tommaso, would it be utterly absurd to ask Donato the same favour twice in six months?"

Tommaso sighed aloud and returned his attention to his work.

In his bed later that evening, Sandro pitched the same question to Fernanda. He recounted everything that he could remember both the cardinal and Father Donato saying. Sandro ushered his wife judiciously down the path of persuasion, only to pull back and tear his own arguments to shreds. He repeated this pattern over and over, until—on perhaps the fourth repetition—Fernanda rolled over, pulled the bedsheets over her head, and declared that no one could make this decision for her husband but himself.

The next Sunday was the final weekend in October. Sandro decided to take his thoughts out for a long walk. Whether he would ask the Carmelite for a second favour or not Sandro did not know; yet, regardless, he resolved to visit the church of Santa Maria del Popolo that afternoon. He was keen to see his old friend either way and was also somewhat curious to witness the painting Donato had mentioned before—this other Assumption painted by the artist named Carracci.

First though, Sandro made his way towards the Piazza Navona, just as he had that sultry Sunday all those months before. All throughout the summer months Tommaso had been visiting the church of San Luigi regularly and had informed Sandro that the bustling crowds had finally gone from the place. Sandro was quite glad of that—not because he desired another visit to see the Michelangelo Merisi paintings of San Luigi again himself, but because he wanted to sit in relative peace in the Piazza so that he might think awhile and remember it all.

Sandro wound his whimsical way towards one of the twin fountains and leaned back languidly against the font. He looked from San Luigi, where Michelangelo Merisi had made his name, to Santa Maria dell'Anima, where his own had sunk. He thought back to the crowds and the noise, the excitement, and the fever... it all seemed so *distant* now. The Piazza was still somewhat occupied by street peddlers and courtesans, families, and gangs of bawdy youths, but it all seemed ordinary once more—sleepy even. It would seem that not even the bewitching talents and scandalous vision of Michelangelo Merisi could keep the people of Rome captivated forever. The human appetite for the new appeared to be quite insatiable. The people walking through the Piazza that day had their attention focussed firmly elsewhere. Indeed, it took a moment for Sandro's mind to register the oddness of their behaviour. A large group was moving south, shouting over each other. Sandro stood slowly and followed them down Via di Pantaleo, where the voices mixed with a larger congregation. Five men of the city watch were arguing with a large group of furious young men, their hands twitching by their sword handles. A young mother was escorting her crying child away from the crowd. Someone among the crowd dared to shout that the Inquisition were brutes, that they were murderous and corrupt. A second voice replied that heathens and devil-worshippers should be burned on Earth as God would surely consign them to burn in Hell.

At hearing the word *Inquisition*, Sandro felt his stomach tighten. His feet seemed to move reluctantly with the flow of people, down Via dei Baullari, as if they were being drawn towards the crowd by some ghoulish and inescapable volition of their own.

The bulk of the crowd were gathered at the Campo de' Fiori marketplace. They seemed angry for the most part, many voices were shouting and jeering, and the sound of shrieking cut through the general displeasure. Sandro pushed forwards and saw that three structures had been erected above the marketplace. They were wooden and crossed at the top, like a crucifix, while the bottoms were fitted with stands. Two of the structures already had people strapped to them—a man and a woman—with their feet on the stands and their arms bound tightly behind their heads. A third figure was being fastened, forcefully, to the last.

Sandro squinted at this last man, convinced even at such a distance that he knew him from somewhere. However, much of the man's likeness was obscured by the iron mask that covered the lower half of his face. The scold was shaped like the twisted face of a daemon and was designed to prevent him from speaking or screaming. The man wore a large iron crucifix too, and both ironworks were blackened, as if they had been burned before. All three were wearing them. Their heads were shaven, their bodies stripped down to their loincloths and their flesh was purple and mangled.

At once, the identity of the men struck Sandro: the one being attached to the third stake was Piazza Navona Youth—the same man who had spent May outside San Luigi, then wearing a tunic and flower garland and proclaiming Merisi's brilliance. Who had, in the guise of an angel, shared a canvas with St Matthew. Who had fed Tommaso wine weeks later, and who had been among those who had beaten Sandro bloody in the street before they had been forced to share a cell together.

The others he also recognised as the blasphemous man who had danced on the taverna tabletop, now missing his left eye, and the mocking Bacchante woman who had laughed at his ragged clothing. They had been held for as long as he had been free and recovering, Sandro realised, they had been tortured and questioned for more than three months.

Around thirty soldiers of the Papal Guard stood in a line between the stands and the crowd. They were a colourful arrangement—almost jovially so—wearing orange and blue striped uniforms and helmets adorned with scarlet plumage. They clasped their halberds to attention in the face of public unrest. When their line was jostled apart, an old man stepped forwards from the centre, coughing to clear his throat as he ran a bloated red hand through his lank and thinning hair.

"Citizens of Rome," began Cardinal Gentile, his voice scything through the general din. "Bear witness to justice! I present a trinity of serpents for your judgement today. These are the devil's agents! They stand accused of blasphemy and heresy against God. They stand accused of duelling and bloodletting in the streets—they are accused of making improper jests! They have confessed fully to each crime and every charge—and, in doing so, they have permitted us this chance to redeem their souls—they have accepted the penance! And yet, they have confessed also to further indiscretions. As I suspected, they serve two masters: Lucifer, and the man they call Michelangelo Merisi da Caravaggio. He is their earthly master! He is their dark prophet! This one," at this, Gentile pointed to the Piazza Navona youth, "this one, is also his lover!"

"Lies!" shouted a woman's voice from the crowd.

"Truth!" Gentile replied, his voice thin and reedy when strained to full volume. "He has confessed to a hundred charges of sodomy and a thousand charges of fellatio—he admits that Michelangelo Merisi and he worship the devil together as they fornicate beneath the silver light of the moon!"

"Torturer!" an old man sobbed, "a man does not confess to the Inquisition; he only begs for mercy."

"He has confessed. They have *all* confessed," Gentile insisted. "They have admitted to me, before several witnesses, that those accursed black paintings serve as Michelangelo da Caravaggio's Trojan Horse. Through them, he invites the devil onto holy ground. By day, the works taint the soul of all that behold them. Lucifer slithers out from the darkness when no one is watching and sprays his acrid seed across the churches of our great city. I hope then, good citizens, now that you join me in knowing the truth of Michelangelo Merisi da Caravaggio, that you also join me in demanding his immediate arrest and trial!"

Sandro heard only a smattering of cheers among the remonstrating crowd. Unmoved, Gentile nodded back to his red-robed Inquisitors who began arranging kindling beneath the stands.

Sandro had seen a man being burned alive before—the same man in fact, burned many times over. That man was called Lawrence, the saint whose fiery martyrdom had been depicted endlessly in both oil and stained glass. Saint Lawrence—whose rumoured final remarks were alleged to have been a droll quip about being well-done on one side had made him the patron of clowns and cooks all over the Christian world—always remained defiant and serene in the face of death: the established vocabulary of the aesthetic ensuring that halos, cherubs, and trumpets were brought forth to demonstrate the futility of Christian persecution and evidence how faith in God can enable man to transcend suffering and to survive death itself.

The faces of people about to be burned were not defiant. They were not serene. All three captives shook against their bondage and stared out with wide eyed and silent horror, before the Capirotes were brought forth. Sandro looked at the Piazza Navona Youth. Tears were running down the young man's face as he looked upwards to the heavens. Sandro could only imagine the poor boy's thoughts and prayers as the red hood was placed over his face.

The flames quickly caught and were soon licking the soles of the captive's feet. The air did not fill with the trumpets of triumphant Heaven, it filled only with burning flesh, blood and organs, a putrid stench of unholy rust that choked the onlookers with its sweet abhorrence.

Cardinal Gentile watched his prisoners burning with a look of glib satisfaction upon his face. Sandro could not bear to look at him any longer. He reflected that the young man cast subversively as an angel by Michelangelo Merisi months before, and now as a demon by Cardinal Gentile did not deserve this fate. That no living creature deserved this fate. He found that he could not watch them writhing and twisting any longer. He forgave his former attackers with all his heart, and prayed that God could hear him, before then slipping back into the crowd before anyone might recognise that he had played even the lowliest, most insignificant, part in any of this madness.

Sandro floundered at first, walking without conscious direction or at least any conscious direction except away from Campo de' Fiori. Around him were the facades of grand churches, smaller churches, and the looming outlines of distant domes, all adorned with wooden crucifixes. Within each church would be paintings, sculptures, statues, and tapestries—the consummated efforts of many generations of artists such as himself, who had used their talents to valorise their faith, and, in doing so, had glorified the Church. He passed the stained-glass likenesses of saints and disciples clutching the instruments and weapons that once slew them, back in the days when the heathen Romans had held all the power and the founders of the faith had been noble of spirit. The position of the Church had changed radically from those early days. The Christians were no longer the ones affixed to the stakes and wheels, they were the ones lighting the flames and breaking the bodies.

For the first time in Sandro's unassuming and dutiful life, a blasphemy expressed itself in his mind. The modern Church, he silently concluded, was unworthy of its own faith. It had become so deeply veined with corruption, paranoia, and duplicity that when its authority had been challenged by reformation and undermined by schism, the skies above had failed to respond with the promised blood and vengeance.

What were these strange feelings in his heart? Was everything that he had ever painted a falsehood? Could a Christian still truly call themselves thus without the Church? These thoughts went against everything he had ever been told and everything he had felt his whole life. Opposition to the Church led only to Hellfire and damnation. He realised then he had no choice but to cross town then. He had to speak with Father Donato—not to discuss the possible sale of his Nativity scene, but about a matter far, far graver than that. His very soul was at stake. That the resolution of this crisis depended upon a different servant of the Church was an irony that was not lost upon Sandro. In Rome all is faith, and yet his faith felt newly uncomfortable, confusing, and oppressive—and God never did answer him.

II.

Sandro found, to his astonishment, that the Piazza del Popolo was teeming with people and loud with voices. The name Michelangelo Merisi da Caravaggio was sounding out once more! As implausible as it seemed to be, the paintings Donato had mentioned must have been finished and installed. He hurried to remember when it was that the Carmelite had visited—around four months ago. If Merisi had painted both planned works, it would mean that he took no more than two months to finish a large painting—an unprecedented speed! Sandro began to wonder if there was something truly supernatural about the man after all.

He marched past the line and approached the door. "Excuse me, signore," he said to the guard stationed there, "I have not come to look at paintings today, my business with a priest inside is urgent—my mind is aflame, my soul tormented!"

"Then I advise you take them both, upon your anguished legs, to the back of the queue to wait their turn," the guard replied. "Or else visit another church. You know, I believe Rome has one or two others."

Sandro could do nothing else. He had to see Donato. He dragged himself reluctantly to the back of the line.

Was there to be no respite from the tattle and fancies that surrounded this accursed Lombardian? As recently as yesterday, this development might have even afforded Sandro some small measure of perverse pleasure: he could have luxuriated in jealous admiration, or even indulged some fantasy of a rivalry between Merisi and himself. But after events at Campo de' Fiori, he refused to listen to any more of it. He closed his eyes but found no refuge there. He saw only smouldering skin and blackening flesh and the sickening stench returned, wholly undiminished, to choke him once again.

When Sandro was finally permitted inside the church, he sighed, for he could not think of a single good reason not to observe the paintings by both Carracci and Merisi. He walked towards the crowded chapel, looked up to the paintings, and there broke into a fit of hysterical laughter. He could scarcely believe what he could see.

Carracci's Assumption was very much like his own. There were differences here and there, of course, but the paintings could well have been siblings.

Michelangelo Merisi's works framed the Assumption on either side. Saint Peter was crucified on the left. The infuriatingly talented artist had rendered the figures brilliantly of course, the image a sad depiction of needless barbarism as Peter, an old man with dirty feet, was crucified upside-down in acknowledgement of his subordination to Christ. On the right, the founder of the Roman Catholic Church lay in the mud, beneath a horse. The painting was dominated by the creature's posterior. And it was *that*, the image of the velvet buttocks of a horse, that seized the attention of the onlooker while pointing to Carracci's Assumption.

More than anything else he had seen that day, or endured that year, it was the casual irreverence of this…*this*…painting that caused Sandro's spirit to finally break. He laughed uncontrollably, until he creased over, his face wet with tears, and until the other people standing near him began to back away and form a circle around him.

Eventually, he felt a hand touch his shoulder directing him away from the crowd, out of the church and guiding him to a quiet space of the piazza to sit him on a stair outside.

"My friend," began a familiar voice, "why do you laugh so?"

"I laugh because Michelangelo Merisi has never seen my Assumption," replied Sandro looking up to see Donato. "He does not even know of my existence. Yet make no mistake—that horse's rump is for me. Those buttocks are a humiliation. They are a thumb bitten, not just at Carracci, but at me, and at every other dew-eyed patsy who has spent their lives propagating the great lie."

"And what lie would this be?"

"That the meek shall inherit. That the humble and the hard-working shall receive their just rewards. That the Church stands for love and mercy… Today I witnessed three people burned at the stake by a cardinal. They were not good people. In fact, they were the very same people who attacked me earlier this year and beat me half to death. Father, the stake is neither justice nor forgiveness. It sickens me to see representatives of the Church dispensing cruelty and death."

"Those burned people are God's children. Let us pray that His judgement will prove less severe."

"They were not even permitted to speak their defence. Their deaths felt like cruelty. It seemed almost personal. Those men claimed friendship with Michelangelo Merisi. It felt like their executions might simply be a way for Cardinal Gentile to hurt him."

"You may be correct. I have witnessed the moral failings of malcontent men many times before, and I am certain that the lack of interest in his exhibition greatly stung the cardinal's pride."

"Father, I recall criticising Michelangelo Merisi's works the first time I saw them. I thought that by using the people of Rome as models, he had failed to paint sacred beings. The observation was accurate, father, though the interpretation was mistaken— sacred and perfect beings are a fantasy—we are unworthy."

"Perhaps we are," Donato reflected as he scanned the rowdy piazza. "However, by using courtesans and bandits to stand for the saints, I believe that Merisi paints something quite interesting. He has found a way to paint the great struggle of humanity: the strive towards divinity, God's calling both jarring against, and mingling with, the latent defectiveness of His children. Perhaps it is that honesty that makes his works so troublesome to men such as Cardinal Gentile."

"And that is my other issue. I participated in the cardinal's exhibition. I knew the people he burned. I have allowed my life to become some twisted lunacy..." Sandro tailed off, "...and all because I wanted to create something great."

"Pride is a terrible affliction. One of the seven mortal sins. My friend, this is not because God would tear down his children, but because left unchecked, pride will pave a gleeful road towards self-defeat."

Sandro took a deep breath, wiped away his tears and forced himself to look at Donato.

"My great work would not have been for myself, Father," Sandro continued, aware that his words were only half-true at best. "It would have been for the city, for the faith, for God."

247

"My friend, this city, and this faith are hardly impoverished. And God is great, He asks only for your love."

"Tell me truthfully: am I a poor excuse for a painter? My own assistant said that I lack originality. He claims that everything I create is merely an echo of better works. And I never could find success. Then this man Michelangelo Merisi da Caravaggio appears, and he has somehow ruined my floundering life. He has done so without meeting me, without even knowing my name or face, but simply by the fact of our mutual existence! You do not understand—I will never know success; I feel as if failure lives within my bones."

"I understand better than you think."

Sandro was unconvinced.

"Very well," Donato continued as he placed his hand on Sandro's shoulder. "Let us consider this man Michelangelo Merisi. Let us consider his name. Here in Rome, he is called "da Caravaggio." Why does he make this association with his place of birth? Because this small village named Caravaggio is some grand place of prestige? No. He calls himself this because God's light casts many shadows. Despite all his obvious talents, despite all that notoriety and scandal, Merisi is also cursed by that very affliction you call *mutual existence*. His name shrinks in this city. In Buonarroti, Rome already has her Michelangelo."

Silently, Sandro considered Donato's words.

"Cardinal Borghese talks of Michelangelo da Caravaggio like some besotted teenager," laughed Donato. "Each time I see the cardinal he talks of him. He says there are many reports of him fighting in the streets. Michelangelo da Caravaggio has allegedly attempted an assassination of a rival and stands accused of deflowering the teenage daughter of a powerful count—and these are just this week's rumours! You yourself know that Cardinal Gentile works ceaselessly to ruin this man. In truth, the cardinal is one of several powerful men who feel the same way. What then is certain about Michelangelo Merisi? Very little. Perhaps only this: his story shall not end peacefully. Sandro Signorelli, listen to these words: your name shall not echo through the ages, but you do have a wife and children do you not?" Sandro nodded dumbly. Donato removed his hand from his shoulder. "Then my friend, is that not success enough? Do you not have some riches? These are riches that a man such as Merisi will never have. You will depart from this life in peace, surrounded by loved ones. Does that vision not have at least *some* merit? Is it not better than being murdered in some futile brawl; or being hung, burned, or strangled by the myriad of enemies you cannot help but make?"

"It does," Sandro conceded, "but merit does not feed my family."

Donato stood. "It is funny how a slight change in perspective can turn a mortal weakness into a saving grace," he said with a final wry smile. "Daily now, wealthy people visit this church. I hear them all talking, fervently wishing that they could possess a painting like those painted by Michelangelo Merisi. If Sandro Signorelli is a painter of echoes, why not embrace it? Why not simply become an echo of a different music?"

Epilogue: Amor Vincit Omnia

Tales of old Rome are told to exhaustion throughout the eternal city. And yet on the morning of the first day of the new year, Sandro listened to his daughter retelling an ancient story with fresh ears.

"The Romans had a two-headed god called Janus," said Ilaria. "Janus stood for both endings and beginnings, for passage, time, and for change. He kept the gate between the worlds of gods and men. The month of January is named for him. It is an invitation to begin the year by reflecting on life both past and future, and to assess one's place on this Earth."

After eating his breakfast, Sandro stood and kissed his children and his wife with a promise to spend time with them in the evening—a promise that he intended to keep.

He stepped outside his house, greeted the pale sunrise, and made his way down to the workshop where two works were developing inside on twin easels. Sandro began his mornings by mixing paints. Now, even the most menial duties were shared evenly within the Signorelli and Marelli workshop.

They shared money too, ever since Tommaso disclosed that he spent several days away from the workshop looking first for a buyer of Sandro's Nativity during the previous autumn. He had found a quiet church near Rome's southern boundaries willing and able to make an offer of thirty-five Scudo for the painting. Sandro had been beside himself with gratitude. He told Tommaso that if he had done this out of guilt for the indirect role he had played in Sandro's attack during summer, then Sandro could only absolve the boy, this time with complete sincerity. He had then insisted that Tommaso take half the money for himself—for not only had he found the buyer, but he had also carried out half the work. Besides which, for the first time in Sandro's life, it had begun to look as if there might just be enough money to share after all.

Tommaso entered the workshop that January morning and hung up his jacket. The two men greeted each other before rolling up their sleeves, taking up their brushes and beginning to paint, side by side.

Tommaso was painting the anguished face of the decapitated St Paul, held aloft by a Roman soldier. In truth, Sandro felt the work to be a little gruesome, yet he had to admit the contrast of light and shadow was very effective. Like the work of Michelangelo Merisi, Tommaso seemed able to bend light around his figures, giving the work a convincing impression of three dimensions within two, while adding both depth and texture to the image. Watching Tommaso's slight and delicate brushwork throughout the process, Sandro had been able to see that the same principle applied also to the faces of the figures within. Tommaso had lovingly and delicately depicted the soldier's emotional battle, vividly demonstrating a face caught between the dedication to his soldierly duty, and the human revulsion the Roman clearly felt in killing such a great and noble man. The effects were both complicated and subtle. Watching the image unfold, Sandro realised that Tommaso had always understood the dramatic potentiality of chiaroscuro, that great interplay between lightness and darkness, in ways that he had not.

On his easel, Sandro was painting a man contemplating a clean and fleshless skull. It was a Vanitas—a depiction of self-assessment—and, although it was of no real consequence to the casual viewer, the man depicted in the scene was himself. He too was experimenting with chiaroscuro. Though the former master would cheerfully admit that his use of the technique was somewhat rudimentary compared with Tommaso's, little more than a plain black background for his figure. Still, there were clear benefits to this borrowed style. Without a detailed background, the painting had taken more than two months to produce—less than half of Sandro's usual painting time.

The work had been bought before it was even finished. Sandro's next painting was pre-commissioned too, with an advance payment delivered to secure the work. Indeed, Father Donato had only spread word of Sandro's switch in painting style for a few days in Santa Maria del Popolo before he had found his workshop was inundated with unprecedented demand. Somehow, the daring and scandalous vision of Michelangelo Merisi da Caravaggio had managed to distort the artistic tastes of the eternal city itself. These days, there was no end to demand for dark paintings filled with morbid and sanguineous subjects. It seemed as if Sandro Signorelli and his family could finally flourish now that he had chosen to position his voice, as lowly and insignificant as it may be, firmly within the profane chorus of the now.

Acknowledgements

Firstly, I would like to thank my wonderful publisher, Archna Sharma, for her belief in this project, and whose support has allowed me to turn a life-long dream into a reality. Thanks too to both illustrators, Simona Slavova and Emily TahaBurt, whose talents have enriched the collection and put faces to characters that once existed purely in my mind.

I would also like to express my deep gratitude to Mr Gareth Ackerman, an inspirational English teacher at my secondary school, whose wit and imagination sparked a love of literature in me, and whose support played a crucial role in transforming my life. I don't believe that anything that came since would have been possible without his understanding, and his endless patience with an occasionally cocky and generally disruptive young man.

I would also like to thank another great teacher in my life, Jane McKie, who supervised writing The Vanitas. Her unwavering support and wonderful insights during the creative process helped to bring Sandro to life. Thanks too to other brilliant academics who have developed my abilities as both a reader and a writer: Jane Alexander, Patrick Errington, Robert Alan Jamieson, and Allyson Stack.

Other people who have helped with the writing of this book include my friends and first readers Patrick Levy and Mark Wilkins—much love to you both. Also, the brilliant Ranjit Hoskote for his friendship and guidance while finishing the collection. My friends in the writing world: Cordelia Harrison, Emily Harrison, Aiyah Sibay, Sukhada Tatke, and the whole "Cool Kids Writing Club" in my hometown of Oxford. Thanks too to the people behind the lit mags and journals, people who spend their free time helping to build platforms for emerging writers and fostering self-belief.

A special thanks also goes to my partner, Colette. After three dates she asked to read something that I had written. I remember the reluctance in that request, as she later told me she was afraid it would be terrible and that would mean that we would have to separate immediately. I am very glad that she did not think that my story was terrible, and that we were able to go on this journey together. She has since become the most supportive and wonderful partner I could hope for, and she has kept the flame of my belief going in several dark times.

Finally, I would like to thank my family. We have always been a close unit and you are the bedrock of my life. I love you all.

ABOUT THE AUTHOR

Jake Kendall is a freelance writer based in Edinburgh. He holds an MSc in Creative Writing from the University of Edinburgh, and his work has been published in a variety of UK and US-based literary journals. One of his pieces was recently shortlisted for the Scottish Arts Club annual short story contest. Jake has had a lifelong fascination with art and art history and is thrilled to be sharing this passion in *The Vanitas & Other Tales of Art and Obsession.*

ABOUT THE ILLUSTRATORS

Simona Slavova is a visual artist from Bulgaria who is currently based in Lisbon. She obtained a degree in Illustration & Comics from a small art academy called Ar.Co.

Emily TahaBurt is an artist and illustrator currently residing between Baltimore (USA) and Cairo (Egypt). Her previous commissions include illustrations for *Lamplight Magazine, Trampoline Poetry*, and several small businesses across Ireland and the USA.

Discover more illustrated short story collections
from Neem Tree Press:

They Fell Like Stars From the Sky & Other Stories
By Sheikha Helawy

Visit neemtreepress.com for information and orders